CW00430083

SMILER WITH KNIFE

Michael Keenaghan lives in London.
He is the author of a novel: *London is Dead.*

ALSO BY THIS AUTHOR
London is Dead

SMILER WITH KNIFE

STORIES FROM THE
DARK HEART OF LONDON

MICHAEL KEENAGHAN

Nocturnal

First published Nov 2023
Copyright ©2023 Michael Keenaghan
All rights reserved

Nocturnal Books
London

A CIP catalogue of this book
is available from the British Library

ISBN-9798852186508

Front cover: Farm N17
Back cover: A406 Edmonton

Ah London you're a lady
Laid out before my eyes
Your golden heart it pulses
Between your scarred-up thighs.
Your eyes are full of sadness
Red buses skirt your hem
Your head-dress is a ring of lights
But I would not follow them.
Your architects were madmen
And your builders sane but drunk
But amidst your faded jewels
Shine acid house and punk.

You are a scarlet lady
Your streets run red with blood
My darling they have used you
And covered you with mud.
It was deep down in your womb my love
I drank my quart of sin
While Chinamen played cards and draughts
And knocked back Mickey Finns.

Your blood is like a river
Its scent is beer and gin
Your hell is in the summer
And you blossom in the spring.
September is your purgatory
Christmas is your heaven
When the stinking streets of summer
Are washed away by rain.
At the dark end of a lonely street
That's where you lose your pain
Tis then your eyes light up my love
To sparkle once again.

'London You're a Lady' The Pogues

5

CONTENTS

TOTTENHAM FOREVER

Early one morning they burst in and got me, trashed the place and found nothing more than a bit of blow I was selling on the side. After twenty minutes on the ground I was hauled up, enduring the stinking breath of some fat copper with a grudge. The bastard thought he knew me well.

'You were there at the Farm that night, you piece of shit. I've been reading up on you, right into your history, mate. You've been keeping your nose clean for quite a while, haven't you, you lowlife cunt.'

The police had reopened the case. And here they were, raiding my flat on a supposed drug bust. Maybe I'd been grassed up for selling a bit of blow, who knows, but in reality this had nothing to do with drugs and everything to do with Tottenham twenty years before.

Broadwater Farm Estate, 1985. The original investigation into the riot and PC Blakelock's murder had been a shambles. Like dozens of other teenagers, I'd been pulled in, stuck in a cell for three nights, taking slaps and threats, no lawyer. They couldn't prove anything – I was released without charge.

I'd thrown a few bricks, run a bit wild, but so had the police. Ammo was coming in from both sides. Tension had been running high after a woman was killed in a police raid. On the evening, the coppers were hemming us into the estate – Get back into your farm you fucking animals – swinging their batons, going mental. Pure provocation. As night fell we responded with our own violence. Shotguns, firebombs, craziness. Even murder. It was worse than Handsworth, Brixton, anywhere. Blakelock was chased and hacked to death with machetes.

The copper thumps me in the belly, hard, and the cunt holding me lets me spill to the floor. His boot starts hitting the back of my head and doesn't stop. I'm concussed and hear him telling me that Keith Blakelock was a friend of his, and though it might be twenty years since the riots, he's going to see the murdering bastards locked up and rotting away if it's the last thing he ever does. A couple others pull him off. 'Get this lump of shit out to the van before I kill the fucker!'

He'd been right about keeping my nose clean. I hadn't been arrested in years. They drove me from my flat in Ponders End the five miles down to Tottenham nick. These days I hated Tottenham. Too many bad memories, too much shit. The manor had gone to pot. Pubs boarded up, rotting away. Dereliction and waste. I'd tried to avoid the fucking place as much as possible for years. Here they were rubbing it right back in my face.

I grew up in Northumberland Park, a good mile from Broadwater Farm. I was into football, knocked around with a Spurs firm. Most of my mates were white. But my connection with the Farm was my mate Kelvin. He couldn't care less about football, saw all the violence at the matches as a waste of energy, white dicks acting like idiots. He was more interested in the benefits of crime. Making money. He'd been through care homes, done borstal, the lot. Kelvin was pretty reckless. My bad influence, you could say.

Once at a party he was building a spliff and this Jamaican started giving it large.

'Hand over the ganja, English boy!'

Around this time there was a lot of Jamaicans coming over, strutting about like they were something to be feared. They thought British blacks were soft. Kelvin whipped out a gun and put it right in the guy's face.

'Who the fuck are you calling English boy, you banana boat nigger?'

The Yardie had been all mouth and shat it. But pretty soon the Yardies gathered their numbers and became quite a force. Soon everyone was picking up the lingo, trying to speak like them, including Kelvin. Ever since, the accent has completely taken over.

It was a dark era. Thatcher's Britain. Everyone I knew was unemployed. That government couldn't give a fuck. Some blokes thought they had won the pools if they managed to get a job plucking chickens or packing meat in a factory. Fuck that. The best thing about the 80s was the IRA nearly doing Thatcher in Brighton. If they'd hit their target there would have been parties in the streets. There was nothing but hate for Thatcher.

The evening of the riot, we went up to Kelvin's flat and took a load of sulph. It was the first time I'd tried it. Things were revving up, little clashes sparking off across the estate. I remember feeling out of it, charged up for anything, kicking the walls as we headed out into the night.

We were fuelled up on news footage, Handsworth, Moss Side, Brixton. Endless war in Northern Ireland. People were coming up from further afield, Stoke Newington, Hackney, even south of the river. Lots of strange faces. Quite a few whites. One paper even said the Russians were behind it. That was bullshit, but I do remember a skinhead bloke instructing some kids on how to make a petrol bomb; sounded like he'd been in the army. Everyone wanted a pop at the police, black, white, you name it. The whole estate erupted.

The Farm is like a maze, a self-contained closed-in world, not open streets like Brixton. Its layout certainly didn't help the police. Everybody seemed to go berserk. Anything I'd seen at the football seemed like kids' stuff. I've seen coppers on the telly visibly cry just talking about it. They took one fucking battering that night.

A year later I did eighteen months for stashing stolen goods. Nothing could have prepared me for prison. At home it was just me and my mum. I had my own bedroom, own space. Suddenly I was bunking up three to a cell with frequent 23-hour lock up. I grew up fast. I did most of my time in Wandsworth, the biggest shithole ever. The screws were brutal bastards, always barking like dogs, going mental over the slightest thing.

In those days, screws were mostly ex-forces, rejects unfit for the field and fucked in the head. One screw was known as The Monster. I hadn't asked why. I should have. He liked to boast about his two suspensions for brutality and was rumoured to have murdered men in the punishment block. I was a new boy when he batted me across the head for not having my shirt tucked in. He started telling me what he thought should be done to scum like me, the lowest form of life, ranting and raving about Hitler and mass extermination. Frothing at the mouth saying he'd like to round up every pisstaking black bastard and bury them all in the dirt where they belong. He said there was nothing worse than a half-a-nigger like me, and my mother should be hung, drawn and quartered.

I butted him in the face with force. A broken nose can be a great leveller. And if anyone deserved it, this cunt did. But I came to regret it.

They dragged me down to the punishment block. It was like a dungeon. I was stripped naked, beaten and put through hell for weeks. My head filled up with so much hate I thought I'd explode. It changed me.

Back in the wing I became a bit of a nutter. I was game for any violence going. It felt good beating the living hell out of somebody, passing on the hate. There was this nonce that we had the eye on. He'd been arrogant enough to choose integration instead of the perverts' wing. He made out he was this big violent criminal not to be fucked with, playing out a fantasy, when really he'd been raping little boys. Three of us grabbed him, ripped his trousers down and threw boiling water over his bollocks.

He was writhing round with his privates on fire when by surprise this Hell's Angel walks in and castrates the bastard. There was blood all over the walls. The biker had been missing his kids and apparently worked in the meat trade. Quiet bloke, never said much. Those are the ones to watch for, I suppose. The nonce was taken away, treated as an attempted suicide. He knew not to grass, even without a dick. The screws couldn't give a shit.

Something else that blew my mind in prison was hearing that my mum had been mugged. She was set upon by two black kids on her way home from a cleaning job. Another implosion.

The first thing I did on release was head to the part of Edmonton where she was attacked. I prowled around the streets looking for revenge. After being locked away, the outside world felt like it was on fast-forward. Edmonton was a mostly white manor in those days, hardly any black faces at all. But one thing was for sure, I wasn't going anywhere until I'd bashed fuck out of someone.

On a bench round the back of some flats, two black kids were passing a joint. They were slouching about, looked well stoned. One of them nodded at me as if to say Alright. I slipped out the baseball bat, didn't ask questions, couldn't really give a fuck. One went down without a hitch, the other had enough of his marbles to start waving a knife about, missing my face by an inch. I laid into him hell for leather, carried on even when he was out cold, couldn't care less if I killed him.

Soon afterwards, my mum was diagnosed with cancer. She passed away before I knew it. I found it hard to accept, started losing my mind. Prison was nothing compared to this. Friends would knock around and I'd tell them to piss off, throw punches. I was ripping cupboards off the wall, carving slices up my arm. I hardly left the house. Then one day I snapped out of it. Carried on as if nothing had happened. Thankfully nobody mentioned anything. I appreciated that. I started going back to the football, getting hammered, being stupid. But it wasn't the same. It seemed more like an act, going through the motions. Underneath were a lot of dormant demons. Nobody had to remind me: I'd become a different person.

Leafing through my mum's old stuff I found pictures of my dad. I'd never seen him, hadn't even thought much about him. I couldn't miss what I never had. The pictures intrigued me. He was a sharp dresser, confident-looking. I stared at his face trying to read into his thoughts, his life, what he was about. My mum's line had been that sometimes people just don't get on, so it's better for everyone to split. You can't argue with that. I wouldn't want some bastard hanging around the house slapping her about. Some of my mate's dads were right arseholes, gamblers and drinkers that were nightmares to live with. Sometimes I'd counted myself lucky. But these photos drew me in.

I found the divorce papers. When they broke up he moved to Willesden. I wanted to find him. I went to the address, a decrepit looking place near Willesden Junction. Looked like it had turned into a squat. It was no surprise that he wasn't there. I knocked on every neighbour's door. One old woman actually invited me in for a cup of tea, must have needed the company. She remembered him, said he was a big drinker, used the pubs in the area, but had moved years ago. The pubs were all black and Irish. I was relentless, asking around with my photographs, buying people drinks. Some remembered him, but it was as though he had disappeared.

I started checking dosshouses, spread the search over a wider area. I'd go up to down-and-outs around Notting Hill, Camden

14

Town, give them a can of Tennents and a bit of change, get them talking. Finding the old man wasn't even difficult. I followed all the predictable routes and it paid off. I first met him in a drinking den in King's Cross. It was full of crims and alkies, cards and dominoes going. It smelt of prison.

I was shocked when I saw him. He was standing at the makeshift bar with a wasted thousand-yard stare. A million miles from the suave Jamaican in the pictures. I had imagined him to be a fairly big bloke, tall like me. But here he was in the flesh, small and frail, haunted-looking. He looked like he needed a wash. Some self-respect. I was embarrassed. I wondered what my mum ever saw in this wreck.

For a second I considered maybe leaving things be, walking away, leaving history alone. What's done is done, move on. Instead I walked up and blurted out those words. I'm your son.

He looked directly at me, then he started laughing, slapping my back. I joined in, my arms around him.

Then suddenly he turned deadly serious, basically told me to stop having him on. I think he told me to fuck off. It took me quite a while to get it through to him. He went all quiet and I felt like I was dragging up something horrible from the past. I suppose it was the shock. We stood drinking and watching the cards, meditating over the situation. Didn't say much. For me, the anti-climax set in fast, almost immediately. Finding the man had been a little obsession of mine, but now that I had I could see only a vast empty space before me. Looking back, I know that at this period I filled in this space with booze. Like father, like son.

After that I'd meet him fairly regularly. King's Cross, Camden Town, anywhere. We'd sit in a quiet corner of a pub, the drinks on me. To get to know the man somehow seemed necessary. A shrink would have said I was trying to get to the root of myself – find out who I am. They would have been right. But I wasn't thinking about all that. I just got on with it, did what

I had to do. My head was in a mess. It was hard getting anything out of my dad. His mind seemed half stewed; he was always pissed, and on medication.

I learned he'd been in and out of jail. Minor stuff. Making a nuisance of himself mainly. He told me his cellmate, an IRA guy, had been battered to death by screws in front of him in Brixton Prison. My dad had jumped in. It explained his broken teeth and lazy eye. I wondered had they beaten the senses out of him as well, left him mentally ill. He'd never asked about my mum once.

One night I showed him some photos, told him how I felt now that she wasn't around, the only person I had. His reaction wasn't what I wanted. He'd seemed more pissed off about his IRA mate. I felt like shaking some emotion, some response out of him. She's dead, you bastard, dead. But I left him sitting there, staring into space, headed out into the night.

I remember kicking over a load of bins, a tart asking did I want business, telling her to fuck off, and doing the same to some geezer asking did I want drugs. I heard him mutter something back; I lunged in, fists flying. A knife appeared, but I got it off him, slashed him across the face – one, two, three. He clutched his wounds, blood everywhere, screaming in shock. Suddenly I thought, what have I done? I almost felt like helping him, but there were witnesses now, people coming forward, and I ran off, headed back to Tottenham.

I saw my dad one more time. He was dossing in a squat down the end of Caledonian Road. The place was a tip, almost uninhabitable. We were playing cards, working through a bottle of whisky, heavily pissed. An argument started. I can't even remember what it was about. But the subject led on to my mother.

I couldn't believe what I was hearing. He started slagging her off, cursing her name, saying how that bitch had ruined his life etc. I was stunned, knew the marriage had ended in a bad way, but he was taking the piss. I knocked the hat off his head, told him to shut the fuck up. There was a big scar across his scalp like somebody had tried to lobotomise him. He went crazy, mouthing off in a thick patois I could hardly understand.

If I was smart I would have walked away, laughed it off, some old waster that had lost his marbles years ago. But I didn't. I stayed right where I was, gripping his lapels, glaring into his mad eyes as he told me I wasn't his son, he didn't have a son, he was sterile, my mum had run around with other men, every fucking man in Tottenham and beyond, got herself pregnant and made a fool of him. He'd left and hit the bottle, turned into a wreck. She'd ruined his life and he should have killed the rarse clart bitch long before the cancer had.

I nutted him straight on the nose, felt the sickening crunch. I went for him again but he was fast, grabbed the bottle and smashed it across my head. When I shook off the shock he was swinging a knife and I could tell from his eyes his intention was to kill me. I managed to get it off him and we grappled across to the open window. I was surprised at his strength; he was fuelled up on pure hate, but it wasn't enough. He was hanging out, his back over the window-sill, my hands around his neck. It was three floors down to the back-yard below. With one hand I grabbed his legs and flipped him overboard. The last thing I heard him call me was a fatherless bastard. He disappeared into the black. I can't even remember how I got home.

Life carried on. King's Cross was a rough old place, and I figured the death of a dosser wouldn't exactly be anything unusual, foul play or not. I convinced myself it had been self-defence, tried blotting it all out. I woke up in cold sweats. Lived in denial.

The council kicked me out of the flat I grew up in, and I moved to a dingy bedsit in Seven Sisters. I'd stopped going to the football and was on strong antidepressants, smoking a lot of grass. I spent a lot of time walking the streets in a daze. Sometimes, in my paranoia, I imagined the police were watching my every move, waiting for their moment. I was wrong. It didn't happen.

I was lost and needed direction fast. Around now the Acid House thing was kicking off. For me it was a godsend. E cleared my head, brought me back to the land of the living. My depression lifted and I put a lot of shit behind me. I'd found a scene where I belonged.

I made some good friends and eventually had the amazing break of being taken on as a roadie with a soundsystem. We'd do all the illegal raves around the M25 and were soon getting bookings up and down the country. It was like I'd been rescued, like somebody up there was watching over me. These guys became big players on the club scene and in the early 90s I was touring all over Europe. I was off my head every night and loving it. Best days of my life.

When it came to an end it was no surprise. On a lot of people drugs were taking their toll. Casualties left right and centre. People turning to the hard stuff. One of the main players had some dodgy dealings with an Essex firm and ended up buried in a gravel pit by the A13. For me the party ended there. It had been a dream.

Back in the real world I got out of London, didn't need the shit, moved out to Stevenage. I took up painting and decorating. I had a decent run of work, nice car, a little flat. I met Siobhan, fell in love, and things were looking perfect. Her family were a Dublin crowd from Luton. Good people. Siobhan and I moved in together, had a daughter, Charlene. It was the perfect set-up. But things took a turn for the worse. The old demons playing up, wreaking havoc in my head. The rows would be phenomenal. She'd insist on seeing her old mates for girls' nights out and I'd be playing the jealous boyfriend, spying on her through the pub window, barging in throwing my fists at any bloke that had even looked her way. I also started knocking her about at home. It was like I couldn't allow myself or those closest to me any happiness.

One day when I came back from work there were suitcases in the hall. Siobhan's old man was standing in front of her. 'If you ever lay a hand on my daughter again, I'll fucking murder you'. He was raging, looking like he was going to burst. Siobhan's face was a mess. I hated myself. Hated my mad state of mind, the demons that haunted me. I watched them go. I didn't see my daughter for quite a while, didn't push it. When it all calmed down, I became a Sunday dad. A few hours doing McDonalds, the park, the cinema. It was all I deserved. As for getting back with Siobhan, I just hoped that one day it would happen.

When the decorating got slack I tried mini-cabbing. You could make money but only if you really put in the hours. I got a job on the door of a club in Luton. It seemed easy work, most of the punters friendly. Regular faces out for a good time. One night we had to throw out a couple of Asian kids that were being a nuisance. On the street one of them starts giving me attitude. I give him a smack and tell him to fuck off. They go, that's the end of that. Half an hour later a car pulls up, the same guy strutting out, his jaws grinding away like he's snorted up a gramful of Dutch courage. I go to belt him again, pissed off now, but he pulls out a gun and points it in my face.

At times like that, the world just stands still. I fought an urge to lunge at the bastard, what the hell. A part of me believed it was worth it, whatever the outcome. But instead I just stood there, unsure, as he played his power game. He dished out some verbal – nigger this, nigger that, don't fuck with the Pakis etc – and thankfully that was that, him and his mates driving off laughing.

But that was the end of bouncing for me. All it took was one skinny little runt out to earn himself some kudos and you were a goner. I walked away. And I was lucky. A couple weeks later one of the doormen took a bullet to the head, survived but was left with brain damage. I'd left London for a quieter life but it seemed as if the city's bad influence was following me. Around this time, the black-on-black killing thing in London had reached a frenzy. I picked up *The Voice* once and saw my old mate Kelvin staring back at me. He'd been blasted away six months before and I hadn't even known, a lot of the murders getting hardly any media. He was one in a gallery of victims. Something like: 'The Shooting Must Stop'.

Kelvin had got into big-time dealing, all the usual shit. After the Carnival he went to a party in Kilburn. A Harlesden crew walked in and blasted him over the balcony. Down on the concrete, he was still alive. The gunman calmly walked downstairs, pumped four more bullets into his head. When I thought about it, I was surprised he'd lasted as long as he did. I was glad to be out of Tottenham. Away from all that shit. In London you had three-year-old kids talking like Kingston gangstas, the cockney thing I'd always known well out the window. I couldn't feel any real sympathy for Kelvin. He'd chosen that path. I had my own problems.

The only good thing about the 90s was that I kept straight, worked like a horse, six, seven days a week. I needed my mind occupied, needed to keep moving on. The nearest thing I did to illegal was sell a bit of puff to my mates down the pub.

In 2004 I moved to Ponders End. It was the wrong side of the M25 if you ask me, way too close in to London, but it was temporary, near to work. Maybe soon I'd move out to Milton Keynes or somewhere. A year on I was still there. That's when the police burst in. That's when my life changed.

Sitting in the cell in Tottenham police station I thought I would face a petty drugs charge. But when they took my DNA the database revealed I was wanted for the death of the man I'd thought was my father. The police on the newly re-opened Blakelock case were over the moon, amazed they'd got me on something so major. I was charged with murder.

Technology had allowed my demons free reign to finally laugh in my face. With the new DNA swabbing, people were getting busted for stuff they'd done a lifetime ago. Pulled in for that girl hitch-hiker they'd picked up and raped twenty years ago. Pulled up on that bloke they'd thrown out the window and tried to forget.

I'm now back in HMP Wandsworth after all these years. I've been offered a sum for a book. The writer has told me to get lots of notes down. There's a market for this sort of thing. He tells me I have a lot to sell: the football hooliganism, early crime, the riots, acid house, the death of my dad. Tells me I could be publicized as an anti-hero. He could be right. I've certainly never done anything heroic. My life seems to have been anti-everything. It's landed me where I am today. But people love a story. Me, though, I'm the bastard who's had to live it.

As I try to piece my life together, separate the fact from fiction, it blurs into one. For years I've been kidding myself, living in denial, convincing myself that I've simply been unlucky. But underneath I wonder is there a psychopath inside me. I wonder if I'm actually evil. Maybe this book is my chance to confront the truth. The horrible reality that lies within the fog of my fucked-up skull.

My father never came at me with a knife at all. In court I claimed self-defence. The judge called me 'a wicked, despicable man'. Maybe he was right. I simply beat the bastard and threw him out the window. It's amazing they never got me right away. Shows how far they were bothered in investigating the death of a dosser.

As for Broadwater Farm, in reality I did more than throw a few bricks. I was in the posse led by Kelvin that chased that copper out of the car park and descended on him like a pack of wolves. We ploughed into him, hacking away. He didn't stand a chance.

21

Yet I tell myself it isn't true. It's all a bad dream. I'm just a normal bloke. I should be with my missus and kid, a regular Joe with a job, a car, an ordinary life. Yet I'm caged away and forced to stare at the walls. Forced to wonder what sort of person I really am. It fucking scares me.

GRAFTER

I'm released from the 'Ville at 7.30am. Then I'm straight round to Jan's in Holloway, knocking on her door, but there's no answer. I'm out on the landing for five minutes, calling and banging, when I finally hear her voice.

'Go away, Mick. You're not staying here.'

'Come on, Jan. I've just been let out.'

'The answer's no. Now piss off.'

She hadn't visited me in my whole six weeks inside, but I'd written to her enough times saying I was sorry. Surely she had some heart.

'Don't be like this, Jan. Where am I going to stay?'

'It's not my problem.'

I carry on begging, but after a while I feel I'm talking to myself. Fuck it then: I'm just going to stand here. I'll wait here all day, I'm not moving. I light a fag and lean by the balcony.

I'm standing there three floors up, taking in the view, the streets about to be pissed upon by rain - when I realise I'm fucked. I've got a see-through HMP bag containing my life's possessions, nowhere to stay tonight, and my missus doesn't want to know me.

Suddenly I feel like crying. But maybe I should've thought of that before I messed up and got nicked again. Me and Jan had the biggest row ever, practically kicking lumps out of each other. Then I went out, got wasted and tried to drive away in somebody's car.

I've got two choices. Either I throw myself down to the concrete below, or I pick up my bag and start walking. Where to I don't know. Probably the nearest off-licence. Something I'd sworn to myself I wouldn't do.

Then behind me I hear the door open. I turn and Jan's standing there. We look at each other, then she shakes her head. 'Come here.'

'I appreciate this, Jan, honestly, I do.'

I settle back in to home life, but it's only a week before I'm back on the drink. Nothing too serious though. A few cans a day, the odd binge here and there. It's controllable. What's more of an issue is money. Jan's working but only scraping by; I'm bringing in sweet FA. I'm making an effort to change, applying for jobs, but it's getting me nowhere. I soon realise that if I'm not going back to doing houses and cars, then I'd better start thinking out of the box.

Pat Murphy is an old mate. He's one of the few of us who'd got out there and made some money. These days he calls himself a businessman, and I suppose he is. He's involved in all sorts. I'm not one to beg, but I've run out of ideas. I give him a call.

'Listen, Mick,' he says. 'I like you, okay. But shall I be polite or do you want the truth? You're a liability. You've been in and out of prison now for, how long? Listen mate, knock it all on the head. It's getting you nowhere. Get sensible. Get a job. A plain nine to five, that's my advice.'

I hang up on him. Murphy might have once been an Islington boy, but he hadn't known struggle in years. These days he had a five-bed house in Barnet, and was just like every other rich working-class fucker in this country. Greedy, selfish, and with no sense of his own history.

I mope around the flat until even Jan is feeling sorry for me.

'Come on, Mick, something will come up. What about that sweeping job with the council?'

'Didn't get it,' I say, slumped on the sofa in clothes I haven't changed for days.

I'm necking back cans, but they're not even doing anything. I need something different. Something to take my mind off it all. I've fucked up in this way once or twice before, but maybe I don't care anymore.

I get my jacket.

'Where are you going?' Jan asks.

'Out for a bit.'

On Seven Sisters Road I see Shane and Jonesy drinking on a bench. I join them. One of Shane's eyes is black and his forehead stitched. I ask him what happened.

'Long story,' he says, so pissed he can hardly talk.

Jonesy's laughing at him. Then he turns serious, asks if I've heard about Johnny boy. He was found dead the other night in some toilets in Hackney. An overdose.

Jesus Christ. I put my head in my hands. I'd known the bloke all my life.

'Listen, I better go.' I head for home. Smack? I can't believe I even considered it.

A few days later the phone rings.

'Is this Mick?' a voice says. 'I've heard you're looking for work. Pat Murphy tells me you're reliable.'

'Yes, I am.'

I'm in luck. Turns out Murphy put a word in for me after all.

Clive is a slick-looking black guy who operates his business from above a shop in Kilburn.

'So, you're Murphy's man,' he says, swivelling in his office chair. 'Cool. I need more white guys around here. Sending black guys out to some of these addresses only looks bad. Attracts heat.'

Clocking my jogging bottoms and sweatshirt, he takes out his wallet. 'I think you need to smarten up a bit. Here, go clothes shopping.'

'Cheers,' I say.

'Don't thank me, it's coming out of your wages. You drive?'

'No licence.'

'Don't matter. You can use the buses and tubes. Probably quicker anyway.'

Clive seems to have his head screwed on. My job is running deliveries to some of the most exclusive areas in West London.

I hit the shops. I get kitted out in a three-quarter leather jacket, black jeans and a decent pair of shoes. There's a bit of sun out, so I add some shades.

'Look who it is - Al Pacino,' he says when I walk back in.

Clive runs a smooth, sophisticated operation. He has a dozen runners working on a shift system, providing twenty-four-hour service, quality to your door. I work noon till night. On the runs I keep the gear down my pants, and carry a machete for security. If the Old Bill pull me I'm fucked. But it's not my manor so they don't know me.

I'm into the swing of things, no problem at all. I'm buzzing around Maida Vale, Notting Hill, Kensington, delivering to flats, houses, hotels, seeing the sights and meeting all sorts, and what's more I'm enjoying it.

I'm finally bringing in some money and Jan's happy, but she doesn't want the details. Just tell me you're not getting locked up again, she says. I tell her there's nothing to worry about.

During work I stay sober, but afterwards I usually hit a pub or a snooker hall with a couple of the boys. Before long I'm nightly coming home blasted. Half the time I'm waking up fully-clothed on the sofa, and Jan's soon getting sick of it. One night I stumble in and she punches me in the face and we start fighting. Next thing I'm pushed out on to the landing and the door is slammed shut. I'm banging to get back in, but she won't relent.

'You're not coming in, Mick - never again!'

I leave her to cool down for a while. I pace the streets. In the end I head into the park and find a bench. I lie down and drop off immediately.

Hours later, I awaken. There's a group of figures around me. One up close trying to check my pockets. I push him off and jump to my feet, viewing the scene. Four youths. Three black, the closest one white.

'Gimme your money, prick,' the white cunt says, pushing me with both hands back down onto the bench.

The others are laughing and whooping, and he flicks out a small knife, turns to them: 'I think this guy needs to learn how we do business round here.'

I whip out the machete and slash him across the face. A gasp goes up, the bloke staggering backwards, and I follow through tearing him to ribbons.

'You want some too, you cunts?'

Bodies are panicking and scattering as I run them like rats. In the chaos one of them pulls him up, the bloke half running, half falling. Figures disappearing into the dark.

Suddenly I'm alone, standing there breathing. The park is silent now, the whole thing like a dream. I look at the blood on the blade and all up my arm. Did that really just happen?

I walk back to the flat. I discover the keys were in my pocket all along. I rinse the blade and give my jacket a clean. Then I throw my clothes in the washer and have a shower.

When Jan gets up, she sees me watching morning TV. Tired, she snuggles in with me on the sofa. Last night is forgotten.

Work continues on. I'm grafting hard, staying out of trouble, and one night Clive calls me into his office. He's got his feet up on the desk and it's the first time I've seen him smoking a spliff.

Word is he hardly drinks, smokes, touches anything. Too sensible.

'My man,' he says. 'Come in, sit down.'

I take a seat. On the wall there's a business diploma. And next to it a picture of a famous sportsman, signed: *To Clive – keep wheelin', keep dealin'.*

He tells me he's impressed with my work performance.

'Can't say you've put a foot wrong really. You turn up on time, you put in the graft, you get the shit done. It's not exactly rocket science, but you'd be surprised with some of the dicks I have to deal with. You want to do some overtime tonight?'

'Yeah, why not.'

He opens a drawer. 'You might need a tool for this run though. You'll be carrying a heap of cash.'

'Don't worry about it,' I say, opening my jacket and showing the strapped-in, sheathed machete.

'Not bad,' he says. 'But I'm thinking something a bit more instant.' He takes out a handgun. 'I usually do this run myself but I can't be arsed tonight. I need some zeds.'

He passes me the gun. 'Any fucker tries to rob you,' he smiles, 'shoot 'em straight between the eyes.'

'Is it loaded?'

'Full clip.'

'Nice one.'

'Here's the funds,' he says, handing me a small sports bag. 'Bring it straight to your boss.'

'My boss?'

'Yeah, Murphy.'

'Oh right, course.'

'You know his yard, yeah?'

'Yeah. Up in Barnet.'

'Nah, not that kind of yard,' he laughs. 'His timber yard - in Cricklewood. Just ring the buzzer. He's doing a late one in the office.'

'No problem.'

I leave with the gun and the bag, not even knowing where I'm going. Everyone thinks I'm well in with Murphy, but truth be told I hardly know the bloke these days.

Luckily on the street I see Sean, one of the other runners I drink with, a local QPR boy.

'Sean mate, listen. You know the exact street of Murphy's timber yard?'

'Yeah course. I thought you were one of Murphy's lumps on loan?'

'I am. Should have that tattooed on my forehead. But I've forgotten the road. You know how it is, too many doobies lately, mind all scrambled.'

'You crack me up.' He tells me the street, then nods to the bag. 'You doing the money run?'

'Yeah, Clive's knackered. He's up there puffing on the weed. Maybe I'll just make a dash for it. Straight to Heathrow and tomorrow I could be lying on a sunny beach somewhere.'

'A rainy beach, more like. Thames estuary. Washed up, minus your testicles.'

'Oh well, back to the daily grind I think.' I slap his shoulder. 'Catch you later.'

I take the bus along Kilburn High Road and Cricklewood Broadway. I get off near Staples Corner and head into the industrial estates. The streets are deserted this time of night, but nobody's following me so it's all good. I turn a corner and see the timber yard up ahead. Reaching the gates I'm ready to ring the buzzer when cold steel touches the back of my neck.

'Stop right there or I'll shoot.'

I turn to look and I'm gun-butted to the ground. A car door opens, another figure jumping out, and I'm grabbed and thrown into the back of the car. All in, the driver burns rubber.

'Is this all of it?' the two men next to me keep repeating, but I'm clutching my bashed-in head, the pain so bad I can hardly

29

think.

The driver tells them to shut up. 'Give me the bag up here,' he says, and they place it in the front seat. With one hand he has a feel of the cash. 'I think this little lot will do us just fine,' he says. 'Get him out of the car.'

The door opens and, with the motor moving at a steady pace, I'm thrown straight out.

I roll and land by the gutter. Slowly I pull myself up and sit by the kerb. I'm hurting bad. I feel for the gun and the machete – both still there. Then I put my head in my hands. Jesus Christ...

Back at base Clive is in front of me, fuming.

'You expect me to believe all this shit?'

'It's the truth - look at the fucking state of me.'

'What car they drive?'

'I don't know, it happened so fast.'

'You tell anyone about the run?'

'Course I didn't, why would I do that...?'

Then I remember I did tell someone. Sean. Who must have made a phone call. I say nothing. But Clive's heard enough. He punches me in the face and I stagger back onto a leather seat.

He grabs me up. 'You better bring me back that cash, and don't show your face till you do!' He pushes me towards the door. 'Now get the fuck out of here!'

I head to Sean's place. Marching into his block of flats I kick his door straight off its hinges. In the bedroom, he's up on his feet clutching a baseball bat, his missus sitting up shocked in bed. I grab the wood off him and throw him naked up against the wall.

'Where's the money, Sean?'

He's pleading his innocence, but I'm in no mood for it.

I grab the fucker by the neck and start squeezing. His missus is trying to pull me off and I kick her away.

30

'You made a call, didn't you - phoned some of your mates!'

Both my hands are around his neck now, strangling the life out of him. His missus is back on my case, screaming and pulling, and Sean's face turning blue, when he finally nods.

I let him go and he crumples to the floor, gasping for breath.

'Okay, I made a call... but I had to, I owe people...'

I pull out the gun and point it at him.

'Okay, okay!' he says. 'I know where it is. I can get it. They use my lock-up as their slaughter.'

We drive over to Acton. At the wheel he's almost in tears.

'These men don't mess about, Mick. They find out it's me, they're going to kill me.'

'That's better than what I'll do, Sean. I'll chop off all your limbs, pour salt on the wounds and let you live. Try that.'

After a while I shake my head. 'Why me, Sean? Why did you do it? I thought we were mates?'

He just shrugs. 'Money rules the world, Mick. It runs all of us, what can I do?'

The next day I walk into Clive's office. I put the bag and the gun down on his desk.

'It's all there,' I say. 'Sorry for fucking you around.'

He zips it open, has a look at the cash.

'You made the right decision returning this, Mick. Because you know stealing from me just ain't an option.'

'Listen, I didn't steal anything from you.'

Then I say it. I grass.

'For your information it was Sean. He saw me yesterday on the way out and put in a call. I had to half strangle the bloke last night to get it back off him.'

'Sean?' he says, surprised.

I nod.

'Okay. Leave it with me,' he says. 'Go back to work.'

31

For days afterwards I'm feeling nervy. Sean hasn't once shown his face. Then Clive comes up and speaks in my ear.

'I made some enquiries,' he says. 'Turns out his friends gave him an ultimatum. Return their cash or things get physical. Which must have shook him up pretty bad. Because his woman found him lying in a pool of blood. He'd slit his own throat.'

Smiling, he pats my back and walks away.

That night, I'm half-dozing in front of the TV, and Jan's reading the local paper. She asks if I've heard about the boy that was stabbed in the park. For weeks he'd been on life support, but now he's dead.

'Gang kids,' I say. 'Thick as shit. They can't spend five minutes without killing each other.'

'No, they reckon this one was a stranger. Totally random. God, the amount of psychos out there is getting scary.'

'Tell me about it,' I say.

Out doing the rounds, I'm not feeling myself any more. I feel people are watching me. Since the whole business with Sean, I'm paranoid to fuck. I'm dipping into the wares, trying to take the edge off things, but it's doing me no good at all.

One day, in broad daylight, I throw a bloke up against a wall, holding the machete to his neck.

'Are you fucking following me?'

He's shaking his head, begging for his life, and suddenly it occurs to me I might just be imagining things.

I let him go. 'Look mate, I'm not with it today. Here, take a few quid.'

He doesn't want to know, runs up the road wailing.

Things are getting too much, the state of my head not improving. One day when Clive calls me into the office, I realise this is my chance to come clean.

I sit down and before he can speak, I tell him I want to resign.

'I'll work till the end of the week, or until you find someone else, but either way I want to go.'

He stares at me, swivelling in his chair.

'Your call,' he finally says. 'Go ahead.'

'You mean I can just walk out now?'

'Yeah, go. Walk out that door,' he says. 'But one thing I want to make clear. If you do, I can't say I can guarantee your safety.'

'You what?'

'People can't just come and go in this business, it ain't in my interest. Look at the intel you've got on this place.' He points his finger. 'And you've already pulled the wool over me once already.'

'What are you talking about?'

'Letting me believe you were one of Murphy's trusted men. But it turns out that ain't really the case, is it?'

'Murphy got me this job.'

'He mentioned you, yeah. But I like to know the dudes I'm dealing with. And now after a little chat, he's turned round and been honest. Turns out he don't think much of you at all.'

'Now listen...'

'No, you listen to me,' he says, slamming the desk. 'You're going nowhere. You're going to keep grafting, keep pushing my product till I say so, you understand me?'

I stand up. 'Fair enough. But I want a holiday. I need a break. I've been working my bollocks off around here and it's doing my head in. I need two weeks off or I'm going to be of no use to anybody.'

He looks me up and down.

'Okay,' he says. 'Two weeks.'

So that's it then. Me and Jan are going away for a bit. I've got money saved, no problem. If I have to keep working for Clive when I get back, fine, I'll do it. I'll be clean by then. Recharged. And anyway, let's be realistic, what other job can I do?

I'm turning into the estate, all ready to break the news to Jan and get the fuck out of London, when a ten-strong squad of police storm out of a parked van and come straight at me. I'm thrown face-down onto the ground, cuffed and relieved of the machete.

'Michael Murray, I'm arresting you on suspicion of murder.'

'Murder of who?'

'The bloke you almost cut in half in the park, you scumbag.'

And that's how they got me. How I landed myself back inside, and this time for the long haul.

In court they tried painting me as a psycho, saying I'd taken delight in the attack. But what can I say? I did what I thought was necessary. They asked if I was sorry, but of course I'm not sorry. The bloke was a mugger with a stabbing conviction himself.

What drives me most up the wall is Jan. She spent all my savings on a lavish holiday. Then she met another man. Wasted no time at all.

The police want to move in on Clive and Murphy and the whole operation. They've been watching things for quite a while. They're questioning me regularly. Tell me if I play the game I could get my sentence halved on appeal. That would mean parole in only a few years.

So yeah, I'm singing away. I'm giving them everything.

I've got nothing to lose.

LIAR

I stared down from the public gallery, my bredrin Jermaine in the dock, and the jury about to announce their verdict.

J looked like he was carrying the weight of the world and I felt for him, I really did.

The guy was innocent. He didn't deserve this crap.

I'd known him for time. The charges were pure bullshit.

Then I heard: 'Not guilty.'

We roared and jumped in the air.

The judge was calling for silence but we didn't give a shit. The courts had finally got something right for a change. But what about the nine months J had spent on remand in Feltham, not knowing if he'd be looking at life? It wasn't fair, the whole system was rigged and it angered me. But right now J was a free man and that's all that mattered.

Outside he put a hand on my shoulder. 'You've been good to me Mark and I won't forget it.'

I felt like hugging him, shedding a tear even, but I suppose it isn't the way. We bumped fists. 'No probs J man, it's nothing.'

We were both the same age, but J always seemed older. He'd grown up in care and was streetwise from an early age, chasing girls and joyriding bikes when I was still talking little-boy stuff. He always had my back though. Like the time some Tottenham boys tried to stab me up and he flew in with a bike chain, scattering the lot of them. Supporting him through all this shit was the least I could do.

In truth, J was no angel. He'd got up to plenty bad stuff. But this? Dragging some girl into the bushes, repeatedly raping her, then battering her with a brick and leaving her for dead? That was serious sick-in-the-head shit. It was mistaken identity. A classic case. Lazy policework. Some sick fuck still walking the streets out there laughing about it.

The girl's family were staring over, giving us eyes, and when one guy started shouting insults the boys had to hold me back. It ain't worth it Mark, allow it. I wanted to knock the man down, I swear it. The girl was led crying to a car. No offence to her, going through what she did and that, but maybe if she'd got her facts right the guilty party would be safely locked up now.

We had a drink in a pub up the road, J's lawyer buying the whole house a round. Then we took the party back to Edmonton. Bare people turned out, quite a few girls too, and it was music and drinking and whatever else till the early hours.

It was almost dawn when I was up in J's bedroom, just me and him, the whole of downstairs littered with wasted bodies now. J was snorting up some coke as I asked him that age-old question.

'All that time inside - what was it like?'

'Easy really,' he said, rubbing his nose.

But he was kidding me, surely. Even if you're king of the wing, you're still restricted, still living with a hundred per cent men under lock and key. Can't be that nice.

He offered me a line, but I wasn't too into that stuff. I just wanted to drop down and sleep now. Soon I'd be heading home. J leaned by the open window while I sat on the bed, the morning outside a shadowy blue.

'Do you think they'll ever find the guy who did it?' I asked.

He shook his head, blowing smoke out into the air.

'Grow up,' he said.

'What?' I looked at him in confusion.

He turned to me.

'Bitch deserved all she fucking got. Look at what she put me through, man.'

'What are you saying?'

He looked me up and down like he had zero respect for me. During those nine months in prison he'd pumped himself up pretty big, and coupled with the weird glint in his eyes, I was suddenly seeing a Jermaine I didn't know.

'I'm saying what I'm saying,' he said. 'Because Mark man, you need to start wising up to things, serious. Stuff happens. That's life.'

No way. I stood up. 'Are you saying you did it? Is that what you're fucking saying J?'

He stepped closer, and for a few moments we locked eyes. Then suddenly he started laughing, slapping my shoulder, doubling up.

'You crack me up, fam - look at yourself!'

I stood there unsmiling as he pointed at me. 'I'm winding you up. Giving you a bit of face, a taste of prison. You asked me what it was like and I just showed you.'

J was fucking with my head and I didn't like it.

'Listen,' he said, putting his arm round me. 'You were there for me - visiting, sending me shit, doing this and that – and don't think I ain't going to reward you either.'

'Get off me.' I pushed his arm away.

He shrugged and walked back to the window. He tossed out his cigarette. Then he turned to me.

'Maybe it's time for you to head home now. I'm gonna grab me a girl from downstairs and be putting this bed to use - so I won't be needing an audience round here, you get me?'

Walking home I felt I'd been punched in the brain. All the sick shit described in court, did J actually do that? No way, he couldn't have. But who knows. I was baffled - I didn't know what to think. I just felt I didn't know the guy anymore.

My older cousin Tony had an office job with a building firm, and he got me some labouring on a house renovation. He said it might get me thinking about learning a trade. I was coming home each night knackered, so for a few days I saw none of the boys. Jermaine was messaging me repeatedly, but I didn't answer him. I didn't want to think of the man right now. If he was some kind of secret nutjob, then me and him were over.

One evening I was walking home when someone grabbed me from behind and threw me in towards some garages. What the fuck? I sprang up off the ground and saw J standing there laughing, sparring on the spot. Maybe once I would've seen the joke and fought back, but instead I just dusted myself down.

'The fuck you doing, J?'

'I was going to ask you the same question. How come you're not returning my calls? I thought it was always ride or die with me and you. Blood brothers innit.'

I pushed past him and walked back along the street.

'Come on Mark, speak to me,' he said, following along. 'You're acting like a girl, I swear it.'

I stopped and looked him in the eye.

'That shit you were chatting the other night. I want to know the truth.'

'Jeez,' he laughed. 'So that's what this is all about. I was coked, man. Probably talking non-stop bull all night. Ain't that what people do at parties? Chill blud, you're getting all strung over nothing.'

I stared at him – and saw the old Jermaine looking back at me. Suddenly I felt I'd been over-reacting. What exactly had he said anyway? I'd been on the weed and brandy myself that night so maybe I'd just blown things up. I started to feel a little so maybe I'd just blown things up. I started to feel a little embarrassed.

'Come on, allow it,' he said, shaking my shoulder.

I nodded and we walked on, and before long we were chatting and running jokes just like old times. On the corner we bumped into Pepe and G-Man, a blunt going round, and there was so much laughter and good vibes I couldn't believe I'd actually felt hatred for the man.

After a bit we carried on walking, J laughing at the state of my boots and the plaster in my hair.

'Humping shit on a building site? Never thought I'd see the day.'

'Money don't grow on trees you know. Some of us round here have to earn it. I ain't frightened of getting my hands dirty.'

'So you say,' he said. Then we stopped outside my house.

'Listen, you know I was gonna do you a favour? Well, I might have a proposition for you. Something big. Lucrative. Plenty men round here would be queuing up for a job like this. Join the team and you're gonna walk away loaded.'

'Nah, no thanks J. I'm doing fine at the moment. I mean, I've got to make a few changes in my life you know. Come September I might even go back to college. Maybe try to learn a trade or something. I don't want to jeopardize that.'

'Fine. No probs,' he said, his eyes going up and down on my face.

'Look J, I appreciate it, but...'

'Nah, you're cool. I understand.'

We bumped fists and he said he'd catch me later.

I watched him walk away. At one point he turned round and we met eyes. When I went into the house, my mum asked me something and I snapped at her. She told me I wasn't too old for a slap you know, and I said I was sorry. I realised I wasn't feeling good. Not about J and not about the whole thing.

*

I carried on working. I quite liked it. I was keeping fit, the sun was shining and I was earning decent notes. One day as I was running rubble up into the skip I stopped to chat to a girl who worked in the cafe down the street. One more chat and I'd have her digits I reckon. It wasn't the first time the foreman caught me having a break, but I thought nothing of it.

That night I got a call from my cousin. He told me the foreman had had enough of me and I was sacked - why hadn't I tried harder? Tony was one of these straight no-bullshit types, lecturing me down the phone how I was going to end up on the scrapheap unless I knuckled down and started taking my life seriously. After a while I hung up on him.

I went up to my room and lay on my bed. I couldn't believe it. Ever since leaving school I hadn't been able to hold down a single job. Now I couldn't even get through a couple of weeks' donkey work. I felt like a total wasteman.

J was making up for lost time, playing Romeo with his various girlfriends, so I didn't see him for a while. Then by the time I did I was absolutely broke. I was moping about the house, my mum doing my head in, and one or two of the boys said I should be getting myself out there on the roads doing business. They said they could put in a word for me. Shotting Class As wasn't my style, yet finding a viable alternative wasn't proving too easy right now.

'You on for the job then?' J said, both of us coming out of the dole office - except J had a hot-looking girl waiting for him in the car.

I stood there thinking about it, when he said:

'I'll take that as a yes then,' and I found myself nodding.

He told me he'd fill me in later. 'Be good,' he said and I watched him drive away.

Three nights later, what the job entailed was still unclear to me when a car picked me up at the end of my street. I sat in the back next to J, and up front were two guys he'd met inside, Fats and Drilla. Fats, who was driving, looked just like his name, while Drilla was wiry and shifty-looking, a brother to watch. I instantly disliked the pair of them.

I told J it was about time he told me what was happening tonight. He took a handgun from his waist and slammed home the clip. 'Two rich yuppies, one big house.'

The other two laughed. 'He only just told you now? Rah! Boy's totally green, man!'

J's power-playing was beginning to piss me off. Drilla threw me some gloves and a balaclava.

'There, you'll be needing that shit.'

Then Drilla took out a sawn-off shotgun, playing around with it trying to impress me, so I turned to the window just to piss him off. Guy was a clown. So was Fats, chuckling away as Drilla held the gun out from his crotch saying: 'I'm gonna slam some pussy so hard tonight bitch will be begging for mercy I swear it.'

We headed down through Tottenham, then turned at Seven Sisters towards Finsbury Park. I didn't even know where we were going, and by now I was regretting the whole thing.

Suddenly J pushed his gun into my side:

'Bam!' he said, and I jumped.

'What you doing!' I said and he just laughed.

I stared at him. What a prick. I kissed my teeth and turned to the window. Suddenly he grabbed my face back with his hand.

'You fucking cool?'

'Course I'm cool,' I said, shaking him off.

J had problems. He wasn't the same person these days. He had an attitude, an arrogance about him. Maybe prison did it, or maybe he'd been that way for years and I just hadn't seen it. I thought of all the times I'd done him favours, storing boxes under my bed for him, weed, stolen shit, God knows what, thinking nothing of it when in reality I could've done time for that crap. It's like the man had been using me all along.

We parked on a street near Highbury Fields, fancy townhouses lining each side. J pointed out the target house; a stash of top dollar jewellery inside, untold goods. We masked up.

'Let's do this.'

We hid at the sides as J rang the bell. When the door opened we flew in, a posh-looking guy in his thirties backing up with Fats' shotgun in his face.

'On the floor! On the fucking floor!'

A woman appeared, heavily pregnant, and Drilla was straight over, pulling her by the hair, the sound of everyone shouting and screaming on max now. For a moment I freeze-framed. What the fuck was I doing? Shotguns? Pregnant women? Was I really a part of this shit? Then I snapped out of it because regrets seemed pointless now. The best I could do was just co-operate and we'd be out of here as soon as possible.

'Where's the jewels! Where's the fucking jewels!'

The guy was on the floor, J and Fats beating him with their guns, while Drilla pushed the woman up the stairs, ignoring her pleas, grabbing her up every time she fell.

'Get up there, bitch!'

No way... this was as fucked-up as it gets. I ran up telling him to calm down and he almost pushed me down the stairs – 'Fuck you, pussy!' He disappeared up into one of the rooms with the woman. Then J came up telling me to help collect the loot from the main bedroom, while Fats stayed below with the man.

We were pulling out drawers and cupboards, filling our bags with anything that looked valuable, then J started looking under the bed for any hidden goods and told me to get cracking on the next bedroom.

I opened the door to see Drilla standing with his trousers down and the woman crying on her knees as he forced her onto him.

'Ain't gonna give a guy no privacy, no?' he smirked.

Without a second thought I lunged for him, but just then J appeared behind me, pulling me backwards out of the room.

'Yo, Drill,' he said, sticking his head back in. 'You better be saving some of that for me, man,' before closing the door on him.

He shoved his gun in my face. 'What's your problem, Mark, you getting all righteous again?'

'Get that thing off me J, I'm serious.'

He left it a few beats before lowering it. 'Get the fuck downstairs.'

I waited down with Fats, fifteen minutes like an eternity as he kicked and poked and shoved the sawn-off into the now semi-conscious guy's mouth like some kind of crackhead nutcase.

J and Drilla finally came strutting down the stairs, J fastening his belt, joking to Drilla about it being 'that bitch's lucky day', and I looked at him, unable to believe I'd spent nine months supporting the fucker when he was nothing but a scumbag rapist. He threw a loaded bag at me.

'Job done, let's roll.'

Heading back in the car little was said. At one point J told me he'd get onto me about my share but I ignored him. I didn't want to talk to him, see him, or even have him in my headspace anymore.

Once again the messages came rolling in, but I ignored every one of them. Then I was walking on the street one night and, deja vu, he jumped me. But this time I fought back. I got in a few punches, but soon he was all over me so I pulled out the blade I was carrying - a blade with his name on it.

He grappled it from my hand and threw me up against a wall.

'So you want to shank me now, yeah?'

'You're a freak, J. You should be rotting inside with all the other sex fiends.'

He backhanded me round the face.

'You better watch your tongue, I'm warning you. And if you've got any fancy ideas of chatting shit to people then your little sister might have to start losing her looks, you get what I'm saying?'

'Touch my family you die!' I shouted, but he just laughed.

He let me go.

'You're a prick Mark, do you know that? Here I am coming to deliver your earnings and you're acting like an immature schoolboy. Anyone tell you that attitude shit is old? Us brothers are playing the game now man, making money these days. It's time for you to start growing up.'

He threw a wad of notes at me and walked away.

Back at home with the wad on my bedside table, I sat and had a think. That dough was blood money, pure and simple. I thought about maybe shoving it in a church box, or even going back and bunging it through that couple's door. But my prints were all over it, and what good would it do now anyway? In reality I had debts to pay and I was skint. I needed it.

J got in contact again and this time, reluctantly, I answered. He told me to be at the end of my road at 8pm sharp. Another job.

'No way,' I told him, but he'd already hung up on me.

Again they rolled up in a stolen car, except this time Drilla was in the back. I climbed in with a stone-face and Drilla straight away slapped me across the head. 'Boy here look like he got lemon on his tongue!'

At the wheel Fats kissed his teeth, while next to him J said, 'That's coz he's a dickhead innit.'

I sat there fuming. I wanted to batter all three of them.

We drove to a new housing estate in South Tottenham. We

were robbing the home of a drug dealer called Killa B. From that name alone it didn't sound like a good idea, but what say did I have in the matter? Parking in, everyone masked up. Drilla took out two machetes, jacketing one and handing me the other.

'Any complications, lick off the guy's head.'

At the door a woman answered, black, twenties, and we rushed her down the hall.

'Where's the cash! Where's the fucking cash!'

She was struggling so much that Drilla and J got to work tying her to a chair in the kitchen. Fats, shotgun in hand, checked the rooms. He found the guy and chased him up the stairs.

A minute later, the woman bound and gagged, we heard a single shot.

'Looks like Fats wasted him,' J smiled.

He tucked his gun into his waist, and was about to head up to see when Killa B appeared in the doorway wielding a .44 Magnum.

Drilla let out a scream and Killa shot him where he stood, blowing half the head off his shoulders, a mess of blood on the wall as his body dropped.

J whipped out his automatic and shot Killa B twice in the arm, the gun flying out of B's hand as he tumbled backwards.

In panic we ran out the back door and across the garden towards the railway beyond the fence. Climbing over I turned to see Killa staggering out of the house, aiming his gun. A bullet whistled past my ear but J was struck twice.

He fell from the fence, rolling down through the bushes of the embankment.

I ran down and stood over him. One of his hands clutched his bloody stomach, the other was stretched out to me.

'Mark... please, help me...'

In the eyes of that balaclava I saw the old J again, the J I'd thought was my friend.

But the moment passed. I ran.

45

*

It's three months on now, and being the mystery man who got away that night, I'm still looking over my shoulder. It turned out Killa B is a serious player out there and Jermaine messed with him at his own peril. Everyone's in agreement of that and nobody seems to miss him. But words travel, and the day I tell anyone I was involved is a day I won't see the end of.

THIEF TAKER

In the morning we have a coffee, then she tells me she's got a few things on today so I take the hint. The night before we'd gone for a meal and had a few drinks, then she'd invited me back to her place. Not a bad first date by anyone's standards.

So by the door I say, 'So what do you reckon then?'

'About what?'

'Us - you know, me and you.'

'I'll message you,' she says, and already she's closing the door on me.

'Hang on a minute,' I say, putting my foot there. 'I'd like an answer actually.'

'I just think we're different people, okay. Now can you take your shoe away from my door?'

I push it further open. 'That's not what you said last night darling. In fact in the bedroom back there you couldn't get enough of me.'

'Well maybe I was drunk. Can you please go now?'

'One more date, come on.'

'I can't do it…' Then she says it: 'I can't go out with a police-man.'

'Oh, I see. Anyone but a copper, eh?'

'It just wouldn't be appropriate. With my job and everything there's no way I could possibly...'

'Save it, I've heard enough. You types fucking love yourselves.' I look her up and down. 'You suck a good cock though, I'll give you that.'

I remove my foot and the door slams shut in my face.

'Chauvinist bastard,' she shouts, so I give the door a good thump just to spook her. Then remembering last night's post-coitus joint, I have a word through the letterbox.

'With drugs on the premises I'd watch it if I were you. I've got friends... everywhere.'

Laughing I hit the street and head for the overground. It's my first Saturday off in months and within the hour I'm back in Enfield, home soil, and meeting my mate Colin, a postie who spends half his life in the pub. I bring two pints out to the beer garden where he's sitting rolling a doobie.

He asks how it went with the posh bird last night and I tell him the story.

'If you got a shag out of her then what's the problem?' he says.

'If I wanted a one-night stand I'd fucking buy one. I was hoping for more. A hopeless romantic, aren't I?'

'Did you tell her you were a copper?'

'Yes – while I was smoking that shit,' I say, watching him light up. He takes a toke then offers it over but I shake my head.

'Up till then she'd thought I was a common or garden office bod. A nine to five cog in the machine, no problem at all. Then like a spanner I throw reality into the works and that's it, sayonara.'

'What was her problem?'

'She was a fully paid-up liberal, Colin. All police are racist, all muggers need a cuddle. She worked high-up in the council. Last night telling me all the holidays she goes on, three or four a year. Fucking coining it in. There's more socialism up my arse mate. The fiddles that go on behind Town Hall doors you wouldn't believe.'

48

'Where did she live?'

'Hackney. You know the score, knobs in the houses, scumbags in the estates. Mind you, hers was a snazzy new-build place, so they probably demolished a whole council block for that one. I used to work down there when I was a probationer. Homerton. We broke into a flat where an old man had spent the whole summer dead and rotting in his armchair. Neighbourly round there, aren't they?'

'Jesus.' He shakes his head. 'I was at a rave down that way once. Back in the day. A big warehouse. Your lot raided the place and I got a truncheon over the head from a prick on a horse.'

'Probably deserved it you cunt.'

'It all went off. One minute peace and love, next thing there's bricks flying, running battles, the works. The Old Bill were well naughty, I remember that much. There was half a dozen of them giving this bloke a right kicking.'

'Different times now mate. Wouldn't happen. Fucking cameras everywhere.'

'You can't get any digs in no more?'

'Not as easily, no.'

'But you still can?'

'Depends on the situation. But mostly there's no need. There's plenty worse ways to piss somebody off, believe me.'

'You fucking love it,' he laughs.

'I don't actually. The Job's fucked. You've got one doing the work of five, wages are shit, perks non-existent. The gyms, section houses and canteens have been sold off - if you couldn't kick some civilian arse now and then there'd be no incentive whatsoever.'

'You crack me up.'

'Anyway,' I say, changing the subject. 'What's it like living back with the missus? It's got to beat six weeks dossing on my sofa.'

'Think I preferred the sofa actually. What about you and

Debbie, you said you might be getting back with her?

'Did I? Must have been drunk. That shag a while back when her bloke was away has done more damage than good I reckon. Which reminds me, I'm picking up my son at three. I've got a few hours with him. Every time she hands him over it's the same thing, no words, just this icy look. I blame the fucker she's with.'

'Same old shit with my ex.'

We sit in silence for a bit. Then Colin says, 'I've been thinking.'

'About what?'

'Australia. New Zealand maybe.'

'Go on.'

'Well, it'd be a new start, wouldn't it? You know how it is, this country's finished.'

'Right barrel of laughs you are, I tell you.' Then I head to the bar for another round, because if I don't, he won't. The cunt's even more skint than me.

Walking up Debbie's path, her bloke Kevin is at the window arms-folded staring at me. He works for a loan company, hence the spanking new Audi A8 in the drive. Should be in prison the crook. Him and all the other banker cunts.

Debbie answers the door.

'What are you doing here? I've told you already, Alfie's got a cold and he's not leaving the house today.'

This is news to me, but she insists she left a message. I check my phone and there it is. Then Kevin is on the scene sticking his oar in.

'You're in no fit state to look after a child anyway,' he says. 'I can smell the drink from here.'

'What did you just say?'

'You heard me, *officer*.'

I lunge for him. Only weeks ago my son had asked if he could start calling me Jack rather than Dad as he felt he had a new dad now. I made little of it, but I knew where it was coming from. Debbie gets between us, and I stop when I notice Alfie on the stairs crying. Deb rushes to him.

'Go on, Alf,' she says. 'You tell Jack what you told me earlier.'

'You're not my dad,' he says, unable to look at me. 'I don't want to see you anymore.'

I'm standing there in shock. I knew I'd let him down these last few weeks due to work, but I never expected this. I step back, the front door closes and then I'm walking away, eyes welling.

Me and Debbie had spent our marriage if not all over each other then rowing like nutters. Maybe it was just our method of stress-release, but it can't have been nice for Alfie. My own parents had fought like cats and dogs too, except with violence thrown in for good measure. My old man was a drinker until he died, then despite a peaceful home for the first time in an age, my mum soon pined away.

It's probably why I became a copper. To somehow try and help people.

It seems laughable now.

I get home, sit back and crack a can of Stella. Perhaps the whole thing's nothing to worry about. Little Alfie's stubborn, that's all. Just like his mother. Just like me. It'll blow over. I get a text from my workmate Kermit. A police party tonight, somebody's birthday. I'm not in tomorrow till 4pm so a break is just what I need.

I roll into the nick fifteen minutes late, hungover to fuck. I kit up then head to the briefing room where twelve colleagues are enduring mugshots of the usual uglies. I mutter a quick sorry and thankfully the Inspector keeps talking.

'Finally boys and girls, we have this gentleman,' he says, pointing to a close-up of Mike Tyson's more vicious-looking twin. 'Wanted for rape, arson and a nasty assault on a stranger who remains in a coma.'

'Nice,' someone says to some chuckles and the guvnor rounds it up. 'Okay, now get out there and bring me some bodies.'

Then he points at me. 'O'Leary, get your arse in on time you lazy bastard.'

We head out to the car park, Kermit and Rambo telling me how hammered I was last night, happily filling in my blacked-out final hour. Apparently I started a fight, got kicked out of the venue then walked across several car roofs shouting how some loan shark called Kevin was a dead man. I tell them I've heard enough and make for the fast-response car where Mack is already in the operating seat. I climb in behind the wheel.

'What's this I hear about you kicking off last night?' he says.

'Not you as well,' I groan. 'Look, whatever you've heard I don't want to know, because as from now I'm officially off the drink.'

'That's what you said after the Christmas party when you—,'

'Please, don't remind me.'

There's phone-snatching, shoplifting and two drunks trying to kill each other on Camden High Street. All the usual fun and games. Then it's dark when we're called to a stabbing near Queen's Crescent market. We pull in behind the flats, a small crowd by a teenager who'd been chased and stabbed. His ankle's twisted and he's got two nasty gashes on his thigh. I begin first aid as Mack clears the scene. I tell the bloke he's lucky the blade didn't sever an artery, but when I probe for info he fails the attitude test.

'I'm suffering here man, I need help not an interrogation. Go catch some criminals instead of harassing me - now where's this fucking ambulance?'

Again I ask if he knows his attackers and he tells me to piss off and quit the inquisition. I shake my head. Here I am down on my knees playing Mother Teresa when I'd rather be stamping on the fucker's leg and watching him scream. I ransack his pockets and pull out his wallet. Inside, along with £470 quid, are twelve wraps of crack.

'Surprise surprise.'

'No way, that's for personal use. I've got addiction problems, I'm the victim here.'

'Course you are.'

I check his ID on the system which reveals a list of robbery and dealing convictions. An ambulance pulls in, then the Trident boys arrive to take over. I hand them the wallet, drugs intact, cash four hundred short. Fuck the cunt.

'A dozen rocks,' says the detective. 'And he didn't even try tossing them?'

'Nope. They get more clever every day.'

I'm in a pub-restaurant in Covent Garden, my date a blonde called Nicki.

'So how long have you been single?' I ask.

'Six months now. I won't lie, I caught my boyfriend cheating on me. All men are bastards,' she laughs.

'A lot perhaps, but not all,' I say, and the way our eyes meet confirms I might not be sleeping alone tonight. Nicki works in admin and rents in Stroud Green. She likes running, swimming, hiking. A country girl lost in the urban jungle and looking for a mate.

I tell her I'll be running the marathon again this year. Used to be a gym freak, big into weights, but these days prefer the great outdoors, good ten milers to run off the stress.

'You don't work in accounts at all, do you?' she says.

I shake my head and come clean.

'So you're a policeman,' she shrugs. 'Big deal. Why the big secret?'

'A lot of people don't like the police. They think you're never out of uniform, always on the look-out. But it's not like that at all.'

Outside she suggests her place and we jump in a taxi. We're snogging away like a pair of teenagers until we come up for air near Finsbury Park. Stuck by the lights I notice an altercation. Two men grappling. Somalians. I see the flash of a knife then repeated stabbing motions. Instinctively I jump out of the car.

STOP POLICE.

The knifeman pauses, tosses his victim aside and legs it. The chase is on. A patrol car pulls alongside me, I shout that I'm Job and point back to the victim, keep running. The man tumbles into a bystander, loses his blade but rolls straight back up and keeps going. He turns down an alley then takes a right along some garages. By the time I turn the corner he's gone. He's hiding somewhere. I edge through the dark. Out of habit I reach for my baton but it's not there. My CS spray wouldn't go amiss either, but weighed down in my full kit I'd have lost him long ago.

Then I hear a noise by some dumped rubbish. I close in.

'Okay mate, it's over. Come out with your hands where I can see them. Police will be everywhere in a minute, you've got no chance.'

A mattress upturns and he jumps at me with a lump of timber. My left arm takes the blow, right smashing him hard in the face. He staggers, drops the wood but comes back at me and we're rolling on the ground. The man's putting up an energetic fight but he's all skin and bone, and eventually I'm on top, punching him repeatedly until he submits.

'About fucking time,' I say, out of breath, turning him over and kneeling on his back, angry now because not only has he binned my romance for the night, but I'm absolutely covered in shit.

I search the fucker. Three phones, a bit of weed and six hundred quid in cash, which goes straight in my back pocket.

Drug-dealing scum.

Four plod come running, ask if I'm alright.

'Never felt better,' I say, wiping blood from my lips. 'But I think our friend here might beg to differ.'

Back at the stab scene there's police everywhere. The victim has been rushed to hospital, serious but stable, a pool of blood on the pavement. The Inspector slaps my shoulder, says good work, then a uniform shows him a bag containing the knife.

'Excellent,' he says.

He turns to me and asks if I managed to retrieve the cash.

'Cash?' I say.

He tells me what happened. The suspect had robbed a late-night grocery, the victim worked there and chased him out, hence the fight on the street. Suddenly the wedge in my pocket feels like a dead weight

'No Guv, your officers took over once I managed to restrain him.'

'Okay, no problem.'

I head to Hornsey Road nick for the debrief and inevitable form-filling, immediately stashing the dough behind a radiator in the toilets. I message Nicki to apologise, but the whole thing seems to have freaked her out. Great.

Hours later, finally ready to go home, I'm approached by two suits from Professional Standards (i.e. the Anti-Corruption Squad) for an informal chat. Jesus, do these cunts ever sleep? We sit and the female of the two tells me the stolen cash still hasn't been found.

'And?'

'We thought that perhaps you could enlighten us?'

I scrape back my chair and stand. 'Is this a wind up? Off duty and unarmed I took down a violent criminal tonight and you're insinuating that I'm a common thief?'

'We're not insinuating anything,' she says. 'But I might as well inform you, there are also questions about undue force being applied. Not only is the suspect's face a mess but he collapsed during an interview. He's been taken to hospital with a suspected fractured skull or worse. Now if that turns out to be the case, do you realise the implications, constable?'

'You people are unbelievable. I most likely saved a man's life tonight and all you can do is stir up shit.'

They look at each other.

'Er, I don't think you've been informed.'

'About what?'

'The victim. He didn't make it. He passed away two hours ago.'

Debbie tells me I can see Alfie again. She even admits he's been missing me, which cheers me up no end. I take him to London Zoo, something I've promised him for ages. I wouldn't say I'm a massive zoo fan as it's humans who deserve locking up, but we have a pleasant day out and I feel we're bonding again.

The only fly in the ointment was an incident as we walked back along Parkway to Camden tube. A BMW slowed alongside us, the driver giving me a gun sign. I recognised the scum instantly. Desmond Daniels. I'd nicked him last year after he'd skipped bail for the rape of a girl he'd been pimping, and here he was, back on the street after no time at all and taunting me in front of my son.

I told Alfie it was just a man messing around, but the following night after work I paid a masked visit to Daniels' current address and keyed both sides of his car. He was number one on my shit list now, so could expect these little hassles on a regular basis. Maybe I'd take it further, put a word in and get his flat raided. The options were endless. It was looking to be fun.

I'm out in the car with Golden Boy, a newbie who's rapidly proving himself in the school of no-nonsense policing. He's disarmed a gunman, talked down a suicide and made an arrest that led to a shitload of Class As, and that's all in the last few weeks. He's good, but he's got a rocky road ahead. These days young upstarts who make waves don't always tick the right boxes. We slow down to eyeball a group of scrotes loitering by an estate. Message received we keep going.

'I can't believe Standards think they can treat you like that,' he says.

'Start believing. We used to be a force, now we're a glorified PR firm. Forget criminals, it's us versus the management. To be honest though, it's looking like a lot of hot air now anyway. Turns out the fucker's skull was fine and at the hospital he even tried to escape. He'd obviously tossed the money during the initial chase. I feel bad for the victim though. Clean record, well liked in the area. If I'd got there a few seconds earlier he'd still be alive.'

'That's London for you. A fucking shithole. The sun goes down and it's Night of the Living Dead out there.'

I turn to him. 'So says the fucker who's from Luton.'

'Shut up, you Spurs supporting tosser.'

'London born and bred pal, so course I support Spurs. Only a cunt wouldn't. Yid fucking Army mate.'

Just then a call comes in. Naked man with axe smashing up cars in Gospel Oak.

'Right, the fun begins,' I say, changing gears. 'Disco lights and va-va-voom.'

'Your round,' says postie Colin, planting down his empty glass.

'You're having a laugh,' I tell him. 'I bought the last one.'

'Who's the man pulling out the big wads nowadays, you or me?'

I walk to the bar. Suppose he's got a point. The other day I was at a mansion flat in Hampstead where an old man had died in his sleep. A loner, no family. Waiting for the undertakers Mack sat with his feet up watching TV while I had a wander. In a biscuit tin at the back of a cupboard I found four grand. Whoa. I gave this one some thought. But ultimately the gent had peacefully departed this world, I was still here and on my salary money wasn't too plentiful.

'So how's the dating game?' Colin asks, supping his fresh pint.

'Over, hopefully. I've had a proposition.'

'Oh yeah?'

I lean in. 'Debbie and Kevin aren't such a happy couple any more. They're rowing all the time, Deb told me as much. Kevin's away at a conference tomorrow and she's asked me to fix her washing machine again, and you know what that means.'

'You dirty rascal.'

'She's my wife, we're separated not divorced. This could be my in-road. It's what I want. What I've always wanted to be honest. Back in the family home where I belong.'

'Knowing you mate, you'll get what you want.'

I take a lug of my pint and place it down.

'I always do, Colin. I always do.'

CALLY BLUES

We were together on the sofa watching TV – until suddenly the window went in, glass flying everywhere and a lump of concrete landing right in front of us.

Liz screamed, but I was on my feet and straight out the front door wanting to murder the bastards.

'Nonce!' they shouted as they disappeared around the corner. I stopped and returned to the flat.

'Don't worry Liz, they're gone. The same bunch of toerags. Just bored kids, nothing better to do.'

'I can't stand much more of this Terry, I'm serious,' she said, holding her chest. 'Next thing they'll be trying to burn us in our bed.'

Hugging her I promised things would soon be okay. Then I went to fetch her pills before she gave herself a nervous breakdown.

As I boarded the window, the bloke next door started giving me gip about the late-night hammering. I almost went for him, but Liz held me back. I had to behave. I'd only been out of jail for five weeks and one bit of trouble I'd be back serving the rest of my sentence.

After this I stayed in for a few nights, didn't go out cabbing. But soon I was so skint that I had no choice.

'Look, I'll only be a few hours, I promise.'

I set off in the car and picked up two punters outside a pub in Upper Street who looked like they were waiting for a taxi. I took them over the river, made twenty quid, then did the same outside a pub in Bermondsey. Nice trick. But it's outside the clubs you make the real money. Not tonight though. After a promising start I was soon wasting my time.

Back in Islington I headed to O'Rourke's on Caledonian Road for a few swift ones. I did the secret bell ring, the door buzzed open and I headed upstairs into the drinker. Groups were gambling at the tables while Frank Ryan, one of the few friends I had left, was seated as usual at the bar.

'Here he comes, my favourite kiddie fiddler,' he laughed.

'Not funny, Frank, not funny,' I said, taking a stool.

'Chin up, Tel. The coppers get you for whatever they like these days, we all know that. Anyway, how's life?'

'Shit,' I said, taking one of his cigarettes. 'For one thing I'm skint. For another, I've got bricks coming through my window. It's getting out of hand.'

'Get off that estate of yours, it's not good for your health.'

'It'd be the same anywhere. Words travel.'

'How's Liz coping?'

'Her nerves are shot, Frank.'

He mulled over his whiskey for a while, then said, 'How long do we go back?'

'Since forever mate, why?'

'Well, you've helped me enough times when I've been in the shit, so let's just say I owe you a favour.' He winked but refused to elaborate.

The next evening I noticed a blacked-out van parked across from the flat. The following night it was there too. Then the kids were back outside, chucking stones and mouthing off.

'Come on out and we'll fuck you up.'

Another chanting: 'Pee-do, Pee-do!'

I was debating whether to grab my samurai and take a run for them, when four masked bruisers emerged from the parked van wielding bats.

Most of the gang ran, but several didn't make it, and I watched as the men beat them to the ground, working mercilessly. Job done the van sped off, the injured youths only dragging themselves away at the sound of the sirens.

By the time the plod knocked on my door there was only an empty street and puddles of blood. I don't know what you're talking about officer.

A few days later I saw four youths loitering by a wall, all cuts and bruises, one with his arm in a sling, another with a full leg cast. How they could parade themselves in public in that state I didn't know.

'Alright lads,' I smiled as I walked by.

They stared, said nothing, but when my back was turned I heard: 'You're a dead man.'

I spun around. 'Am I now? Well, I feel alive as fuck mate. Happy as Larry in fact. How about you, how do you feel? Not too healthy by the looks of things.'

Phoning Frank, I told him I owed him one.

'No worries Tel,' he said. 'Those boys love it.'

The trouble ceased. Not that it stopped Liz from fretting. She never left the house now, and most of the time sat medicated in front of the TV, staring at the screen like her life depended on it. It was good she had the distraction I suppose. But if a neighbour slammed a door she'd be shaking and panicking, fearing all hell was breaking loose. I told her not to worry. Our problems were over now. Frank had sorted it.

I carried on cabbing, and one night I picked up four pissed-up girls from outside a club in Camden.

'You're licensed, yeah?' the girl in the front said, knockers spilling out of her top.

'Of course,' I said.

Then I had to listen to their cackling all the way to Hendon where I finally dropped three of them off.

The girl next to me wanted to continue on to Mill Hill. When they asked if she'd be okay she said, 'What, you think I'm frightened of him?' and they laughed.

I drove on. The car was silent now, the suburbs thinning out. I found myself sneaking glances at the girl's jugs.

Then she noticed and pulled up her top. 'Eyes on the road okay.'

I turned on the radio. Dire Straits. Started tapping along.

'You like this then?' she said.

'Yeah, I do actually.'

'I'm not listening to this crap,' and she turned it over, singing along to some pop shit.

I switched it back onto 'Sultans of Swing'.

'What are you doing?' she screamed, but I caught her hand before she got to the dial: 'My car, my music.'

She pulled her hand away, staring at me. 'You've got a real problem, do you know that?'

'Listen, you tart, you're pissed so just behave okay.'

'Did you just call me a tart? You bastard!'

'God, I don't know how you kids are brought up these days, but you need taking over the knee and given a serious slap.'

'You sexist piece of shit. Let me out of the car right now.'

'No skin off my behind darling.' I pulled over. Then she was out and tottering away along the road. I jumped out. 'Er, I think you owe me some cash, don't you?'

'You can dream on if you think I'm paying you a penny.'

Bushes and trees lined each side of the road, cars flying by. She was staggering along, clearly out of it, but this was no joke now, I wanted my money. I grabbed the handbag off her and started rooting. She went ballistic, hitting and scratching me until I pushed her to the ground. 'I want my cash, okay!'

At one point a car pulled over, some busybody asking if everything was alright. 'It's a domestic,' I told him. 'Now piss off.'

Off he went.

'You've broken one of my heels, you bastard,' she hiccupped, unable to get herself on her feet.

I stopped for a moment, took a deep breath, reminding myself to calm down.

'Look, I'll ask you nicely okay. Just give me what you owe and I'm out of here.'

She started screaming and suddenly I was dragging her aside into the bushes.

'You want it like this do you?'

I slapped her round the face. Then she was biting my hand and I was hitting her harder, and everything about her, the way she was dressed, the way these slappers always dressed just made me fucking angry. She was struggling and trying to scream and then I was on top of her, hand over her mouth... and I suppose I got carried away.

Afterwards I stood over her. The girl was groaning, only semi-conscious now. Jesus Christ, what had I done? I backed towards the car and got the hell out of there.

Driving back I was cacking it. At one point I pulled over to get myself in check. If the girl called the police I'd be heading back inside and this time for a stretch.

A brainwave hit me. Maybe the girl would still be there, unconscious in the bushes. Perhaps I could drive back and kill the bitch. Why not? I had nothing to lose. Toss her in the boot, bury her somewhere then torch the car, problem solved. But what was I thinking? Murder, killing people? I was losing the plot.

Two knocks at my window and I jumped in fright. It was the police.

'Evening sir. Could you step out of the car please.'

I got out. Two of them.

'Everything okay with you sir?'

Then I noticed the breathalyser and it clicked – it was just a routine breath check.

'Fine,' I said, perking up. 'I just pulled over to make a call. And you'll even find I've stayed on the orange juice tonight.'

The test was negative, everything was in order and within minutes I was off on my merry way. In fact, I was so relieved that I almost forgot the whole thing. And once a few days passed without incident, I more or less did forget it.

Why kill myself over it? After all, it takes two to tango, doesn't it?

One night after a quiet shift, I sat in O'Rourke's with Frank. The topic of conversation was money, the both of us pissed.

'I remember the days when you were making dough here, there and everywhere,' he said. 'Fingers in every pie going.'

'Yeah, but those days are gone, Frank,' I said, staring into my drink. 'I brought the car out tonight and hardly made one fare. A man can't even make a few quid from an honest graft anymore. It's fucked, Frank, the whole thing, whole country, it's finished.'

'Old news,' he said.

'You know what happened last week?' I went on. 'I had some tart in my car who brought me out to the sticks, then just walked off. No money. Go fuck yourself.'

He leaned in with a grin. 'I'm surprised you didn't make her work for it.'

I stared at him. 'And why would I do that?'

'Er... no offence Tel.'

I turned away. 'None taken.' Then I looked at my drink and pushed it away. I'd had enough. I stood up.

'Off already?' he laughed. 'It's only 4am.'

'Yeah, nice early night for a change.'

I set off along the Cally, the only soul out walking. I passed one boarded up pub, then another. Once it seemed there were laughs to be had on every corner. What's happened to the manor?

I turned into the estate looking forward to hitting the sack and waking up in a better mood when I heard the sound of car doors. Turning, I saw the four youths I'd had words with coming straight for me. I ran but I wasn't fast enough, and soon I was on the ground and they were kicking away.

Then they stopped, one of them hovering over pointing a gun and the other three saying: 'Do it, shoot him!'

The boy's hand was trembling.

'No, please...' I begged.

He pulled the trigger and there was a flash of light as the gun exploded. He screamed, clutching his bloody hand, then his mates grabbed him and they ran back to the motor, burning rubber.

I sat there in shock. The dodgy gun lay next to me, and so did two of his fingers.

'Listen,' I told the police. 'I haven't slept in forty-eight hours, can I go home now?'

They'd accompanied me to the hospital for a clean-up then escorted me straight to the nick.

'Four youths attempt to blow your head off and you don't even know what they look like?'

'Correct. I just want to go home okay.'

One of the detectives leaned back. 'Last of the swingers, hey? The no-grassing rule doesn't exist anymore Tel. It's dead and gone. It was all a myth in the first place. Name a single face from history and I'll tell you right now he was a grass. You help us, we'll help you. You've been in and out of the system your whole life Terry, so don't play naïve. And look at your last bit, a fucking nonce conviction.'

I slammed the table. 'I'm no nonce and you know it.'

'Okay, I'll be straight with you. The toerags have been brought in, we've got them. One of the little cunts is related to a face I've been trying to put away for years. For now locking up his favourite nephew will do. But only you can make that happen. So I need a positive ID, a signed statement and you testifying in court.'

'Are you having a laugh?'

'Fair enough - back to you and the kiddies then. Maybe we need to start looking into your lifestyle a little closer. We can discover all sorts of things these days you know. A nice little raid on your flat and who's to say what we might find? You fancy another stretch Tel?'

I shook my head. 'You cunts.' Then I told them everything.

Back at home, things with Liz were going from bad to worse. Finally she moved out to her sister's in Essex for a while. It would have made sense me going with her, but her sister hated me. I'd have to sit this one out alone.

One day nipping out for some fags, a car screeched up beside me. Two heavies jumped out, bundled me in the back and we were off.

'What the fuck's going on?' I shouted.

The bloke riding shotgun turned to face me, his ugly mug a sight I hadn't seen in years. It was Mad Kenny Kane. We weren't friends then and it didn't look like we were now.

'No friendly greeting then?' he said. 'Last time we had dealings you were flogging my wares to loved-up rave kids, making yourself a packet. Then you run off with a stash and lucky for you I'm carted off for an eight in Wandsworth. Convenient that, don't you reckon?'

'Come on Kenny, that was a long time ago. And as far as I

remember I only lost it because I was nicked myself for GBH.'

'You, GBH? The only people I've heard you assault are underage kids. Bad news, Terry.'

'That's bullshit. Believe the police and you're a bigger mug than them.'

'I think you better watch your language, don't you?' he said, his face hardening. 'You've got a court case coming up I hear.'

We pulled over on a backstreet overlooking the railway. They pulled me out of the car. Then grabbing me they lifted me over the wall, suspending me upside-down by the legs. I screamed as a train rushed by below.

'Are you going to testify?'

'No!' I yelled. 'No..!'

'Can't hear you,' he said, repeating it until they were dangling me by only one leg.

'I WON'T TESTIFY, I SWEAR TO GOD, PLEASE!'

They pulled me back and dumped me on the ground. I lay there sobbing and shaking while they laughed.

Kenny came down close. 'One word and I'll have you strapped to a chair, wired up and screaming for your mother, have you got that?'

He kicked me three times in the ribs and I heard the car pull away. I lay in agony.

How had I got myself in this mess?

It all began with a prostitute called Tina Bryne.

I'd been driving round the back of Euston one night and the urge just took me. She climbed in, twenty for oral and got working away. Then afterwards I realised I had no cash. The row spilled out onto the road and by the end of it she was on the ground wiping her bloody face and swearing I was going to pay. I drove off and thought no more of it. Then a few days later I was arrested for rape.

She'd told them I'd forced her down on me then kicked the shit out of her. When they said she was underage I couldn't believe it; she looked twenty-five at least. But I suppose crack and heroin can do that. I just lost my rag on her. But I denied everything. Told Liz it was just a row over a fare and she believed me. But the jury didn't.

With my ribs aching like a bastard, I dragged myself home. Then I went with my brief to the nick and told them I wanted to retract my statement.

The next day there was a knock at my door. Through the spyhole I saw the two detectives.

I grabbed my samurai. 'You're not coming in. I don't care if you've got a fucking warrant!'

A laugh came through the letterbox. 'Put it down Zorro. Just come out and we'll have a little chat. No hassles.'

We walked around the block in the rain. 'Nice day for a stroll, don't you say?' the big one said. Then passing some garages he suddenly punched me in the face and his mate twisted my arm and got me on my knees.

'Please, I'm an injured man.'

He came in close. 'Play silly bollocks with that statement and your life won't be worth living, that's a promise. Are you looking forward to prison again Tel? A nice ten this time for drugs, guns, kiddie filth - our choice. Is that what you want?'

I had three days to get my arse down to the station and get the ball rolling, or else.

I sat in O'Rourke's downing the whiskies.

'I'm fucked, Frank. I really am. What am I going to do?'

I watched him mull it over. 'Well,' he said, nodding to the next room where a big poker game was in progress. 'I don't want to raise your hopes, but old Ray McKenna's in tonight. And I might be able to have a word with him.'

Frank and Ray had history, Ray a copper based at Hornsey Road. An inveterate gambler who would sell his own mother for a flutter.

'Do you think he'll be able to get the coppers off my back?'

'Well, you know what the Adams boys used to call him – Mr Magic. But he'll want paying and it won't be cheap, I know that much.'

The next day Frank got back to me. McKenna wanted seven grand.

'I'd help you out Tel, but I'm a bit short at the moment. Raise the cash though and the coppers will leave you alone, he guarantees that.'

'I'll raise it, Frank, don't you worry about it.'

After a long hard think there seemed only one option. A short, sharp bank withdrawal. I got hold of an imitation gun and headed off the manor. Kilburn High Road seemed about right.

I barged into the bank masked up and screaming blue murder, civilians hitting the deck and the cashiers working quicktime as I waved my piece about, swearing any funny business a customer dies. Job done I was out of there and down the backstreets before you could say Flash Gordon.

Somebody up there was finally looking out for me. McKenna was paid off and the whole case was quietly dropped from lack of evidence. Result. I got no more local hassle, and Liz was even talking of returning home. Life was good again.

Then one night I was having the craic with Frank when the police came bursting through the door. I thought it was a raid on the club, but instead my two favourite detectives came straight for me.

'Terry, you're under arrest.'

'What for?'

'For the rape of another 15-year-old girl. Mill Hill, remember that one, do you?'

'No way!' I shouted as they put the cuffs on me, reading me my rights. Then I leaned in, seething: 'I paid you lot seven grand, you cunt.'

'You'll need a lot more than that to get you off this one, Tel mate. Our files are bulging with unsolved rapes. Seems to me you've been a busy man.'

I turned to Frank. He looked baffled.

'It's a lie,' I told him. 'Don't believe a word of it. I swear to you Frank, it's bullshit!'

He just kept staring at me, looking me up and down.

DEATH OF A PARTY

It's the end of a three-day binge and time for me to go. Si's trying to get me off the floor, saying his girlfriend's coming round, which I know is bullshit because she left him last week after he blacked her eye. But I'm not going to argue. Si had got hold of some cash and we'd spent the whole weekend smoking it up into the air. But when it's time to go, it's time to go. I stand up, squinting at the daylight.

'Sorry, Mac,' he says. 'I just need to clean the place up, get myself together and that.'

'No worries Si. I've got a few things on anyway.'

I take the lift down with a pram-pushing teenage girl, one of her kids eyeing me warily from behind her legs.

'Boo,' I say and he jumps.

The girl turns round.

'Only joking,' I say. 'No harm done.'

'Take your jokes elsewhere,' she says, moving out of the lift.

'Nice to be nice,' I call.

I take the backstreets to Kentish Town Road then head towards Camden. It's a sunny day and there's music in my head, but within minutes the craving is kicking in, my system threatening a revolt.

By the tube I bump into Roadie Ron. He stops begging the

moment he sees me. Alright Mac, he says. I tell him he's looking sharp in his new leather pants and he says he can get me a pair for thirty quid. No thanks Ron, my rock 'n' roll days are over I think. Then he's trying to sell me a methadone prescription. Back in the 80s he'd worked for AC/DC, Motorhead, the Pogues. But shit happens.

'No, I need the real thing mate. I've been round Si's on the pipe for days, I'm fucked.'

'Is Simon at home? He'd take this off me for definite.'

'Leave him Ron. I think he needs a bit of time to himself.'

'I heard he threw his bird down the stairs or something.'

'Don't know about that, but it wasn't pretty, put it that way. She's left him and he's torturing himself about it.'

'He needs to forget all about her. I saw them once up the road and she was kicking him in the head trying to get him off the ground. I had to pull her off him.'

'Yeah, well.'

I tell him I better get on. Things to do. Which isn't a lie.

I make a beeline for Sainsbury's. Check the security - go. I mingle with the paying customers, then I'm straight out the back door with a jacket full of men's shaving goods and four organic steaks. I head to Benny's place in the Clarence Way Estate, the bloke standing in his doorway taking the piss.

'Come on Benny, that's prime beef there. And look at all these razors. I could go round the pubs and make a killing on this lot.'

'Don't let me stop you,' he says, closing the door on me.

'Whoa,' I say, putting my foot there. 'Okay, twenty it is.'

I head for the betting shop in Queen's Crescent to get myself fixed. Then I sit in a stairwell shooting up. Instant relief. I sit forward, elbows on my knees. I hear the sound of schoolkids in a playground. A ball being kicked against a wall. A radio playing an old Oasis song.

Music was once my life. I was the guitarist in a band, playing the circuit, looking for a break, but it wasn't happening. After too long doing the rounds of the Robey/Falcon/Bull & Gate the band fell apart. I was signing on, working weekends in Camden Market and going nowhere. It was the summer of '94. Trying to form a new group in the Velvets/Stooges/Sonic Youth-vein was proving difficult. Bands were packing away their fuzz pedals and getting out their Kinks and Beatles songbooks, aiming no lower than *Top of the Pops* and actually getting there, fast.

Around the pubs I met Si. He was the singer of Leatherette, an indie-glam-pop outfit that were going places. Si was a classic frontman; a mockney torch singer with mod hair, a retro suit and the kind of heart-throb looks young girls die for. Watching him at a packed Dublin Castle blew me away. I'd forgotten just how fun pop could be. I became a helper of the band, hanging out at the Good Mixer then piling back to Si's for more. A&R men were at every gig. Finally they signed to Polydor and PR firm Savage and Best.

Si's dream had seamlessly happened - start band, get signed, live the rock 'n' roll dream. Mine hadn't, but I was in the thick of it having fun at least. Then one day he told me to meet him in the pub, he had some news for me. I watched him walk in with a grin.

'Welcome to Leatherette, Mac. You're coming on tour.'

He wasn't kidding. Their bass player was out after refusing to give up his high-flying day job, so with me being an all-round cool geezer, he said, the decision was unanimous. The band were supporting Gene on a 31-date UK tour and I had three days to pack my bass and get my shit together. I was over the moon.

Being on the road was a whirlwind, with all the excess I'd imagined. But headliners Gene were consummate pros which tempered us somewhat from gloriously fucking up. Every night we belted through our set, Si winning over the audience each time. Back in London we played some raucous gigs at the Garage and the Electric Ballroom, and had spreads in the *NME, Melody Maker*, even *Smash Hits*. Our single made no.18 and we played on *Top of the Pops* alongside the Boo Radleys and Supergrass, the Britpop thing in full swing. It was all happening. Photoshoots, interviews, radio shows. We headlined our own tour, teenage girls fainting and being dragged out of the pit. Our next single reached no.12.

'I'm a fucking pop star!' Si shouted one night in the Mixer, albeit ironically because in-house that night were several big players. Louise Wener from Sleeper told him he was a one-hit-wanker and he turned to show her his arse. Kiss that, he said.

We cut our first album, then it was off to Japan for eight dates with Marion and Salad. The Japs were bonkers and Si even gained his own stalker. She'd be at the front of all the gigs and outside the hotel at every city, sending him crazy notes. It culminated in Osaka when she ran at him with a knife, our tour manager and two porters holding her back. On the plane home we were laughing saying he was going to die like John Lennon.

We were living on coke and Stella, but doing well on it. One night after a cracking performance on *TFI Friday* we were looking for somewhere to go. Someone suggested a flat where a few of Elastica were staying, a 24-hour party zone. We jumped in a cab to Camden, the arse end of Royal College Street, council blocks everywhere you look. Walking in we saw three quarters of Elastica and half of Menswear with the tin foil out doing heroin.

'Let's get out of this dump,' I said to Si. 'Place is full of fucking junkies.'

'Hang on geez, I might stick around,' he said, a barely-dressed Anita Pallenberg-alike walking up the hall smiling at him.

'In that case I'll leave you to it,' I laughed, slapping his shoulder. I'd had enough anyway. I walked back home.

Our album was released to rave reviews and we set off for another tour. UK and Europe. France and Italy loved us. Then we were booked to try our hand at cracking America. Six club dates along the East Coast and a final night in LA. Polydor were talking of big things, putting a lot of money behind us, and if all went well there could be amphitheatre dates supporting the Cranberries, perhaps even REM. This was a whole new level.

But stateside was our first taste of failure.

Our first night was in Boston. We were checked into the worst hotel in the worst part of town. Oh well, crack the beers open, have a line, carry on. Then we played the gig in a half empty sports bar. Si took his act down to the bored seated punters, pulling Elvis moves in front of guys in work clothes more interested in their bottles of Bud.

Someone soon lamped him one and we jumped down to help, the fracas becoming a free-for-all until our tour manager hustled us out to the van just before the cops pulled in. I had a black eye, Si had a gash on his head where he'd been bottled, Pete our guitarist lost a tooth and drummer Dan had knuckles so fucked that for the next few nights he could hardly hit his snare.

The LA show was cancelled so we played our final night in New York. We were announced as Leatherface from Manchester, England, and two pissheads were constantly heckling and throwing nuts. When a full bottle flew, Si walked off and our rugby-playing drummer jumped down and nutted one of the drunks. Another night, another brawl and again we had to be rescued from the chaos. At JFK airport Si got caught carrying a forgotten stub of a spliff and we were all dragged in, strip-searched and delayed for hours. Si was the last to be released.

'Now get your pot smoking ass back to the UK,' they told him.

'I will,' he said, 'with pleasure.'

In London we were back in our element. More gigs, more parties, more drugs. We mimed our latest single on Saturday morning kids' TV after caning it all night with Jarvis Cocker and the boys from Supergrass, off our heads talking to hand puppets and curiously loving it. Si took home the female presenter and they spent the weekend shagging in his new Delancey Street flat.

As for me, I was now living in Primrose Hill with a posh blonde who did PR for Creation. It was a cushy flat and she didn't rent, she owned. When she'd be working away I'd bring back female company, playing the lad down the pub laughing about it. But perhaps I should have kept quiet.

I came back one evening to find her over the kitchen worktop and a bloke with his trousers down giving her one. As Sarah vocalised her pleasure, the man turned to me, carrying on. It was Liam Gallagher. Understanding sweet revenge, I took a beer from the fridge and went inside to watch TV. We had an important gig in Germany next week supporting the Oasis fuckers so I could hardly rock the boat, could I? But when Blur came on the telly I turned the volume up loud. An hour later with Laughing Boy gone and Sarah fresh from the shower she told me to pack my bags and get the fuck out of her flat.

We hit the studio to record our second album. We were aiming for a larger sound incorporating strings, but even getting the basics down seemed difficult. Nothing was sounding right. We just couldn't pull it together. After thirty takes of a vocal Si kicked over a guitar and stormed out. He'd been temperamental lately, but the pressure was on so it was understandable. Polydor wanted big sales on this album or they were threatening to renegotiate our contract. They were still pissed off at us about America, and more worryingly had signed a lot of new bands, but I was keeping my head together about it. A few years ago Blur had been threatened with the same thing. Then they released *Parklife.* Our new material was the best we'd ever written. We just had to catch that feel on tape. Thing was, we were on our second producer and still having problems.

'Don't worry boys, I'll go and get him.'

I headed out of the studio expecting Si to be pacing about in the yard having a fag. Instead he wasn't there and we didn't see him for two days. I checked all his haunts, even phoned his parents in Oxford in case he'd done a flit back there. Nothing, no sign. Then I thought of one place I hadn't checked: the party flat on Royal College Street. Nobody answered the door but I could hear the radio on so I broke in through the side window. Sure enough there he was on the floor, strung out amongst several other bodies.

I dumped him home. Then next day he called me round to his flat for a talk. He still looked terrible and suddenly I was no longer angry at him, but worried as a friend.

'I've been doing it on and off for quite a while, Mac,' he said, sipping a glass of JD beneath a poster of Bowie's *Low*. 'But I'm finished with it, I honestly am. I've made the decision. I'm going to pull myself together.'

Back in the studio we began making headway, working night and day, pouring our hearts into it. Si got his vocals down then slipped off for a spell at the Priory.

I was drinking in the Pembroke Castle in Primrose Hill one day when I noticed Liam Gallagher in the corner with a group of hangers-on. After a while he swaggered over.

'Hey, knobhead,' he said. 'How's your smackhead mate? Heard he's in the loony bin.'

That was it. I lunged for him, we wrestled and suddenly there were people pulling us apart. Liam was straining at the leash, shouting how he was going to rip me to pieces as his entourage dragged him out of the pub. I stood there shaking my head. Why nobody had yet smacked the fucker I couldn't fathom. But the following week I heard that somebody did. His own security guy. The hulking ex-SAS monster had enough of him and put him flat on his arse. It earned him instant dismissal, but I reckon it was worth it.

With Si clean and a new single due from the forthcoming album, we set off for our most extensive tour yet. UK, Europe and Japan. Four months. But before long there were problems. Constant coke, alcohol and lack of sleep was finally getting to me. On stage I'd be losing track of what I was playing, wondering where I was, sometimes who I was. Si was back on the smack and Pete our guitarist had joined him. Even the hired keyboardist was dabbling. Our drummer, strictly a beer and spliff man, was missing his girlfriend and new-born baby and complaining how he was surrounded by fucking drug addicts.

For all of us touring had become exhausting. We were on a conveyor belt - another gig, another hotel. Here we were, doing what we'd always dreamt of doing and were we enjoying it? Not one bit.

With heroin all around me I finally succumbed, using it to come down off all the coke that I needed to perform. It took the edge off, but it was strictly temporary, something to help me get through the tour, then back home I'd fuck it out the window. Finally we reached Japan. This time it was one long trippy nightmare, brown being hard to find. We couldn't wait to get home.

Back in London there was bad news. Our new album wasn't shifting enough units. Reviews in the weeklies could have been better, but we blamed the record company. They'd hardly advertised it. Other bands were being promoted with full page ads, why weren't we? We sat watching bands like Mansun, Kula Shaker, Ocean Colour Scene break through to centre stage while the album we'd put so much into slipped further down the charts. Our next single reached no. 56. If this was our demise then it was happening too fast. We played some dates around the country, finishing with a lacklustre gig at the Astoria 2. Afterwards we ended up at a flat in Hackney doing crack and heroin.

'I'm out, I can't do this anymore,' our drummer said, walking out halfway through a rehearsal.

'Fuck him,' Si said, lounging on a chair in the Ray-Bans he now never took off. 'Let him go. The bloke's a wanker anyway.'

Within a week we'd found a new drummer. We needed to get things up and running again, start banging out the goods. But by now 'musical chemistry' usually meant sitting around a rehearsal room chasing the dragon.

Times were changing. All around us Britpop bands were falling away. In Cool Britannia unless you were selling like Blur and Oasis you were in trouble. And if worries about being dropped wasn't enough, we were also completely skint. Where was all our money? Noel Gallagher was sipping bubbly with Blair at No.10 while we couldn't afford the rent. We met up with our accountant who explained where all our earnings had gone. Record label, publishers, licensees, agents, PR firms, the list went on. Basically we'd been generating cash for everyone but ourselves.

Then it happened. We received a fax from Polydor that contained one word: Goodbye. Almost overnight the party invites dried up and people we'd thought were friends were blanking us on the street. That was it. Freefall. Pete our guitarist vanished back to where he came from, and me and Si moved to a flat above a greasyspoon in King's Cross; crack and heroin the order of the day.

Time passed. A year, two years. Between us we cleaned up, went back on it, cleaned up again. Si even got back into the biz for a while, managing low-level bands. I travelled. Did this, did that. Washed up in Southend, more of a drugs town than London. After involvement in a warehouse burglary I did some time in Chelmsford prison. Then I ended up back in Camden.

I met Si again. Both of us were back on the gear, but Si wasn't doing too bad. He'd got himself a council flat in Kentish Town and was in a relationship with a girl called Holly, an on-off user like himself. It was serious, he loved her. Maybe together they'd give up for good. I was glad for him. Si was the best friend I'd ever had. He might have got me into the band, but he hadn't got me into drugs. You make your own choices.

A few months later I got into a bit of trouble with a dealer called Wayne. I'd done some selling for him, and was left with a sizeable stash of his gear while he did seven weeks in Pentonville. I'd sold most of it and smoked the rest. Now he was back and asking around for me.

'Get out of London, Mac,' Si told me. 'The bloke's a psycho. If he finds you he'll fucking kill you.'

'I'll be okay. Besides, I'll have some money in a few days. He'll get his dough.'

Si shook his head; he knew me too well. Around this time very little scared me. In jail a lot of the supposed nutters had been full of nothing but mouth. In time I'd learn and get wise, but that day hadn't come yet.

For a while I simply kept my head down, avoiding the estates around the Queen's Crescent area. Then one night I was down in King's Cross with Si. We'd just scored and were heading back along the canal to Camden. It was raining and we were chatting away when Wayne stepped out from nowhere.

He chased me back along the towpath, catching me by the York Way bridge. We fought on the ground, until he wrapped a bike chain round my neck and pulled me up against the wall. Si was nowhere to be seen.

Wayne pulled out a blade saying he was going to carve me like a pig, when Si flew from the shadows stabbing a jagged bottle into his neck.

Wayne fell gasping to his knees, his severed carotid artery spurting over the cobbles.

Shocked we stood and watched, fixed to the spot until he finally dropped.

Si spoke first. 'I'll check his pockets.'

He found a wad of notes, passed me half then pulled out a bag of rocks that we'd later sit smoking in his flat. 'Okay, give me a hand,' he said.

We dragged him to the edge of the water and dropped him in, his body like a pile of rags among the floating debris.

*

80

Back to the present day. Sitting in the dingy stairwell of some flats near Queen's Crescent NW5.

I hear voices and realise I've been dozing. Two teenagers in school uniform are shouting at me, telling me to get the fuck off their stairs. Junkie cunt. State of you man. Get off my block you fucking tramp.

I jump up, flicking my knife from my back pocket.

'Whoa, calm down!'

'Easy bruv, easy!'

Another feint forward and they're running like rats.

Fucking little cunts.

I start walking. Malden Road down to Camden Town. Then on past Mornington Crescent to Eversholt Street, to the place I call home. A squat I share with five Portuguese vegan anarchists who want me out. I get in, open my bedroom door and there's a couple I've never seen before shagging on my bed. What the fuck? I head down to speak to Pedro who's watching TV with his girlfriend Marcia. I ask him what's going on and he tells me they're the new residents, I told you a month ago no fucking junkies, and then we're shouting and pushing each other, his girlfriend trying to get between us until two of his mates rush in and pull me back, one wielding a baseball bat. I see they're not fucking about and back down.

'Your shit will be outside in black bags tomorrow. Now go.'

'Fuck the lot of you,' I say, kicking over the cat litter tray as I leave.

I mope about the streets wondering why it's all happening today. It's evening now, people eating al fresco outside the cafes, my eyes scanning the tables for any lonesome mobiles, when a copper calls from a car at the lights.

'Keeping out of trouble I hope, Mac.'

'Course I am. Clean as a whistle.'

I spend a couple hours by Camden Lock having a few cans with some Irish blokes I know. Then I admit the inevitable - I've got nowhere to go tonight but back to Si's. Si will put me up for a few nights. That stuff about his bird coming round was bollocks. He'd already told me when he was out of it. She wasn't coming back.

I'm outside his flat for an age shouting through the letter box but there's no answer. He's in though because I can hear the TV on. I lean by the balcony for a minute wondering if he just doesn't want to see me.

Then a dark thought hits me.

No way.

I stand back and take a kick at the council-issue door. Two more and it smashes open.

I find Si in the kitchen hanging from a rope.

GHOSTS

I was fourteen when a girl cornered me in the school playground and said she liked me, had liked me for ages, told me she wanted to go out with me. I looked at the ground, didn't know what to say, the girl coming in close, her eyes, her warmth - I'm not joking you know, I really want to go out with you. Moving slowly forward to kiss me. Then just before our mouths met she said DREAM ON and laughed out loud, her mates suddenly right there all laughing. Word got to the boys that I'd tried to kiss her, kiss Melanie Smith, and at home time they followed me out of the gates. Who does he think he is? Fucking cunt. Their voices trailing behind, getting closer. They jumped me, kicked me on the ground, then pulled me by the arms towards a puddle, my trousers tearing as they dragged me, loosening to my knees, somebody coming up and ripping my underpants down, everyone laughing, and somebody else coming up and kicking me in the head.

School wasn't easy. Each day I'd walk home through the park, sit on a bench and stare across the green. My mum was always busy working, and my dad was dead three years now and I still hadn't got over it. One day a stranger sat next to me and started to talk. I could have easily told him to piss off and leave me alone, but I didn't. And when he invited me back to his flat, I thought of the dangers but went along anyway, over to the tower block, the man making me tea just like he said he would, and we sat and watched TV. For once in my life I felt relaxed, just sitting back and forgetting the lot of it.

It became a regular thing. Trevor telling me of his years in the merchant navy and his travels around the world. The bullet he dodged in a bar in Brazil and the stabbing in Argentina that left him with his permanent limp. And I opened up about my dad and how close we'd been, Trevor listening, always understanding, treating me like an adult, offering me a beer or a whisky perhaps, words and advice, and it was as if things happened naturally, with no manipulation at all, Trevor talking about girls and if I'd had sex yet. Sometimes we'd watch videos, drink a little whisky and things would happen; nothing harmful, just practice, a part of growing up. And I never questioned whether I was being used or not, simply enjoyed the company, somebody who didn't judge me, who cared whether I lived or died.

Then one day I turned up at the flat and there was no answer. The same happened the next day and the day after that, until eventually the council re-let the place, and each day after school I sat on the bench waiting for him, the only real friend I had, but he never appeared. Somebody mentioned prison, another saying he'd simply moved away, until it felt as if it had all been some kind of trick - as though Trevor had never existed.

I turned fifteen. Then sixteen. I was in my final year at school now, growing bigger and taller, people leaving me alone, and sometimes I'd bunk off and hang around the park, searching for that same company, same warmth, somebody to come along and whisk me away, a silly ridiculous dream lined up by the urinals with the men, not even knowing what I was doing. One day three skinheads burst in and raided the place - Queer fucking cunts - locking myself in a cubicle, hearing the kicks and gasps, one of them hanging over the partition saying he was going to kill me, another kicking the door in and ripping me out onto the floor - Dirty fucking queer - curling into a ball as three pairs of boots laid into me. Then they were gone. Only the groans of the beaten men around me and blood across the tiles. I staggered out into the daylight and vomited into a bush. Then I got myself together and made my way home. I wasn't a queer. I'd never been a queer. I liked girls. I'd always liked girls. What was wrong with me? My mum sent me straight to hospital. I had two cracked ribs, heavy bruising and a head cut that needed stitches.

Six months later I left school. Freedom at last. The summer of 1991 drifted by, but by autumn I'd got myself a job working the nightshift packing shelves in a supermarket. Afterwards, some of the blokes would go to a pub that opened early on the sly, and often I joined them. The months went on. I had my routine, was making a wage and couldn't complain. As I'd clock out, some of the day staff would be coming in, and there was one particular girl who'd smile and I'd smile back, and before long it became a daily thing, waiting for that precious smile, and if I somehow missed her my day wouldn't feel complete. At last we talked. Her name was Lisa.

We both agreed that work was crap but better than school any day. Lisa talked of the places she liked to go at night, and I told her I usually went for a few morning pints with the men and she laughed, couldn't believe a pub would be open at this time, but was impressed, liked a drink herself. Suddenly I was asking her out, if she wanted to go somewhere at the weekend, almost unable to believe it myself. But then she was saying yes, she'd like that, writing down her phone number and telling me to give her a buzz to arrange a time. She kissed me on the cheek and smiled back at me as she walked away.

All the men turned as I walked into the pub. Who put a smile on your face this morning? I told them I'd just asked out one of the till girls and she'd said yes, no problem. They got me a drink saying they didn't know I had it in me, but I obviously did, and from then on they called me the Dark Horse.

On Saturday night we went to the cinema, getting tipsy on a bottle of cider, and halfway through the film we kissed. Afterwards we went to a pub and it was as if we'd known each other for ages. I brought her home on the bus and we kissed on the stairs of her flats. Walking the six miles home I was buzzing. I felt like a new person. At the weekends we'd go out, and during the week we'd meet in the playground on Lisa's estate. Lisa knew everyone. Before work I'd bring a can or two, or there might be a spliff going round, everyone having a laugh. Her friends welcomed me, no questions asked; I was Lisa's boyfriend and that was good enough for them.

Soon we wanted to take things further. One night she led me off the estate and towards some trees. We slipped through a broken fence and along an overgrown path to a clearing by an old factory wall. We kissed and one thing led to another, but when she removed her jeans and lay back I was suddenly nervous.

'What's wrong?' she asked.

I told her I'd never done it with a girl before, had never done it with anyone. Lisa smiled and told me not to worry. Then kissing me, she told me to lie back and relax.

Afterwards we lay side by side.

'So, what's it like not being a virgin anymore?' she asked.

I smiled but thought about it. In truth I hadn't really been a virgin at all, at least not a proper one, but that was unimportant now. Anything I'd done before had just been a part of growing up, a mistake best forgotten. Lisa pulled on her jeans and lit a cigarette. Under the moonlight she looked so perfect that for a second I wondered if the whole thing was a dream. She seemed too good for me, and I was jealous of the other boys she'd been with, wondering if they were local boys I'd met and spoken to. But that didn't matter either, that was the past too. She came down close to kiss me. All that mattered was now, the two of us together and nothing could taint that.

The next weekend we went to a club near Lisa's. The place was packed, Lisa in a red top, wearing the necklace and earrings I'd bought her, the most stunning girl there, the drinks flowing, the two of us moving on the dancefloor and the hours rushing by. Until some bloke edged in and started dancing with her, speaking in her ear, Lisa smiling, looking into his eyes, the two of them moving together.

I tried to edge my way back, but kept getting shouldered away and it was as if she'd forgotten me now, wasn't interested at all. Finally I stood off to the side watching them. The bloke looked me up and down, said something in her ear and laughed.

I charged forward and pushed him in the chest. He pushed me back, Lisa getting between us telling us to stop. In the end he called me a wanker and walked away.

Lisa was angry now, asking what was wrong with me, a rave anthem kicking in as we argued by the side of the floor. The bloke and his mates were staring over, eyes flashing under the strobes. There was an atmosphere to the place now. Lisa said it was probably best we left.

Walking her home I asked who the bloke was.

She said she didn't know him, but I knew she was lying. I kept on until she admitted it was Jake, her ex.

'We used to go out, we don't anymore, are you happy with that? I know loads of people around here, what's it got to do with you?'

We walked in silence. Then I didn't want the night to end like this and said I was sorry. It was the drink. I'd got carried away. In the end we agreed to just forget about it. But heading home I felt terrible.

The next day I phoned her, but she was tired and said she'd see me during the week. She'd got a job closer to home at Boots and tomorrow was her first day, so I understood she needed to relax. But the thought of things being different between us worried me.

On Monday evening I phoned her again, but her mum said she was out with friends. I got the bus to her estate hoping she'd be in the playground, but it was deserted. I called at her door but she was still out. It was dark now and I sat on a swing staring over at her block. When some kids passed by I asked if they'd seen her. They hadn't. It started to rain. Still I waited. Where was she?

Suddenly I got up and headed towards the trees. I went through the fence and up the path to the factory wall. Rain poured through the branches, mud beneath my feet. I reached the clearing. It looked different now, littered with beer cans, a burnt-out motorbike on the spot where we'd lain. What was I doing? I hurried back to the swings. Sat waiting. Eventually I saw her, coming along the close under an umbrella. I stepped out from the dark and she jumped in shock.

'Jesus, are you trying to scare me to death?'

'Where were you tonight?'

'Are you checking up on me?'

I asked her again, shaking her by the arm. She pushed me off saying she'd had a drink with some girls from work, and you know what, you're mad in the head, do you know that? Look at yourself. And I'm getting sick of it. Now go home. I watched her go. Then suddenly I rushed forward saying I was sorry. I'd never meant to upset her, but I'd been waiting hours, I was worried - tears forming now. She looked at me. Shook her head.

'It's okay.'

We hugged beneath her umbrella. Then she told me I'd better hurry off to work or I'd be late. She was right, I'd forgotten all about it. Packing the shelves that night I knew I had to stop over-reacting. There was no need for it. We were both in love. What was there to worry about?

At the height of summer we went for a weekend away in

Brighton. We found a cheap hotel and hung around the fair and the beach, and at night the pubs and clubs, and the days just whizzed by. On Sunday night we ran up the hill for the last train back to London, catching it just in time. It was the best weekend of my life.

One morning after work and a few drinks, I took a long route home, walking through the old park. The night before, Lisa's family had been out and we'd spent two hours in her mum and dad's bed. I sat on a bench. The sun was beaming down, not a cloud in the sky. I hadn't been here in ages. I thought of when I'd sit in this very spot and how grey it seemed back then, but now the flowerbeds were alive with colour and the birds singing in the trees. That lonely and confused fourteen-year-old now seemed like a stranger to me.

Looking back I should have maybe stuck up for myself more. Not have let so many people push me around, take advantage. But it was the death of my dad. It affected me. Left me vulnerable. I'd started secondary school the same year and retreated into a shell, and not a very protective one. But what was the point of going over it? These days I looked forward. The past was dead and gone. I lifted my face to the sky and closed my eyes. I was listening to the birds and the bees, enjoying the day, when a voice sounded next to me. I turned to see a stranger in his sixties.

'I remember you,' he said. 'From a while back. You knew Trevor, didn't you?'

I stared at him as he sat rolling a cigarette. Trevor had been in prison, he continued. Some trumped-up charge about a child. A load of shit really, but that's the authorities for you, always condemning people. But now he was back and asking around. Asking if anyone had seen his young Richard these days. His old friend. And of course you've changed a bit, grown up and that, but I never forget a face.

Suddenly I was on my feet, grabbing him off the bench

saying I didn't know what he was talking about. I don't know any Trevor and my name isn't Richard. Are you listening to me, you old cunt? He was croaking at the throat, and I said if I ever saw him again I'd kill him and that goes for Trevor too.

'Leave him alone,' a woman with a pushchair called over. 'What's he done to you? He's an old man.'

I dropped him back onto the bench, my mouth dry, mind in shock.

The sun was killing me now. I walked away vowing I'd never enter that place again.

It was a Friday and that night Lisa suggested we go on a double date with her friend Claire and new boyfriend. We went to a pizza place then on to a late pub. The pub was loud and busy, yet we found a table and slotted in. With Lisa and Claire catching up on gossip, I was left with Darren. We had little in common but conversed anyway, Darren doing most of the talking (or shouting over the music) while I nodded my head or gave the odd interjection, even sometimes when it made no sense at all. Because no matter how hard I tried, I just couldn't get the park incident out of my mind.

Afterwards Lisa made us wait for their night bus, the girls laughing and joking, Darren and I now sitting at the bus stop saying nothing. I was thinking of the things I'd done with Trevor, and then with other men in the park toilets. Had I really done those things? Yes I had. But why? I stared at Lisa's legs, the way her top clung to her chest. I stared at her hair and her face and the way she smiled. Why had I done those things?

Once they'd gone Lisa put her arm in mine and we walked. She said she was sorry she'd chatted so much to Claire tonight and left me out, but she hadn't seen her old friend in ages.

'You didn't mind having to chat to Darren, did you?'

'Of course I didn't,' I told her.

We headed off the main road.

'Are you okay?' she asked as we came out from under a railway bridge. 'You seem weird tonight. Spaced or something?

'Let's go in here,' I said, turning into an overgrown alley.

'What are you doing?' Lisa said as I pushed her against the wall. I lifted her top, kissing her breasts. 'Steady on,' she laughed.

'Let's do it. Now.'

'What's wrong with you? Someone might see.'

'There's nobody around.'

We did it against the wall as the trains clattered over the bridge. I was moving as hard as I could, yet I felt nothing, felt numb. Still I somehow finished fast.

'I've never seen you like that,' Lisa said, pulling down her skirt.

We walked home.

Outside Lisa's flats she looked at me. 'Seriously, are you okay?'

'I don't know, maybe I'm coming down with some kind of flu.'

The next day, I lay in bed for hours thinking. I had to put the past behind me once and for all or it would drive me mad. Hearing Trevor's name had been a shock, but I had to move on, leave the past where it was. My life was different now. I was a different person. The past couldn't touch me.

I started to feel a lot better. One evening I spent a few hours over at Lisa's. Her place was always busy with nowhere to really be alone, but it was nice having a chat and a cuddle on the stairs, Lisa in her dressing gown, fresh from the bath. At last we said goodbye and I headed off towards the bus stop. At one point I noticed a group of youths by a wall across the road, but thought nothing of it. Then a minute later I heard my name being called from behind.

'I want a word with you, cunt.'

It was Jake, Lisa's ex. Jake's mates stood further back. I thought I recognised one of them from school, but that made no sense, this was miles away. Jake came closer, the gold chain over his Arsenal top glinting off the streetlight.

'My cousin back there tells me you're a queer. Remembers you from school. Tells me you're a cocksucking little nonce. A dirty poof who's now trying to go straight, is that right?'

I stood there frozen, Jake right in my face now.

'Come on then, gay boy, think you're hard do you?'

He pushed me in the chest. Then he pushed me again. Finally I lunged for him, but he came back with a flurry of punches, the two of us wrestling on the ground. Just then a police car swerved over, all lights and radios.

'Break it up, what's going on here?'

They questioned us by a wall. We told them we were just mates messing about, and after a bollocking we were sent off in different directions.

I went home. I didn't go to work. I hardly got out of bed for days. I was waiting for Lisa to phone, but she didn't.

Finally I phoned her. She told me she'd heard stuff from friends. I think we better meet, she said. We met in McDonalds. Lisa ate a cheeseburger and chips.

'Is it true?' she finally asked.

'Of course not.'

'I suppose it doesn't matter anyway,' she said, pushing away her wrappers. 'All that matters is now I suppose. The best thing is probably for Jake to just shut his mouth.'

We walked along the empty high street, all the shops shuttered and closed. There was a chill in the air. Summer was over. At the bus stop I asked when I'd see her next. She told me she didn't know. She kept stepping out onto the road, looking for her bus.

'Do you love me?' I said.

She looked at me, her bus approaching in the distance.

'Of course I do.'

At work Keith the supervisor asked me where I'd been for the past three nights and why I hadn't phoned. I told him I was ill, but it wasn't good enough. He gave me my final warning.

On the shop floor I couldn't focus. Everything I did was wrong. In the end I let slip a jar of pickled beetroots. Keith stood watching as I mopped up the mess.

'What fucking planet are you on?'

'You do it,' I said, tossing him the mop and Keith jumping back in shock.

I went to get my jacket, Keith shouting behind me that I was sacked. I took the last bus up to Lisa's. It was late but I didn't care. Alone on the upper deck, I thought of the future. The two of us getting away. Escaping from the lot of it. Starting up somewhere else. Starting afresh.

'She's not in,' said Lisa's mum in her dressing gown. 'And what sort of time do you call this?'

I asked where Lisa was. She told me she was staying with a friend.

'What friend?'

'Look, I'm not getting involved. If you two have had a row or something then sort it out tomorrow. It's late and you've got me out of bed.'

Lisa was with Jake, I knew it.

The next day I turned up at Lisa's work. She was behind the make-up counter, shocked as I walked up to her.

'What are you doing? Keep your voice down,' she kept saying.

I grabbed her: 'You were with Jake, weren't you?'

'Get off me ... Leave me alone.'

A guard rushed over and pulled me away. He was all ready to call the police, but Lisa pleaded with him to let me go.

That evening I phoned her house. Her dad answered.

'Go within a mile of my Lisa again and I'll break your legs, have you got that?'

I appeared at the playground. Familiar faces were around the frames. When they saw me, one tried whistling a signal around the corner to where Lisa and I used to kiss.

I marched forward. Sure enough, there they were tongues down each other's throats. I ripped him off her and started kicking him on the ground.

Lisa was screaming at me, trying to push me back, and Jake shot up and flew at me, fists flying. Next thing I was down and he was over me repeatedly punching. At last some of the others pulled him away.

I stood up. I was swaying on my feet, blood across my face. Lisa was next to Jake, in tears. I looked at her. I still loved her. I took a step forward but she clung closer onto Jake, people jumping in the way telling me not to even think about it.

Jake was breathing heavily. 'Show your face around here again and you're dead.'

I walked away.

I lay in bed staring at the walls of my room. Then the next day, I went back to the old park. I sat on the same bench. I stayed for hours. Finally in the twilight I saw him. The man who had mentioned Trevor. I came up behind him and bundled him aside into a bush.

'Where does he live now?'

'Who?' he said, terrified.

'Trevor, you stupid old cunt.'

I stood outside Trevor's block. I headed up the stairs to the third floor, walked along the balcony to the last flat. I rang the bell. I stood waiting. The door opened. Trevor seemed half-pleased, half-confused. I stared at him, holding the knife behind my back.

Sensing something, he quickly tried to close the door. Too late. I pushed in and plunged the knife in deep. We staggered down the hallway as I repeatedly stabbed him.

The date was 13 September 1992. That day my life changed. I was charged with murder and faced a long prison sentence. You could say a chapter of my life neatly ended, but of course things are never as simple as that. Life goes on, with its challenges, its ghosts and memories that never recede. Life in prison wasn't easy. Nor were the years afterwards. But that's a story for another day.

BENT

The bastard was laughing at me. He was taking the piss.

'I'll ask you one last time,' I said. 'Where were you on Friday 8th June at 10.30pm?'

The burglar who had beaten an 84-year-old man half to death, said: 'Up your fucking arse.'

I turned off the tape and lunged for him. DC Burns held me back. 'Easy, Rob, easy!'

He and another copper had to pull me out of the room.

I was up before the boss. The way I'd been handling stress had become something of a talking point.

'I'll let this one go,' he said, after giving me the bollocking of my life. 'But between you and me, you need to take a holiday. And I'm not suggesting, I'm telling you.'

'Yes, Guv.'

I'd got off lightly. But using up a fortnight of my holiday time to sit in my flat talking to the walls was probably the last thing I needed. It wasn't as if I could fly off to the Bahamas - I was skint, up to my eyeballs in debt. For too long I'd been drinking too much and hitting the cocaine, and financially it was crippling me.

Driving home I phoned Cat. She was a nurse at the Royal London and we had an arrangement. At the moment she was working nights.

'Are you at home?' I asked her.

'Hang on a minute.' I heard a door opening and closing. 'You certainly choose your times,' she said, her coarse Dublin accent instantly cheering me up. She told me to hold on for a while as Steve hadn't left for his shift yet.

Steve was Job and a mate. I'd known him for years since a stint at Stoke Newington. But from what Cat had told me, their marriage wasn't exactly made in heaven, so as far as guilt was concerned there wasn't any.

I parked up the road from the flat waiting for Steve's Audi to pull off. When it did I made my move.

I started for her the second I walked through the door.

'At least let me finish my coffee,' she laughed.

'Fuck the coffee,' I said, putting the cup aside. We made for the bedroom and within two minutes flat I was banging her on the bed.

I'd joined the force ten years ago. Within four years I was a detective. That was good going; I was working in specialist squads, moving up, heading places. I met Trisha, a constable in Plaistow, and we were married within months, loving each other one minute, plates flying the next, both too similar, too mouthy for our own good. Trying for a baby, losing it, trying again, then one night she stepped out in front of a speeding car and it was all over.

I finished and rolled away in a sweating heap.

'God, you needed that, didn't you?' Cat said, pulling the duvet off the floor.

She was right, I did. One thing sorted I suppose. I got up and headed to the fridge, coming back with a cold can of Stella.

'Is that what you do with all your women,' she asked, 'steal their husband's beer?'

'I'm a one woman man, Cat, you know that.'

'So you say,' she said, getting up and putting on her dressing gown.

She stood looking at herself in the mirror.

'Steve says I'm getting fat.'

'Don't listen to him. You look great.'

I preferred a bird with a bit of shape anyway. So did most men I reckon. The girls growing up now were brainwashed.

She headed to the bathroom, and it was just as well because I'd probably have had to grab her for a second round. That was the coke that was. It was turning me into a raving sex maniac.

'How's work?' she asked when we were dressed and respectable in the kitchen.

'Don't ask. I've just been forced to take some of my holiday time.'

'Lucky you.'

'Maybe if I was heading off to the sun, yeah, but on my wages?'

'Try mine, then you'd really have something to moan about.'

Just then we heard a noise. Keys at the front door.

Shit. I rushed back into the bedroom, standing behind the half-open door that I hadn't had time to close. Steve was already in the flat, heading up the hallway. He was saying he'd had to drive all the way back to collect some files. I heard him move from the living room to the kitchen.

'Has someone been here?' he said, crushing the empty can in his hand.

Cat told him her brother had popped by, and with some good news as well. His girlfriend's pregnant. Is that grand or what? He was just passing in his van and popped in to tell me. He was so excited.

'Tell Dom congratulations,' he said. 'And another thing, tell him to stop nicking my beer. And to change his aftershave - it stinks.'

They laughed and he kissed her goodbye. I took a peek through the crack and watched them hug. He had both hands on her behind and they were whispering sweet nothings like a pair of lovebirds.

When he finally left I stepped out into the hall.

'Jesus Christ,' she said.

'That was close.'

Most surprising though was just how lovey-dovey they had been.

'I thought you two were on the verge of splitting up?'

'Look, you just better get going before he forgets something else.'

I checked that his car had gone, then said my goodbyes.

Bill Morgan was an ex-copper and private eye. In the Met he'd been a tough old bastard and had the marks to prove it, a nasty facial scar the result of a boozy police do where he took on five coppers in the car park, putting up a good fight but ending up with his head through a car window.

But that was then. Salad days. These days he had a dodgy ticker and resembled a bloated Alan Sugar. A lot of his police contacts had dried up, so that's where I came in. I'd been blanking him for months telling myself never again, but times were desperate.

He told me to pop by his office, a place above a kebab shop in Walthamstow. I headed up to the first room, and the reception desk where a young secretary usually sat was empty. I knocked on his office door and heard him tell me to hang on. A minute later out popped his secretary, a dirty-looking bird no more than eighteen, giving me a polite smile before sitting back behind her desk.

I walked in. 'You dirty old goat,' I laughed, watching him adjust his shirt over his fat gut.

He ignored me, moving in behind his desk all business-like.

'So, Rob, long time no see.'

I sat down. 'Not long enough, Morgan mate, if I'm honest. But needs must.'

He laughed, tapped a few keys on his laptop, then leaned back in his seat.

'So, how are the Keystone Kops these days?' he said.

'Usual shambles, you know how it is. Lunatics running the asylum.'

'You're making me nostalgic.'

He took out a bottle of Scotch and poured two glasses. He offered me a cigar but I shook my head. I asked him what he had for me.

'Times are interesting, Rob. I'm branching out. Getting a lot of work from some contacts in the press. Big stuff, high-end. After Leveson the hacks are only working with people they trust. People with the experience and know-how to get the job done and make sure matters are conducted in the strictest confidence. You see, the way I operate--'

I put up my hand. 'What's the job, Morgan?'

'Okay,' he said. 'She's a soap star.'

'Who is?'

'The girl a certain red top is paying me to investigate.' He took a sip of whisky and continued. 'She's got a coke habit, big time, and is dealing left and right, on-set, to feed it. But it's a tight circle and no-one's talking. We can't get a thing on her. Believe it or not, she's too fucking clever. So the hacks are willing to settle for a confession rather than an exposé.'

'And how's that going to happen?'

'Well, that's where you step in. You're going to tip her off. Tell her the Drugs Squad have been watching her, know everything and are about to bring down a massive bust on her. An arrest in full view of the press. A police PR stunt, if you like. The Met finally putting into practice the 'don't-think-you're-above-the-law-if-you're-famous' line they've been promising for years.

By now you'll have the tart scared shitless. But tell her there's a solution. A deal can be made to confess all to the press: "How I Got Sucked into the Evil World of Drugs." That way she'll get the public's sympathy rather than scorn, and the Squad will drop it and target some other mug. It should work like a dream.'

I leaned back taking it all in. 'How much are they paying you for all this?'

'Well, let's just say when it's all over I'll be taking a holiday. A long one. And you won't be doing too bad either.'

I thought about it.

'Just give her a talk, Rob. One night's work. She's whisked off crying with the hacks to a hotel for a full confessional, you're walking away fat in pocket telling the taxman to go fuck himself.'

I'd done plenty of dodgy stuff in the past, but this was sleazy, I didn't like it. Anything to do with the tabloid press stank of shit. But money talks a different language.

'I'll do it,' I told him.

'Good man.'

He opened a drawer and took out some powder. He chopped out two generous lines and, toasting our deal, we tucked in.

There was a knock at the door. His secretary stepped in asking if she could be excused for lunch.

'Course you can, darling. Be back at two.'

We watched her totter away: tight skirt and heels.

'Nice arse,' I commented.

'You complete the job and I'll let you have a taste of it.'

I sat in front of the TV. I hadn't watched an episode of the 'nation's favourite soap' in an age, and now that I had, I realised why. It was pants. All the same old storylines and a script that seemed written by cretins. Too many drama school twats prancing about giving it the mockney. But whatever, I wasn't paid to be a TV critic, I was being paid to ruin some tart's life, or at least change it irrevocably, which I had no qualms about whatsoever. Why would I? She looked like a right gobby little upstart.

The job was on. I staked out her flat, followed her to the studios, to a restaurant, a nightclub - but not for one minute could I get her alone. I was living in my car, shoving so much coke up my nose I didn't sleep for days. Then finally I got my chance. She came out of a cab, staggering in her heels a little drunk up the path to her flat - alone for once. I caught her near the door, knowing I'd have to be quick. When she saw a flash of ID and heard the words 'police', 'drugs', 'under arrest' she jumped in fright. Bingo.

I took her arm and led her to the car. She seemed stunned. I put her in the front seat and got in beside her. We pulled off and she took out her phone, saying she needed to call her lawyer.

'Not yet,' I told her. 'Wait till we get to the station.'

She looked at me, suspicious now. 'You're not a policeman at all, are you?' Then she started to panic, shouting, 'Let me out, let me out...'

I pulled over into an empty car park.

'Calm down,' I told her. 'I am a policeman. But no, I haven't been entirely honest with you. You're not under arrest. But I do have some very important info concerning the Drugs Squad that you need to know.'

By the time I'd finished and offered her the only ultimatum, she was bawling her eyes out. I even felt sorry for her.

'What have I done?' she kept saying. 'Things just got out of control...'

I told her she'd better hand over any incriminating possessions, just to be on the safe side. She passed over five grams of coke, some Ketamine, some rocks and a bag of Es. Jesus, she was a walking fucking chemist.

She sobbed onto my shoulder and I patted her back.

'It's okay. I'll make the phone call and the journos will have you in a hotel within the hour. You can get it all off your chest, no more threat from the cops, and you'll be bunged some money as well. It'll work out for the best, you'll see.'

'I'll lose everything...'

'You won't, you'll have the public's sympathy,' I lied, realising my hand was stroking up and down her thigh. I reined it in.

She looked at me, her make-up smudged around her eyes.

'How much?' she said. 'How much to make the whole thing go away?'

'I'm sorry. It's much bigger than that. It's out of my hands.'

She leaned in, playing me now. 'You're a powerful man,' she purred, 'in a powerful position. You can sort it. You can pull strings...'

Her hand was moving downwards. I knew what was happening but I didn't stop it. 'You're that sort of man,' she continued. 'You can do anything. I know you can...'

Before long, my trousers were around my knees and she was working away, both my hands pushing her head up and down.

When my time came I leaned back and, with a groan, shot my load.

She was sitting back next to me now, talking, but I wasn't listening.

'So that's what we'll do, yeah, we'll sort it. My dad has money, no problem. So no police, no journalists, just lots of cash - to everyone if need be...'

Coming to my senses, I zipped myself up.

'No can do. I've told you already, are you fucking delusional? It's out of my hands.'

'You bastard!' she screamed, her fists pounding at me. 'You just made me suck your filthy dick, you bastard!'

I grabbed her arms and pushed her back. 'Shut the fuck up.'

'That's it, I'm calling my lawyer,' she said, mobile in hand.

'Do that and the bust will go ahead,' I told her. 'Look at the Class As you just handed me. Look at what they've got on you already. You're a drug dealer. You'll get ten years inside.'

I made the call and within fifteen minutes a car pulled in opposite. My part was played.

The next day I drove to Walthamstow to collect my money. In the car I phoned Morgan telling him I was on my way, but he told me there were problems.

'What problems?' I said, charging through his office door.

'Sit down, Rob. I need to speak to you.'

'I did my bit, fair and square. If there was aggro at the journos' end, it was nothing to do with me. I want my money.'

'You fucked her, Rob.'

'What?'

'You coerced her into a blowjob, same thing. By law, blackmail and sex don't really go together, do they? And now her lawyer is using rape as a bargaining tool.'

'Her lawyer?'

'Yeah. She took her chances. And under the circumstances I'm not surprised.'

'You're winding me up,' I told him. 'You're full of shit.' But I was starting to sweat now.

'Are you living in reality? Do you want to face a rape charge? You know the rules on these jobs, no fucking sex. I told you this tart was clever. She recorded the whole thing on her phone, to edit as she and her lawyer pleases. The job is fucked.'

'Shit!' I slammed the desk.

He poured two glasses of Scotch.

'I don't get it. I handed her over to the hacks.'

'I know you did. And she told them she'd just been forced into sex by a copper on their payroll and has it all on her phone. Then she disappeared and had her lawyer on the blower saying even stevens or they take it the whole way. The press have dropped the whole thing. For now anyway.'

'Could they find out who I am?'

'Quite easily I reckon.'

I grabbed him by the collars. 'You fat piece of shit.'

'You ever want a penny off me again, you better remove your paws.'

I let him go. Started pacing the room.

'I don't want this coming out,' I said.

'That makes two of us. This could get me fucking closed down. Or worse.'

Then I had an idea. 'Who is her lawyer?'

'Jeff Cohen. Showbiz prick. Corrupt as fuck.'

'Give me his home address.'

'What?'

'Give it to me. Now.'

Night, a leafy street in Highgate. I walked towards him as he stepped out of his Merc. I was wearing a balaclava and holding a Glock handgun. I ordered him back into the car and got in behind him.

'Drive.'

Indoors were his wife and three young children. They were being held at gunpoint, I told him, and if he ever wanted to see them again alive, he better obey my instructions.

'It's done,' I said, walking into Morgan's office, slapping a pink mobile phone down on his desk.

It was after midnight and he was half cut, a bottle of Teacher's in front of him, his secretary long gone.

'And there's no copies either,' I smiled. 'Believe me, I know.'

'Fucking hell, Rob,' he said, sitting up. 'What did you do,

break into his safe?'

'Never you mind,' I said, walking up and down, still pumped.

He poured me a drink and I necked it.

'We had a private word,' I told him. 'It's not likely the bloke will bring up the subject again. It's over.'

But soon Morgan was letting the drink talk, getting arrogant.

'I'm impressed. But it doesn't solve everything. The story's been dropped so I'm out of pocket. And my credibility's not exactly intact either. You fucked up, don't you forget that. And I'm going to lose a lot of work over this.'

I tried to stay calm, but he kept banging on. I was pacing up and down, the sweat pouring off me.

'You'll have to do me some favours for this, Rob, big time.'

I'd had a hard few days, all coke and no sleep, and I felt my anger go nuclear. Suddenly I was pointing the gun at him.

He jumped in his seat, spilling his drink.

'Open that safe now, you fat old fuck.'

'What are you doing, Rob, what are you doing?'

'Get over there and give me the cash you owe me, you cunt, or I'll have this whole place shut down and you serving a fucking ten-stretch.'

'You're out of control Rob, out of control...'

He headed over and keyed in the numbers.

His safe contained more than I even imagined.

'All of it,' I ordered.

'That was great,' I said, rolling off her.

I lay back on the sheets.

'We should go to Spain together. A few days away. A week maybe. Tell Steve you're off with the girls, a hen-do or something.'

'Are you dreaming?' Cat said. 'Steve would find out in two seconds. Anyway, you might have another week off, but not all of us have.'

I reached over to my jacket for a wrap and started snorting.

'Go easy on that, will you?' she said, tying up her dressing gown. 'Steve will notice it on the sheets.'

I laughed, rubbing my nostrils as she headed to the shower.

'Steve Joyce can go shag himself,' I smiled quietly.

Over the next few days, I sat in my flat watching DVDs and hitting the powder non-stop. I'd bulk-bought off a contact in Woodford and it was good stuff, about as pure as you could get. I watched Scarface, Goodfellas, The Terminator on a loop. The part where Schwarzenegger crashes into the cop shop and shoots up all the police was my favourite bit. I had the Glock pistol next to me, semi-automatic, seventeen rounds in its clip, but Arnie's hardware was something else.

I sat back and thought. Perhaps with Morgan I'd gone too far. Though maybe not. The bastard owed me. I'd been risking my arse for the bloke for years and he'd paid me peanuts. No, he deserved it. So did Cohen. He'd had to open his safe too, though of course it wasn't his money I'd been after. He'd sweated from the moment I picked him up, driving him back to his office, the prick pleading and crying that he'd do anything for me, and I had half a mind to get him grovelling on his knees. Snivelling little cunt. I hate lawyers.

Finally I turned off the TV, had a shower and got dressed up. Black suit, white shirt. Reservoir Dogs. There was a police engagement party at a cricket club in Crouch End. A little socialising would do me good. I tucked a wedge of Morgan's cash into my wallet, then looked into the mirror. I looked the fucking bollocks.

'Okay love, I'm off out,' I said to Trisha. It was nothing new, I spoke to Trisha in the flat all the time.

'Are you going to behave?'

'I'll try, I promise. But shit sometimes happens.'

'Another one of those nights then.'

'Hope not, but we'll just have to wait and see.'

I walked into the party, patting a few backs, then headed to the bar. Up walked Steve Joyce. He looked drunk and distressed but I didn't let on.

'Alright, Stevie boy,' I said, but he was having none of it.

'Me and you need a word. Now.'

He led me towards the back door. How the hell had he found out about me and Cat? Cat wouldn't have mouthed, no way. Only one mate knew of the affair, Dave Barker. And sure enough, there he was, across the room, staring straight at me. As our eyes met he turned away.

Outside, Steve stood opposite. Suddenly he headbutted me in the face. It didn't quite connect as expected, but still I dropped to my knees, my cheekbone throbbing.

'What the fuck was that for?' I said, playing innocent.

He pulled me up. There were actual tears in his eyes.

'I'll ask you just once, Rob. Are you sleeping with my wife?'

I looked straight at him - and put on a performance worthy of an Oscar.

'How long have we known each other, Steve? How long? Would I do that to you, a mate, a fucking mate? This is bullshit. Someone's stirring, Steve. Trying to fuck with your head and get me in the shit.'

He took a step back trying to get his head together, and I continued on. 'Cat's no slag, she doesn't shag around, you know that. I've known the pair of you for six years. She loves you. You love her. Someone's trying to make a mug out of you, Steve. Make mugs out of all three of us. Whoever spread this, I swear to God, deserves a fucking glassing.'

His eyes had lost their fire, and finally he started sobbing onto me. 'I'm sorry, Rob, I'm sorry...' He told me he'd just phoned her and she'd told him it was bullshit but he didn't believe her, didn't know what to think...

I held him, patting his back. This wasn't the Steve I knew at all, but that's women for you.

'It's okay mate, no worries. But promise me, whoever spread this shit...'

He dried his eyes then looked at me. 'I'm going to kill him.' And with that he charged back inside.

I stayed where I was, cooling off. I heard the smashing of glass, raised voices, then pandemonium. Maybe I'd leave the party there for the night. I headed around onto the main road and hailed a black cab. 'West End,' I told the driver, then sat back ruminating on how many stitches Dave Barker would be getting down the hospital tonight.

The next evening I woke up on my sofa shattered. I'd spent till morning in a strip club, then had paid for a little something extra off a bottle-blonde from Macedonia. My head was swirling. But I was winning. The cunts couldn't get me. Morgan. Cohen. Steve fucking Joyce. None of them. I was too fucking clever.

Cocaine, beer bottles and fifty-pound notes littered the table in front of me. My throat and tongue were like sandpaper, cheese holes audibly popping in my brain. I'd soon have to clean up my act, get back into the swing, give it all a clean break. But not yet anyway, I thought, snorting home a wake-up dose of the devil's dandruff, letting it blow away the cobwebs of sleep.

I stood up to fix myself a coffee, when the door went in. Two men: balaclavas, guns.

'Down on your knees, now!'

I tried to dive for cover but they started firing. Seven shots. Then they were gone.

I lay on the floor. I checked my wounds. Only two rounds had connected. Arm and shoulder.

They meant to kill me and very nearly could have, but like a lot of hired guns in London they were too low down the chain, wannabes who couldn't even shoot straight. Scummy estate kids who'd watched too many rap videos. Rule number one: once you've floored the bastard you put two good ones behind the ear or you don't bother at all.

I dragged myself up, my arm pissing blood. I hid the gun and the coke and called the cops.

One week later, Private Eye Bill Morgan had a heart attack. His secretary found him slumped over his desk, dead. He and Cohen had obviously put their money together to pay me the ultimate, and once that failed, then Morgan knew it was only a matter of time before I'd come calling. The pressure must have been too much for him. Just as well.

As for Cohen, life carried on for a full five months. Then one night as he parked his car outside his house, he was attacked by two masked thugs wielding a knife and an axe. He never regained consciousness. The police speculated it was most probably an attempted mugging or carjacking gone wrong.

Don't ask me, I had nothing to do with it.

THE GAME

I slammed the front door behind me, threw my gym bag into the car and drove. One more minute in that house and I'd go insane. Dani was doing my head in. I'd warned her, told her a hundred times but she kept banging on, pushing me to breaking point. I'd left her on the floor, but what did she expect? Was I supposed to just sit there and take it?

I turned into the gym car park and some fucker in a VW was in the way, too slow shifting his arse. I slammed the horn and called him a dozy cunt hoping he'd give me something back. But he didn't want to know, accelerating off. Clever man. I pulled into a space and reached for my bag. Then I put it back down and remained sitting. I needed to get my head together.

A group of youths were hanging by a wall pushing each other and laughing. And occasionally a fit-looking bird would enter or exit the gym doors. Dani was lucky. Was I out shagging every night like some people I knew? And didn't I do everything for her?

Then I realised how stupid I sounded. I looked at my hands. The thought of her curled up and whimpering on the floor wasn't doing me any favours now. Maybe I'd over-reacted, been too harsh on her. She'd said a few things and I'd snapped. Jesus, what had I done?

I took out my mobile. 'Dani, it's me… listen, are you okay?'
A few seconds passed then she muttered, 'I'm fine.'

I told her I was sorry, then there wasn't much more I could think of to say. I told her I'd see her later. I'd acted like a cunt, but admittedly I felt a little better now. Besides, I'd make it up to her. She knew that.

I walked into the gym. In the weight room Neil and his new mate Black Sam were flexing their muscles.

'Marty mate, how's things?' said Neil.

'Sweet.'

I got working on the lat bar. I hadn't trained in two days and was near going cold turkey. I banged out fifty reps, then taking a breather Neil came over wanting to talk business, Sam hovering nearby.

'The shipment definitely on for Friday then?' he leaned in, talking quietly.

'Look at you,' I laughed. 'You're fretting like an old woman. If I say it's on, it's on.'

'There's something else I need to talk to you about. Sam here can cut us a better deal with distribution. That lot at the moment are a fucking waste of time.'

'Who says?'

'Come on Mart, you know there's been problems.'

I leaned in, speaking a little too loud. 'You tell Sambo there if he's got anything to say he can tell me himself.'

Sam shot me a look I didn't like. He'd been well vouched for, everyone saying what an asset he'd be. But I wasn't the welcoming type. I pulled on the bar as we stared at each other.

Neil went over to him. 'Marty thinks you're a copper,' he smiled, patting his shoulder.

'Me?' Sam said. 'Are you serious? Do I fucking look like one?'

'Yeah, you do actually,' I said, winding him up.

'Bullshit, blud,' he said. 'Tottenham nigga becomes copper? That'd put me in the history books.'

114

'Don't give me that ghetto talk. This is Romford, Essex mate, round here it won't earn you jack shit.'

He kissed his lips. 'You seriously think I'm one of them?'

'You could be Frank fucking Bruno for all I know pal. I don't know you.'

He turned away. 'Neil man, your guy here's lost in the head,' he said, strutting off in a huff.

'If you say so, copper,' I laughed.

Afterwards the three of us jumped into Neil's van and drove to Basildon. A bar owner called Bill Brady owed Neil some money. It had nothing to do with me but I thought I'd come along for the ride. Anything was better than going home, and it would be an excuse to see Sam in action I suppose. If he impressed me then maybe I'd let him in. If not he could fuck off back to North London.

'How much does this bloke owe you again?' I asked as we headed down the A127.

'Near enough a grand,' Neil replied. 'He's taking liberties Mart, hasn't contacted me in weeks.'

'Is this the same bloke that grassed Teirnan's lot for that lorry jump-up in Thurrock that time?'

'Some say it was him, yeah. Who knows. Wouldn't surprise me though, he's slippery enough.'

'Fucking grass.' Then I turned to our new mate. 'I reckon we let Sam here take care of him. 'What do you say, Sam?'

Smiling he pulled a pair of pliers from his jacket. 'That's what I do.'

We strolled into the place, Sam pushing someone out of the way as we took seats at the counter. It was like an 80s wine bar, except a DJ was in the corner banging out beats. Fucking Basildon. We ordered beers from a nervous teenager with acne who looked like he should be back at home wanking in front of a computer screen. When it came to the payment I just stared at him.

'Get the governor. Tell him some friends have arrived.'

Brady appeared behind the bar, sweating badly. By now Neil was throwing pistachios at the optics and Sam had grabbed the young barman over the counter asking if he could lend him fifty quid from the till.

'Leave it out gents,' Brady implored. 'I've got customers here, I don't want any trouble.'

· 'Looks like they're taking a sudden dislike to the place,' I said as more shuffled out the door.

'Lads, let's be civil about this okay. Give me a buzz and we'll discuss it tomorrow.'

'We'll discuss it right now,' Neil said, standing up. 'THIS PLACE IS CLOSED. EVERYONE FUCK OFF.'

Sam gave the DJ a slap, the music scratching to a halt, and suddenly the remainder couldn't leave fast enough. I bolted the doors closed as Sam went through the till.

'Two fifty boss,' he said, handing me the wad.

'That leaves a seven-fifty deficit,' I said, pulling Brady out onto the floor. 'Now where's our money, cunt?'

I gave him a slap and tossed him to Neil who decked him and put the boot in. Then Sam stepped forward and we took seats ringside.

Driving back we were laughing all the way. We'd ransacked the upstairs rooms and found a bag of coke and now we couldn't stop talking. Sam had tortured the bloke in a chair and it wasn't pretty. He wasn't a guy you'd want to meet in a dark alley that's for sure, but he'd certainly be handy on the team. From his jacket he pulled out the CCTV disc. 'Nice little home movie,' he smiled.

'Sick Sam in the starring role,' I said. 'God, where'd you learn

116

all that shit?'

'On the roads innit. But that was nothing. This guy from Hackney yeah, we hung him upside down from a hook, worked on him all night then fucking castrated him. That's when I was working for the Turks.'

'Fucking hell, I think we'll need to keep a leash on you mate. Lock you up in a cage between jobs.'

'So I'm in then?'

I left it a few beats. 'I think I could consider it, yeah.'

'Safe,' he said, hi-fiving Neil.

'Now what's this I hear about distribution?'

When I got home Dani was asleep. I stripped off in the dark and got in next to her. I had some making up to do. I was also in the mood. Snuggling in she was soon awake and I was warming things up, but climbing aboard and working away she just lay there beneath me like a plank of wood. After I finished, she turned away. I switched on the night-light and stroked her hair.

'I'm sorry about earlier... I really am.'

Then I noticed dried blood on her pillow. I quickly turned her around. One of her eyes was black and her cheek was grazed from where I remembered pulling her across the carpet screaming how she was MAKING MY LIFE A FUCKING MISERY. In the past she'd always cleaned-up and covered any marks in make-up. This time it was worse and she hadn't. My eyes began to well. I couldn't believe I'd done this. What sort of animal was I?

'I'm so sorry...' I begged.

She turned away and I held her.

This was it. I'd change. I'd go easy on the steroids, the drink, all the things that were fucking me up. Never would this happen again.

Falling asleep, I dreamt of my old man. He'd beaten me and

my two brothers rigid, my mum too, and he'd got away with it, dying a peaceful death while my mum's time had been slow and painful and nearly sent me over the edge. Life wasn't fair. The cunts always won and the meek got trampled underfoot and here I was, father like son, the bastard laughing at me, his drunken voice waking me up with a start.

The sun was streaming through the curtains, and Dani was asleep facing me now. She was black and blue, dried blood streaking her cheek. I felt a stab of anger. Why hadn't she cleaned herself up? Why was she rubbing it in like this? I almost felt like shaking her and ordering her into the shower.

I gently touched her. 'Love, I'm going to cook you some breakfast.'

I took up a Full English and set it on a chair next to her. She'd eat and clean up in her own time. As for me, I washed down some growth hormone tabs with a protein shake and had to run.

I picked up Neil and drove to Brentwood to finalise some details with Big Dave about the shipment. This was the big time. A few more loads like this and I'd be looking at a new house and car. Maybe it was time to have some kids, get a family going. Two boys, one girl and a nice four-bed detached somewhere further out, free of scum. Before Romford I'd grown up in Manor Park. My parents before that were Canning Town. But that's what it's all about. Progress.

'So what do you reckon of Sam then?' Neil asked as I stared at the road ahead.

'Not much to be honest.'

'Are you serious?'

'Inner city trash, Neil. Typical cocky Londoner of the black variety. I'll do business with the bloke, but if he pisses me off I'll send him back to N17 with a fucking hole in his head.'

'Bit harsh. He's going to open up new markets for us. And he's a handy bloke to have around.'

'Reminds me of too many men I met inside. All mouth and

muscle but no loyalty. Not even to their own. And don't forget, he's a stranger, we've got to watch the bloke.'

'He'll make us good money, you watch.'

'I hope so. But by then he'll know too much about us and maybe we'll have to disappear him.'

I looked over and saw Neil gulp, then try to hide it. Inside I was laughing. But that's how you play the game.

That evening when I got home all was quiet. Dani was still in bed, her breakfast plate hardly touched. It was like deja vu - all those years ago, seeing my mum like this. I leant down and tried to kiss her but she shrugged me off. I remembered my mum had to go away for a while, me and my brothers moving to my aunt's in Dagenham. We were told she was ill. But my older brother Chris said she was in Claybury and that was a mental hospital.

'Dani, please, talk to me...'

She curled tighter away and I snapped, tearing the duvet off the bed. 'How many times can I say I'm fucking sorry?' I stood fists clenched, but again I realised I was losing my rag, going too far. I placed the duvet back over her and left the house. I got into the car and went for a drive. I took the A12 into London and parked in across from the old house in Manor Park. I'd done this several times through the years, on each visit the house looking tattier, more run down, the whole area gone to the dogs. But what was I doing here? What was I trying to find?

I turned on the engine and slowly drove. Up near Gants Hill the car behind got impatient, flashing his light, so I slowed down just to piss him off. Some young prick with his mate next to him.

Finally he overtook me, giving a wanker sign before gunning onto the A12. That was it. I put my foot down and the chase was on.

The bloke was doing eighty, shitting it now and I was laughing away. Come on you cunt. The pursuit went on for quite a bit, until at last they turned at Romford into Harold Hill. Local boys then. They pulled in by some flats, jumping out, one of them wielding a cosh. Oh, you want to play it like that do you? Heading towards them I whipped out my eight-inch hunting knife and they were off. One disappeared into the flats, the other I chased behind the blocks. He tried scrambling over a fence but I striped him across the arse and he yelped and fell. I laid into him, kicking at the cunt until I was out of breath. Fucking piece of shit.

Walking back past the flats, blade in hand, a cluster of youths had gathered at the sidelines.

'You're dead!' one yelled.

'Anytime,' I answered.

I got back in the car and hit the road. I felt better now. Always did after a fight. Let off a bit of steam and suddenly you can think clearly again, the world a better place, less complicated, less of a fucking jigsaw. A minute from home I pulled over and stopped the car. The place was miserable at the moment and I could do without it right now. I phoned Neil to see what he was up to. He said he was in the pub so I headed over.

Neil, Sam, and a couple others were huddled round as I told them my tale.

'You got him straight across the jacksie?' Neil said.

'The bloke wasn't so cocky then I tell you. Screaming like a girl he was, the scrawny little cunt.'

'You're crazy, man,' Sam laughed, getting up to fetch a round.

'And you're not?' I called. 'The dentist, that's what they should call you mate, you're in the wrong trade.'

After a few snorts the three of us moved on to a little strip place. Sam disappeared upstairs with two blondes as me and Neil watched two black tarts on stage.

'You alright Marty?' Neil said after they'd finished.

'Sound, why?'

'You've gone a bit quiet tonight, that's all. Not like you.'

'Fuck off.'

When Sam returned he was all mouth, running through the details of the two 'blonde bitches' he'd just banged, until it felt like I'd been in the room with him. What was it with these schwarzers and white women anyway? I felt like having a word. Though maybe I'd get at him another way.

'Here, Sam,' I nodded. 'You see that big black bitch over there. Once I finish this drink I'm gonna shag the arse off her, mate.'

We stared at each other unsmiling, tension filling the air until Neil tried watering things down: 'I might have that Thai bird there,' he said. 'I feel like a bit of Thai tonight.'

I put my drink down and strolled over. The woman was chatting to a bod in a suit, but I fucked him off and sat with my arm around her, whispering in her ear. As we headed upstairs I gave Sam a wink. Cocky cunt. The more I saw the bloke the more he got on my goat. Neil must be soft in the head inviting a bloke like that onside. But then again, we needed to branch out. Get back on the London scene. The Essex market was over-saturated. Burning bridges wouldn't be clever; it would be self-sabotage. But still.

I humped the heifer as she leaned over the bed. I caught myself in the wardrobe mirror, muscles rippling. I was taking seven different steroids, gear devised for fucking racehorses, and maybe it was paying off. I was two stone less than my peak, but that was back in the day when I'd been training full time. My dream had been to win the dead lift championships, and I was getting there, but then I injured my wrist in a fight with some two-bob mug from Southend and that was it, everything snatched away in a second, out of the game and into a year-long depression that almost crippled me.

I went a bit mad for a while. Did a few jobs. Betting shops, security vans. Queuing up to be just another mug in prison who hadn't used his loaf. Stick to old-school blagging and you might as well book yourself a ten-stretch there and then. I sorted myself out. It was the drug trade or nothing.

The woman was moaning away faking some kind of orgasm. Call me romantic but prostitutes just didn't do it for me. This was robot sex. Nothing but decent cardio. I flipped her over and shoved it in the cow's mouth. I looked around the room as she worked away. What a dump. The Albanians who ran the place needed to pull their fingers out. Why I belittled myself like this I didn't know. I deserved more. A better lifestyle. A better life. Maybe moving further out to Essex wasn't the answer. Perhaps I needed a suntan. Spain, Northern Cyprus, Thailand. There was a whole world out there. Six months from now I'd be making some big decisions.

I had a drink downstairs then I told the boys I was heading off. It was the big day tomorrow - the shipment - and I needed a clear head.

Back home, instead of going upstairs to face Dani, I sat in front of the TV snorting one last line, then another, until it was obvious sleep would be impossible. Fuck it, I'd stay awake and sort out the deal as is. I watched all the morning TV crap, then by lunchtime my phone wouldn't stop. The collect was on for 7pm near Tilbury Docks.

I headed upstairs for a shower, popping into the bedroom to check up on Dani.

She wasn't there.

Shit.

I phoned her number but she wouldn't answer, so I belled her sister Yvonne.

'Where is she?' I demanded.

Yvonne sounded sheepish, wouldn't tell me.

Then her husband Craig took the phone. 'She's somewhere you can't hurt her, you cunt.'

The prick ran a haulage firm in Rainham and I told him I'd burn the place to the ground. He hung up on me.

I stood there in the bedroom, livid. Then I grabbed the king-size bed, upturning it in one. The box containing my sawn-off was right there on the floor staring at me. Dani's cunt of a brother-in-law was in big trouble. I'd shove the barrel in his mouth, fucking fine the prick big money for talking to me like that. But I needed to calm down. First things first. I had to deal with the shipment.

Late afternoon I got in the van and picked up Neil and Sam. We were all ready and set. Fucking raring to go. Pound notes flashing in front of my eyes as we rolled down the M25. I was in a good mood now, the business with Dani a dark cloud I'd managed to push to the back of my mind.

I was just turning onto the A13 when the phone went. It was Big Dave.

'It's off,' he said. 'The load's been pulled.'

'No way.'

'Afraid so Mart. Of all the fucking lorries they had to target our one. It happens I'm afraid. One of those things.'

Finishing the conversation, I threw down my phone.

'What's going on?' Neil asked.

'It's off. The load's been pulled.'

'But I thought the Customs guys were in on it.'

'So did I.'

'Rah, man,' Sam said, kissing his teeth. 'That's bad shit.'

'Bad shit?' I said, turning to him. 'THIS IS FUCKING BOLLOCKS MATE.' I slammed the wheel, almost going up the arse of the van in front.

'Calm down!' Neil said.

'It's this cunt here,' I said, thumbing Sam. 'He's fucking jinxing things.'

'That's bullshit,' Sam tutted.

'Come on Mart, it's hardly Sam's fault, is it?' Neil said, sticking up for him.

'It is if he's been fucking snitching,' I said, not exactly meaning

123

it but not giving a shit either.

'Right, that's it,' Sam said. 'Stop the van. We're sorting this out right now.'

'What are you going to do, get your pliers out?'

'No, I'm gonna kick your fucking arse.'

I looked at him. Then I shook my head and laughed.

'Take it easy, Sam, I'm only shitting you.'

We were back near Romford when my phone went. Again it was Big Dave.

'Marty, listen, there's another load coming in next week. Felixstowe, same shit. You interested?'

'Course I am,' I told him. 'That's good news Dave.'

'Law of averages there should be no problems this time round. You want the same share? You'll make a bit more on this one too, more bang for your buck. I'll call you in a few days with the details.'

Dropping off the boys I felt more positive. I'd lost a lump of money, but nothing I couldn't make back. I'd been pulling in good cash lately with other business ventures so all wasn't too fatal.

As for Dani, I had things to sort on that score but maybe it was best to behave, get things sorted sensibly. Besides, I was hardly the innocent party, was I? I'd drive to her sister's, come in peace, but first I'd go home and have a shower.

I parked the car and walked in towards the house. Suddenly figures were emerging left and right from the shadows. Scrawny cunts in masks and hoods, but a whole crew of them, some wielding bats.

'Easy now lads, we can sort this...'

No use. I grabbed the first one forward, tossed him aside and kicked out at another, but then the whole mob was on me and I was down on the ground taking a pounding.

*

I woke up in hospital with a detective probing me for info.

'Leave it out, copper,' I said, face scrunched in pain. 'I don't even know what day it is.'

'So you're dealing with the young gangs now, Marty? I would've thought you were a bit above all those street-level shenanigans?'

What was this cunt on about? Dani's brother-in-law had obviously hired some young runts to do me. But I kept schtum. I sorted out my own troubles.

'Here, they left a message for you,' he said, reading from a card: '*Congratulations. You've just met the Harold Hill Boys.*' It was found next to your body when you were out for the count. Haven't seen one of these in years. Don't think you'll be on their Christmas card list though.'

'Give me that here.'

I looked at the card and remembered the road rage.

'They broke into your gaff as well,' he continued. 'Smashed the place up. Even left a little treat on the kitchen floor. Haven't been working your usual charms, have you Marty boy?'

I struggled to get up but the pain suddenly shot through me.

'Best to stay where you are. Best place for you right now. I'll be back tomorrow. We'll talk.'

I lay there for an hour seething. Then I must have slept because the next thing I woke up to see Dani's cunt-in-law Craig standing by my bedside.

'Nasty. That's one heavy-duty kicking you took there, Mart,' he whistled. 'Nothing to do with me though.'

'I know,' I conceded. 'But I'm sure you haven't come to offer me your sympathy.'

'No, I haven't.'

'How's Dani? She must be laughing.'

'She's certainly got a right to be. But she's not as it goes. She's sent you a message. She wants a divorce. She's had enough, it's over.'

'What are you talking about?'

Again I tried to rise but the pain held me down.

He leaned in. 'I should've had you taken care of a long time ago. But you know what, we'll draw a line under this. It's in the hands of solicitors now, so stay away. That's a warning.'

'Big gangster now, are you?'

He zipped up his jacket. 'Just heed my words or you'll regret it.'

He walked off and I was ranting and raving at the prick, until the nurses came to calm me down.

The next day Neil and Sam came in to visit me

'So you're gonna do them, yeah?'

'Who?' Neil said.

'The fucking Harold Hill boys, who else?'

'Hang on, let's get this clear,' he said, looking confused. 'You carved one of them, battered him unconscious, then they returned mobbed up. No offence but it sounds pretty much fair and square now Mart.'

'Am I hearing this right?'

'I mean, these boys are local,' he continued. 'They're teenagers. The whole thing could get out of hand. Do we need that kind of attention?'

'Look,' Sam said, butting in. 'We'll look into it, see what we can do.'

'Damn right you will. You'll round them up and fucking torture the cunts.'

I watched them go. Neil and new boy Sam were nothing but a pair of mugs.

Alone in hospital I was suffering the black dog full and strong. My missus had left me and who else did I have?

After a few days I was discharged. My brother Chris drove me home, giving me crap about sorting my life out – and this from a bloke whose van-hire firm went bust and now he mowed fucking lawns.

'I run a landscape gardening business you tart. Big difference.'

'Oh I know, you're rolling in it. I can tell by the motor.'

'I do an honest day's work. Then I come home to my wife and kids. That's all I want and I'm happy. More than can be said about you.'

I didn't answer that one. Then next thing the tears had come and I was covering my eyes. Jesus, what was happening to me?

Chris tried joking through it, saying painkillers had done the same to him when he'd busted his leg, sent his head all over the place. Then he brightened the mood talking of our football days.

We'd been close back then. Running round causing havoc together. Chris had been a hard cunt in those days. Still was I suppose, if pushed. But he'd pulled himself together and settled down. Something I'd never done.

He dropped me off and offered to help with the clean-up of the house, but I told him I'd manage it.

The house was worse than I'd imagined. Shit wasn't only on the kitchen floor, it was smeared along the walls. I stood in the living room staring at the space where the TV had been. They'd taken the stereo too. Even the toaster was gone.

I set about clearing the place up.

Then hours later I sat in my empty house and realised I needed a think. A big think.

A few days later I got a call from a contact called Roger. He was ex-Met police, now a security consultant for Microsoft. His info didn't come cheap, but it was worth every penny.

'Well, what's the score?' I asked.

'Looks like your little hunch was correct,' he said. 'Sam Johnson, real name Terence Lewis. He's on the payroll. Helped on an operation in Felixstowe last year. A big shipment of coke.

Everyone involved was put away, apart from him of course. He's no angel either. Attempted murder, GBH, torture, you name it, but it seems they'd rather have him on the street.'

I packed my bags. Two hours later I had a hefty wad stuffed down my briefs and pretty much everything else I needed. My flight was at 7pm. Stansted to Malaga.

At the airport my phone rang. It was Neil.

'So the meet's on for tomorrow, yeah?' he said.

'What meet?' I asked.

'Felixstowe... you know, the shipment?'

'Don't know what you're talking about. But if you mean drugs, that's bad news. I'm straight these days. Clean as a whistle. And you can tell that to your mate as well. Adios, Neil.'

BROADWATER FARM
BLUES

Riz was sitting in McDonald's watching the door and getting impatient. Slick had said 9pm, just be there, no calls, but it was already half past and he was sucking his milkshake dry.

He phoned the prick. 'Where the fuck you at?'

'Chill,' Slick said. 'I'm approaching Seven Sisters, I'll be there in five.'

Riz wanted to cuss the fucker but he hung up, said nothing. No business meant no money and if the deal he was arranging tonight went smoothly he'd be due a percentage. Not much, but still, another day another pound note.

He headed out on to Tottenham High Road and stood by a doorway. A police van went by and he hung low beneath his hood until it was out of sight. He couldn't be too careful right now as there was a warrant out with his name on. He'd slashed up two crackheads who tried to jump him one night. They wouldn't be trying that again, but he was in no hurry to go rushing back to prison either. He could be looking at years this time. He didn't want to think about it.

He saw Slick's Audi pulling up by the lights, went over and jumped in the back. Slick put his fist out without turning from the wheel and Riz paused, kissing his teeth before bumping it. This got a snigger from the guy riding shotgun, a mouthy light-skinned dude called Benny. Riz ignored him, the car swinging a left up Bruce Grove.

'You bring all the dough?' Riz asked Slick.

'Nah bred, I came empty handed,' Slick said and both at the front started cracking up.

'Laugh all you like, but T-Bone said no credit so if you ain't got the full payment the deal's off.'

They stopped laughing. Then Slick said, 'T-Bone can suck my black fucking dick coz there ain't gonna be no payment.'

Riz almost doubletook. 'You what?'

Slick kept driving while Benny turned to flash him a look of pride. 'T's getting done innit. No niceties.'

Riz was looking from Slick to Benny, seeing only the sides of their faces now.

'Have you two gone fucking batshit?'

'No,' said Slick. 'I'm just taking back what's mine. Remember the product T sold me a few months back? It was leaned on so heavily it was practically legal. I could hardly shift that shit.'

'You're mad,' Riz said. 'Do you think T's gonna be alone up in this flat? He'll have a whole armed squadron with him.'

'You're wrong. He's got only Yo-Yo with him. And you know how I know that? Because Yo-Yo's one of us.'

Slick and Benny started laughing, bumping fists.

'Yo-Yo with the plaits?' Riz asked. 'Scar down his face?'

'That's the guy.'

'No way. I was in Pents with him, he's a snake. I've heard bare tales about that prick, trust me.'

Slick shot him a look, no jokes. 'That's my cousin you're talking about there.'

'I'm just repeating what I've heard. Shit happens you know.'

'Not between family it don't, so shut your fucking teeth.'

Riz sat back, unwilling to debate it.

'Anyway, Yo-Yo's safe,' Slick continued. 'It's the perfect ambush. T-Bone's in for a surprise.'

They turned down a side road. Up ahead two girls stepped out of a car, headlights illuminating a nice set of curves.

'You see the one in the white leggings?' Benny pointed out. 'That's Pantha's sister Lisa. You can look but you can't touch. Break the rule and his posse of machete ninjas will come for your dick.'

'Well they ain't come for mine,' Slick grinned, 'and I've rode that booty bare times.'

'Rah, her arse is bigger than Kim K, man,' Benny's eyes agog as he turned in his seat.

'Even better, it's real – and I know coz I've gripped the ting.'

They passed by, Lisa giving Slick a smile.

But Riz's mind was on more pressing matters. They were on their way to rob one of the Farm's top dealers – T-Bone for fucksake – a job akin to a kamikaze mission.

Riz leaned forward. 'Listen, the whole thing's a bad idea. It's not gonna work. T ain't going to allow it.'

'He ain't got no choice,' Slick replied. 'And besides, do you know how much money we're going to make tonight?'

Riz shook his head... but felt a twinge of curiosity.

'How much?' he asked.

'How does enough to spend the next six months work-free, livin' la vida loca sound?'

'You serious?'

'He's got ten key of pure coke up there. Weaponry, cash, the works.'

'Along with the stash of brown?'

Slick smiled. 'Now you're understanding me.'

Riz was feeling the pull. But he had a query.

'How did you get all this intel, was it from Yo-Yo?'

'Less of the questions,' Slick snapped, kissing his lips. 'Need-to-know basis innit.'

They drove into the Broadwater Farm Estate, a maze of high and low-level blocks. The site of bare fuckery through the years, rioting, cop killing, the works. Riz was a little excited now, which he knew he shouldn't be because not only did T-Bone trust him to set up these deals but he was actually a friend. They grew up together, knew each other since school. But then again T-Bone had been getting flash lately. Strutting about in fancy garbs and sporting a different motor every time he saw him - and here was Riz, still hustling the roads for a few notes like a teenager.

Maybe Slick was right, maybe T-Bone needed taking down a peg.

Then he thought of last year when T's mum was in hospital dying of cancer; Riz, T and T's sister watching her take her last breath right there. T broke down and Riz held him. Then T-Bone dried his eyes and they went drinking. One bottle of Guinness after another, the strong Nigerian shit. He passed Riz half a grand that night, even tried to give him his watch but Riz refused. 'You've been a brother to me from day dot,' T-Bone said, smiling through his grief as he shook his shoulder, and Riz felt so close to him that night. True brethren. Like back at school. Back when they'd been equals, a duo, laughing and joking together, having the whole class cracking up.

But bare times through the years T had snubbed him. He'd seen him struggling and didn't give a shit. Maybe Riz hadn't always let on how tight things were sometimes, but still. He was even getting cocky about this deal tonight. Saying he wanted every note laid down, not a penny less. Talking down to him like he was his lackey or some shit. Boasting how he supplied the best merch in town. He'd moved on up with the shakers, hanging out at fancy parties with big time Turks and white guys from Essex while Riz was left in McDonald's at a dirty table counting his change. It was time to redress the balance. Business was business.

They pulled down into the covered car park, killed the engine.

'You bring tools?' Riz asked.

132

Suddenly Benny whipped out a Magnum .45, pointing the barrel in his face. 'You talkin' to me punk?' he laughed.

In a flash Riz whipped out his eight-inch zombie knife, lunging at the fucker.

'Point that thing at me again and I'll cut you up big time!'

Slick got between them. 'Chill, the both of you.'

'Guy's a fucking dickhead,' Riz said.

'I was only pranking man, playing Dirty Harry innit!'

'I'll be pranking when I'm carving you like Freddie.'

'ENOUGH!' Slick shouted and there was silence.

Both settled back.

'You two better stop the comedy act, I ain't joking. This is work, we're on a job here. Are we a team or what?'

They glanced at each other and nodded.

'Right then, bump fists.'

'What?'

'I said bump fucking fists, you hearing me?'

Benny put out his spud and Riz banged it.

'Playground games over. Now let's roll.'

They got out of the car and Slick flipped the boot to select the hardware. He tucked a sawn-off 12-bore shotgun under his coat then passed Riz a neat little revolver. Brand new and oiled.

'Cool piece,' Riz said admiringly, tucking it into his waist.

'Anyone gets fresh, shoot 'em in the face,' Slick quipped. Then he slammed down the boot and checked left and right. 'Okay, let's do this.'

They walked across the estate, an eerie feel to the place, nobody about. Reaching T-Bone's block they headed up the stairs and along the scruffy corridor, deep beats reverberating from a flat above. Don't care what anyone says, the Farm was still well grimy. Riz had spent his first ten years growing up on this estate. His first ever memory was his dad beating on his mum. He remembered once she tried to fend him off with a saucepan and he grabbed it off her, bashing her over the head repeatedly. He saw shit like that so often it was almost normal. One day his dad drunkenly trashed the place and never returned. Then two years ago his dad got in contact, wanted to meet him. Maybe he wanted to say sorry, clear his conscience – then again Riz was flush at this point after doing a job; maybe his dad had heard and wanted to cadge some money. Fuck knows. It turned out he lived in Walthamstow, only a few miles away. 'Come into the big Paddy Power by the market,' he said. 'Ask for Cedrick, everyone knows me.' Fuck that, Riz hung up on him.

Then a few weeks later when he was feeling down he thought he'd take his old man up on the offer. Riz headed for E17. He walked into the bookies and asked some ancients who pointed over to a little black guy in a hat, going grey at the sides. No way. His memories were of a hulking mad ogre, but then again he was only a kid. Walking up behind him he realised his fists were clenched and felt his breath tight in his chest, and for some reason he couldn't do it, couldn't meet him. It was like he was still scared of the guy. He walked outside and sat on a bench. Maybe he should just go home, leave the past alone. Then he saw him coming out of the bookies. He was with another old guy, but after a chat and a laugh they parted. Just then Riz had a flashback of his old man burning his arm on an electric bar fire. He wondered if he was imagining it, then he rolled up his sleeve to see the scar his mum had always told him was a birth-mark. He got up and followed him.

The man headed down the backstreets, then entered an alley that led to an estate. Riz checked left and right then upped his pace. Reaching him he threw him against the wall and the man put up his arms pleading. He smelled of rum and didn't seem to know him from Adam. Not knowing what else to say Riz shouted, 'Give me your fucking money.'

The man tried pushing past him but he yanked him back and punched him to the ground. He found a pocketful of change and

134

a single fiver, but threw the lot aside, he didn't want it. He held him by the lapels staring into him; he had so many things to say but couldn't form a single word. Then someone was shouting from the end of the alley and Riz ran.

A week later he was at the flat of a friend called Buzzfly. They were watching TV, blitzed out on strong weed.

'You seen this shit?' Buzz said, tossing a local paper onto his lap. Riz was low on the sofa, but seeing his dad's face on the cover woke him right up. *OAP ATTACKED FOR A FIVER.* His old man's face stared back at him, one eye blown right up. Riz read him saying how there was no respect these days and they should bring back national service. Either that or the birch. He felt his anger build and tore the paper in two.

'That's exactly how I feel bro,' Buzz said. 'The suspect's a black man too. Niggas beating on the old folks. There's no respect out there no more.'

Riz got up and told him he had to go...

'You listening?' Slick said and suddenly he was back on the Farm, standing by T-Bone's front door. Slick told him to ring the bell while he and Benny hid out of view. Riz pressed it and soon T-Bone opened up a few inches, peering through the crack.

'You should've texted, blud,' T told him, eyes swivelling left and right. 'Where's Slick?'

Suddenly Slick and Benny sprang from the sides trying to barge the door but it was on the chain. It took several kicks for Slick to get it open, then they stormed up the hall and into the living room, guns pointing left and right but T-Bone was nowhere to be seen.

'Sshh,' said Slick, putting a finger to his lips. 'Stay calm. This might call for commando tactics.'

Slowly they followed him along the hallway and first checked the kitchen. Nothing. Then they tried the bathroom, ripping away the shower curtain. Zilch. Only the bedroom was left. Slick prepared to kick it open... Boom: they stormed in but again the room was empty.

Now even Slick was confused. 'What the fuck?' He was almost completing a three-sixty when T-Bone burst from the wardrobe firing shots at him – one, two, three. Slick collapsed to the floor gurgling blood, then another wardrobe flew open, Yo-Yo stepping out armed and dangerous ordering them to 'Drop 'em – now!'

Riz and Benny obeyed, standing there hands-up. Benny was trembling, mouth pleading.

'Shut up,' said Yo-Yo and pistol-whipped him down onto the bed.

Benny cowered. 'Please don't shoot me, please...'

'End him,' T-Bone ordered.

Yo-Yo stepped forward with a grin. He placed his 9 mil to Benny's mouth.

'Suck it,' he said.

'No... please.'

'I said suck the fucking ting!'

Benny took the barrel in his mouth, head going back and forth.

T-Bone and Yo-Yo were laughing away: Look at this batty-man. What a pussy. T-Bone turned to Riz nodding at the scene and Riz couldn't help but give a chuckle too.

Then Yo-Yo said, 'Fuck this,' and blasted Benny in the head, the contents of his skull pasting across the wall.

'Rahhh,' said T-Bone, impressed. 'What ammo you packing, Yo?'

'Hollow point innit. Explode on impact,' Yo-Yo said, blowing the tip of the gun.

'Nice.'

Finally T-Bone turned to point his gun at his old friend Riz, shaking his head in sadness.

'Who would've thought it? Me and you fam. Fucking blood

brothers and you pull this stunt on me?'

'You're wrong, T,' Riz tried. 'I came here to set up the deal – on my mum's life. I knew nothing about this. You can blame these two dicks,' nodding to the bodies of Slick and Benny.

T-Bone turned to Yo-Yo who was chewing on a matchstick, looking Riz up and down.

'Don't believe him,' Yo said. 'He knew the score.'

Yo-Yo stepped forward to pick Riz's revolver off the floor.

'That thing loaded?' T-Bone asked him.

Yo-Yo checked the spinner, looking baffled. 'Surprisingly not.'

'You see?' Riz said jumping at the chance. 'You think I'd come on a job with an empty piece? These fuckers sprung this crap on me the moment you answered the door. I didn't know jack shit.'

Yo-Yo began playing with Riz's gun, menacingly pointing and clicking it in his face while T-Bone stood wondering if there was a grain of truth in there somewhere.

'You know what,' T-Bone said, nodding to Slick's body. 'I wouldn't put it past this clown to play a game like that.' Then he turned to Riz. 'And I wouldn't put it past you to fall for it.'

'Nor would I,' said Yo-Yo, adding: 'If it was the truth, that is. But it ain't.'

Yo-Yo put the revolver to Riz's forehead, clicking off another empty shot, Riz feeling the pressure now. Yo-Yo came in close. 'You would've stood by watching us get wasted, guaranteed,' he said, tapping the barrel to his own temple in emphasis: 'Do you think we're fucking stupid?'

Yo-Yo must've pressed the trigger, a slug in there somewhere because BANG! - suddenly he'd blown his own brains out. A mist of red filled the air as his body collapsed sideways.

Riz lurched back in shock and T-Bone was surprised too - 'Huh?' - eyes wide, going from a dead Yo-Yo to Riz and back again.

Finally T-Bone shook his head, tucked away his gun and

stood holding his chin.

'Oh my days.'

They sat in the living room, T-Bone opening two bottles of Guinness. After all that drama in the bedroom Riz needed it. A dating show was on the telly and some of the women were hot. 'I'd take the chunky one man,' T said. 'I like that, a woman with a bit of meat. Nice set of curves and ting.'

'Nah, I'd go for the blonde. Nice legs and that.'

'Yeah but you need some curvature in the mix, complete the full picture you know.'

Then a new couple was introduced on the show. Two men.

'Is this for real?' T-Bone said, screwing his face. 'Fucking bumboys, man. I ain't watching this shit,' and he turned it over in disgust. He started building a spliff.

Riz put down his drink and sat forward. 'T, listen. What are we gonna do about, you know?' He nodded to the next room.

'Them three? Fuck knows. Nothing's happening tonight, I know that much. I need to chill after all that fuckery. Tell you what though, I'll make some calls in the morning. I know a guy who works in disposal. A waste site in Essex. He owes me a favour. That should do the trick.'

Riz felt eased a little. At least T had a plan.

'Don't know about you, but I need a night in,' T-Bone said, lighting up and inhaling. 'But no worries there. There's a caseload of Guinness here and as much ganja as you can smoke.'

Which got Riz thinking...

'You've got other shit too,' he winked, already feeling the pick-me-up.

'You mean coke, crack and that?' T laughed. Then he shook his head: 'Uh, uh.'

'But what about the deal?'

'All jackanory mate.'

Riz was lost for a moment. 'But if there was nothing to deal...

138

that means you and Yo planned to ambush Slick and Benny all along?'

'That's right,' T nodded.

'Then, what about me?'

'What about you, you're safe blud. You and me are the last men standing. You should feel grateful, I do. That could be me or you on the floor in there. It's life – it's a dangerous game.'

Riz mulled on that for a few seconds. Then he shrugged, couldn't be bothered stressing himself.

T-Bone shook his head. 'Must admit though–Yo-Yo shooting his own brains out. I never saw that one coming.'

'Nor me. But the guy was trouble anyway. I was in Pents with him. He caused nuff ructions on the wing.'

'And he wasted Burgerman,' T told him. 'And I liked that guy. They had a row over a pair of Nikes. Then next day Yo walked up to him as he sat in his new BMW down Turnpike Lane. He was there munching on a take-out when Yo says, Hey Burgs, nice car, and shoved a screwdriver through his neck.'

'I heard about that. Didn't know it was Yo-Yo though. I thought it was a guy called Spiderman.'

'Spider from Hornsey? He got shot in the arse last night. Up Leyton or somewhere. He was round Dessie's girl's house to get the slug pulled out coz she's a nurse. She told me he was screaming like a girl. Though I heard he killed a guy up Ipswich last week, did him with a blade in the heart. Some county lines shit. Niggas are dropping like flies these days.'

'Tell me about it. Look at Fatty B the other week, gunned down up Wood Green. They shot him in the shoulder, he tries running into the barbershop and next thing he's got fifteen youngers swarming in and raining machetes down on him. I heard they had to hose the place down afterwards.'

'That's like Biggie C. He was visiting his baby mum up Edmonton way. He walks in and sees her tied up on the sofa, baby in the cot crying away. Next thing ten Somalians jump out swinging blades and by the time they're done with him the place is like a butcher's shop, blood all over the ceiling. He'd been ripping people off left and right though, taking the mick. Even tried it with me once the fucker. Still though, he was one of us, knew him from way back.'

'His mum was good to us back in the day too. Used to bring us in for cakes and drinks and that. Always trying to get us to go to church. You remember that?'

'Yeah, old times fam,' T laughed. 'The good old days.' Then he shrugged his shoulders. 'But there you go. Life is cheap in this game.'

Just then T's phone rang. It was one of his women giving him hassle.

'Yeah yeah, whatever...'

Finally he hung up.

'Fucking bitches, man. Always on my case.'

Then Riz remembered he'd better text his own woman. He had told her he'd be round later which wasn't happening now. He patted himself for his phone but he didn't have it. He stood up.

'Where you going?' asked T.

'Must've left my phone in the bedroom.'

'Well don't go waking anyone in there,' T giggled.

Riz opened the door and what a scene.

It was like a mini war zone, blood and bodies everywhere. But guys like this wouldn't be missed, that's for sure. In fact there'd probably be a few parties in celebration. Riz spotted his phone on the floor and stepped over Slick's corpse to retrieve it when Slick's not-so-dead hand gripped his leg.

Riz jumped in fright, almost falling over as he kicked himself free. Then he saw Slick leaning up on one elbow, face covered in blood, wielding his sawn-off shotgun.

'Die fucker,' he said and BOOM! - a spray of buckshot blew the Rizlaman straight backwards.

Riz was crumpled on the bed, gripping his burst-open torso, vision gone psychedelic as he watched Slick drag himself upright, leaning by the wall, shotgun gripped in both hands, waiting for T-Bone to come calling.

T was bang on cue. 'What's that fucking noise?' he said before Slick blasted him in the face.

Job done, Slick dropped his weapon and slid down the wall to join the other bodies littering the floor, some already dead, some heading that way.

THE MEAT TRADE

We're rolling up the A1 out of London, young Dwayne in the back of the van holding a gun to Smithy's head and telling him to stop the fucking crying.

'I'm telling you now, man,' he says, 'you better shut your mouth or I'm gonna make things painful for you, trust me.'

I'm at the wheel thinking of other things – why not, it's only a job after all, nothing personal - when a police car appears alongside us on the motorway, the copper riding shotgun clocking the state of the van.

I stare ahead and grip the wheel, try to stay calm, praying for a miracle. Getting pulled for the mistake of pulling off some work in a battered old Transit is a mistake I'd never forgive myself for. Then suddenly they're off, lights flashing, speeding ahead to attend to more important matters. Thank fuck for that.

I should be relaxing now, but Smithy's incessant whining is beginning to grate.

'Come on lads,' he's pleading. 'I've got a wife, three kids that'll be left fatherless…'

Then he's addressing me solely. 'Gal, please, we're mates, how can you do this to me?'

I'll tell you how, I feel like telling him, because I'm getting fucking paid mate, that's how. I might've grafted with the bloke now and then, but we're hardly lifelong buddies so it's time he turned off the waterworks.

I'm surprised at him, I really am. Usually so full of himself, prancing about, the big I-am. Now look at the cunt. Rabbiting on, giving me a bloody headache.

And another thing, if he didn't want himself tugged he should've thought twice before sticking a knife in Nick the Greek. Everyone knew the bubble was working for the Family, it was hardly a secret. Take out one of the brothers' good earners and you pay the price. Smithy knows the rules.

'Will you shut the fuck up,' Dwayne says, gun-butting him but he only starts screaming louder. I squint as the decibels begin to deafen me. The bloke sounds like a stuck pig.

'Right, that's it - that's fucking it,' and I hear Dwayne cocking the gun.

'Take it easy D,' I warn him. 'No dramas. Not till we get there anyway.'

Then Smithy starts struggling, trying to kick his way out of the van even though we're moving at a steady seventy.

Dwayne is shouting, trying to control the mad cunt, then suddenly: BAM!!!… and there's silence. The van fills with the acrid smell of cordite.

Jesus Christ. He's just shot the fucker.

'Gary,' Dwayne says. 'I know you said not in the van but the guy was doing my head in.'

I exhale. Then I say, 'Well, at least you got him to button it.'

Dwayne kisses his teeth. 'The fucker's splashed his blood all over me,' he says, wiping himself down.

'Don't worry about that. Once we're finished everything's getting burned, our clothes, the van, the lot.'

'You think I'm binning my new Nikes for this prick?'

I turn around. 'You fucking are mate.'

He leaves it a beat then laughs. 'Bruv, I'm joking. Jeez.'

I turn back to the road. Yeah, I think to myself, and I'll be joking when I'm smashing your head with a hammer.

It's the first time I've been paired with the youngster but already I'm hoping it's my last. The boy might be handy with a shooter on the back of a bike, but this is real work. Work for the adults. I'll have to have a word with Mad Mick. Next job, no Dwayne.

Half an hour ago we'd picked up Smithy from a café in Finchley. All arranged, a supposed business meet with a contact up in Hatfield. But before we even reached the van he sensed something and tried to run for it. Dwayne chased him down a back alley and, fair play to him, caught the bastard as he tried scrambling over a wall. He kept him on the ground while I drove the van in. So far so good.

But now Dwayne had killed the fucker. The three of us were supposed to walk into the flat in Hatfield and Smithy would get a bullet in the nut. The flat was all set out for the purpose. A quick, easy death. Then we'd have the whole night to work on disposal. But not everything runs smooth in this game. Especially not with a young street chancer in tow. Now we'd have to risk our arses dragging a dead body up two flights of outdoor steps. Thanks Dwayne.

I take the turn into Hatfield and soon we're pulling into a passage behind some shops. I climb into the back of the van to check the state of things. Smithy's skull has a fist-sized hole, blood and gore leaking all over.

'What ammo did you use?'

'Dum-dum bullets – powerful slugs.'

'That's clever. Explains why you've got half his brains still down your face.'

'What?' He touches his jaw. 'Fuck, man.'

'I'm having you on.'

I grab some tarp and twine. 'Come on, let's get him sealed up or he'll be spilling his mess everywhere.'

The alley is dark and deserted, and we get him up the steps

no problem. Inside the flat we dump him in the bath. Dwayne is looking around at the floor-to-ceiling plastic sheeting. Then he notices the hacksaws, knives and cleavers.

'So this is what Mad Mick meant by disposal.'

'What else did you have in mind?'

'Don't know. Didn't really think about it to be honest.'

'We're jointing him. Reducing him down good and proper, then storing it all in the big freezer you'll find in the kitchen. What happens then is somebody else's job.'

'You mean he'll be buried or something?'

'Maybe. More likely he'll end up at a pig farm or meat plant. It certainly makes more sense.'

'Are you telling me next time I buy a kebab it could be human fucking meat?'

'It very well could be, yeah. Definitely has been at points in the past, I can vouch for that.'

'This is sick.'

I stop and look at him.

'You've never done any heavy stuff before, have you?'

'Are you kidding me? I've done plenty shit. I fucking buried some guy alive once. Epping Forest. Got him to dig his own grave and everything.'

'Okay, I believe you. But anyone can toss a bit of soil over somebody. Dismembering a human corpse is on a different level. Separates the men from the boys.'

'What are you saying?'

'I'm saying you don't have the fucking balls for it.'

'Bullshit. Come on then, try me - let's do this.'

We shove on boiler suits and fair play to him, he gives it a go. But half an hour in, he's face down in the khazi regurgitating his Kentucky.

'Come on, let's have a break,' I say, snapping off the gloves. 'I fancy a cup of tea and a sandwich. With lots of tomato sauce.'

In the living room we sit watching TV.

'So how many of these jobs have you done?' he asks.

'Cutting jobs? Half a dozen I reckon.'

'Jeez... all for the Family?'

'Who else. Mick might give the orders but it always leads back to the Family.'

He nods to the bathroom. 'What do you reckon the guy did to piss them off?'

'Could be anything,' I say, not mentioning the business with Nick the Greek as it's none of the boy's concern. 'Knowing Smithy he was probably throwing their names around for his own ventures. He fancied himself, thought he was bigger than he was. But that's coke for you. Mix it with the steroids and away you go. An inflated ego can be a dangerous thing.'

He mulls on that for a while, then says, 'How far up do you reckon the Family go?'

'Right to the top I reckon. And I'm talking the very top. No reason why not. The higher you go the more criminal it gets. But they're clever. They're not attention seekers. That's the trick. Be quiet, respectable, blend in with all the other grey suits. And always keep your own hands clean.'

Dwayne puts his feet up.

'That's what I want to do,' he says. 'Become a businessman. Get hold of some serious cash and invest. I can just see myself behind a big desk, minions at my beck and call. And women... yeah. A nice secretary to cater for my personal needs. That's the masterplan. I'm hitting twenty-two next month so I'll have to start fast-tracking. No way do I want to be your age and doing jobs like this, never... no offence though.'

I don't answer that one. Leave Dwayne to his dreamworld. He flicks the remote and settles on a crime doc. The Met doing raids on a housing estate.

'Rah!' he points. 'I know that block, that's Tiverton. I used to be hanging out round those flats night and day.'

We watch the coppers storm in, get the suspects on the floor,

147

one escaping through the window all to get his arse chewed by a K9.

'You a Tottenham boy then?' I say.

'Grew up there bruv. That's my roots. South T for life. Where do you come from?'

'Tottenham.'

'You serious?'

'Why wouldn't I be? Tower Gardens. North T.'

'That's near the Farm, I know bare gangstas from up that way.'

'I remember when they built the fucking Farm.'

'Jeez, put it there, old G,' he says, holding out his fist.

'Less of the old,' I say, bumping it.

I leave him in front of the TV. 'Right, I'm cracking on. But don't get too comfortable because I might need you at intervals.'

'No probs, but the less the better,' he says.

'Just be ready, that's all.'

I head to the bathroom and glove up. Time to open the rib rack and separate the organs.

I'm working swiftly through the job, until two hours later I decide on a bit of sport. I creep up behind him holding Smithy's arm.

I wave the bloodstained hand next to his face and he jumps up out of his seat shitting himself.

'Jesus fuck!' he says, standing there clutching his chest.

'Classic,' I laugh.

'You're a freak.'

'Too right I am,' I say, walking away.

Lazy arsed fucker. Sitting there watching dating shows while I'm here sweating my bollocks off.

I carry on working away. But after a while I need his help.

'D mate, I need you,' I call.

'I'll be there in two,' he answers.

'You'll be here now, just like Oasis mate,' I shout.

He appears, does the bare minimum to help, then skulks off back to the room to put his feet up.

I soldier on. By the time I've got the body cut and bagged, it's 5am. I did a neat and thorough job if I say so myself. The neck and elbows were a bit stubborn, but that's the human animal for you. Not an easy beast to butcher.

'Come on Dwayne, you're needed,' I call. 'We need to get this little lot in the freezer.' I get no response. 'Shift your arse. Where are you, you skiving cunt?'

I walk into the living room and sure enough he's stone asleep.

I go back to the bathroom, de-bag Smithy's head and return holding it by the hair in front of his face, a hollowed-out death mask.

'Wakey-wakey.'

He opens his eyes, pauses, then leaps out of his skin.

I'm laughing like a dog with two dicks when he pushes me in the chest. 'Don't fuck around like that!'

I stop, glance down at my chest, then look at him.

'Hey, I'm sorry,' he says. 'But you scared the living crap out of me with that thing.'

'Here, catch.' I toss it and for a moment he actually does, before it drops and rolls across the room.

'Jesus, don't do that!' he says.

I pick it up and chuckle my way back to the bathroom.

Fucking cunt pushing me.

I pick up two bags.

'Come on, young man, give me a hand with this shit. We need to pack the freezer with produce. Then we can go and get some breakfast.'

After torching the van by a derelict factory, we climb into a little Toyota and set off back to London. Breakfast first then we'll drop the car at Mick's to tell him job done.

'Why do they call him Mad Mick anyway?' D asks in the car. 'He don't seem like no psycho to me, just an ordinary Joe working in a garage.'

'He's mad alright, trust me on that,' I tell him. 'The ones who don't flaunt it are often the worst.'

'I know much madder men out there. Madder and badder full stop,' he says. 'I reckon the guy's tame. He likes giving orders, that's about it.'

I shake my head and turn on the radio. Even Barry Manilow beats the rubbish Dwayne's coming out with.

In the cafe Dwayne nibbles on a bacon roll while I scoff a Full English. But that's no surprise. He might've helped on a few street hits in his time – or so I've heard - but in every other respect he's a one hundred percent pansy.

'Here, you want a bit of egg with that?' I say, forking up some yolk and holding it out to him, but he just rolls his eyes, stroppy now because he hasn't had his eight hours beauty sleep.

We pull into Mick's garage round the back of Kentish Town. We sit waiting while Mick paces up and down on the phone having a row with his wife. Clicking off, he comes over.

'I went and forgot my lunchbox, didn't I? I'll forget my fucking head next minute. Anyway, it's all cleared up now, the missus is bringing it round. Cheese and pickle. And an apple.'

He wipes his hands with a rag, then nods me towards the office leaving Dwayne sitting playing on his phone.

'Okay,' he says, sitting behind the desk. 'How did it go?'

'Done and fucking dusted, Mick.'

'Thank God for that,' he says, finally relaxing. 'I really appreciate it Gal. You've never let me down, not once. How was the new boy, work hard did he?'

I'm about to go with the flow, keep him happy, but that push in the chest the prick dished out is still riling me.

'To be honest Mick, he spent half the night sleeping in front of the telly. I did all the work myself.'

'You what?'

'I don't want to be too hard on him, but it's just not his scene I suppose. Youngsters, you know.'

'The lazy fucking cunt. Sorry about that Gary, I tried to get Sledgehammer Steve to help you but he's fucked off to Holland. You won't be working with Dwayne again, I tell you that.'

'The job's done so what does it matter. Piece of piss. I'd rather you not mention anything.'

'No worries there, Gal. I'll get at the cunt some other way.'

He stands up, claps and rubs his hands together. 'Anyway, business over. How's the wife, all good?'

'Yeah - still complaining though, you know how it is.'

'I know well mate,' he laughs.

We head back out, Mick saying I'll be getting an invite to his daughter's engagement party.

'Event of the year I promise you. I've booked a Bee Gees act for the adults and a Katy Perry for the young 'uns,' he's saying when we both stop at the sight of Dwayne standing flirting with his missus.

She walks forward and hands Mick his lunchbox.

'Lovely young man,' she says, thumbing back at the boy. 'How come you never compliment me like that?'

'I'll see you later,' he says bluntly.

'Okay, be like that then,' she huffs, walking away. As she passes Dwayne, he gives her a wink then returns to his mobile.

Mick's face has turned to stone. Cold hard stone.

The last time I saw that expression was when he walked up behind Spider O'Mullen from the Cally and slit his throat. Spider had been telling a light-hearted joke at Mick's expense. He can be pretty sensitive like that.

'Take this,' he says quietly and hands me his lunch. 'Now close up shop.'

151

He heads back to the office and I walk to the entrance and pull the sliding shutters.

Dwayne looks up from his phone. 'What's going on?' he asks.

In unison we turn to see Mad Mick standing in the middle of the floor wielding a shotgun.

The youth jumps to his feet, but the force of the blast sends him crashing back against the shutters. He lands sprawled on the deck with a gaping hole where his heart should be.

'Another job for you,' Mick says. 'Now get rid of this,' and he throws me the gun. 'And get rid of that,' he says, pointing at Dwayne.

THE HAND

No way. No cunt takes the piss like that. I've packed my samurai and I'm heading straight over there. Mate or no mate, he's getting it, the junkie fucker. Eight hours banged up and when I get home - my gear – there's no sign of it - someone's been in. Think I don't know it's you, you little prick? This time I swear it, you're getting taught a lesson. Had it too good from me, that's what, too many fucking times.

I get to the junction of Turnpike Lane and by the High Road there's police cordons, crowds, the lot. All I need. I make a wide berth and hear someone say it was a gang fight, some kid shot dead or something. Nothing new there then. But with all this filth about I've got to watch it. Getting done with a weapon is the last thing I need. I press on. Hit the backstreets towards Tony's place.

I bang on the door – 'Open up. Now' – Then there he is greeting me in his boxers – 'Alright mate' – like butter wouldn't melt.

'You pisstaking cunt!' I belt him in the face and down he goes. I'm kicking him down the hallway – 'I want my fucking gear!' – when suddenly his girlfriend appears, notices what I've just whipped out of my coat and starts screaming, running straight past me out of the house in her bra and knickers.

153

'That's right you tart, fuck off!' – kicking the door shut – then I'm moving back to Tony, on the floor by the stairs shitting himself now.

'Mikey, I swear it, I don't even know what this is about.'

'You lying little wanker,' I say, lifting the sword.

'No, please...'

'You've been round my gaff Tone. Ripping me off again. Last time I'm with you I lose my wallet, now this – letting yourself in!'

'Honest, I swear it Mikes, I've been here all day. Honest...'

'SHUT UP! I know it was you, you cunt, I fucking know it.'

'No... No...' He's crying now, tears flowing down his face. 'I swear it man, on my mum's life...' and look at him: he thinks he can turn on the waterworks and each time I'll let him off. No fucking way.

'UP! Get up! On your feet, now! You're going to take this like a man, you wimp...' I'm pulling him up but he's trying to stay down, face screwed up, pleading away...

'I SAID GET THE FUCK UP!' – booting him in the gut but he's crying even more...

'I ain't saying this twice Tone. Just stand up and hold your hand out, you'll get a stripe and that'll be the end of it. You're getting taught a lesson.' I'm poking him with my foot... 'You fucking listening to me?'

Then to my surprise he's staggering to his feet. Tears, snot – the state of him. Blubbering away. Same old shit since we were kids. Pathetic...

And I don't know... I feel like maybe leaving it. Like I've tortured him enough. I mean, what can you do with a fool like this. Maybe he knows next time not to go robbing my gaff... after all, it wasn't much really... only a gram or two... well gone now I'm sure... and luckily I did find a bit of spare...

Yeah, fuck this... maybe I'll just nick something and leave it at that.

But then he fucks up. Tries grabbing for the sword, the silly cunt. Never learns. I belt him with a left hook, and he slams back against the wall, should fall and that should be that - but then he's coming at me again, grabbing for the sword.

How much has this cunt got to learn? I clout him, one, two, and he's down. 'God, when are you going to FUCKING learn?' – for emphasis swiping the samurai a few inches from his face, a little gesture so he knows not to mess. But fuck-up number two: he puts his arm out, right in the line of fire and – Whoosh! – the samurai takes his hand clean off!

I'm stunned. We both are. Frozen in shock. His arm still out and the severed hand palm up on the floor. Suddenly Tony starts screaming all high pitched and I almost jump. He's clutching his wrist, panicking, looking up to me and back at the stump in disbelief.

I drop the sword and it thuds to the floor. Fuck. He's a mate. I've known him all my life. What have I done?

'You bastard! My hand! My fucking hand...!' Tears are flowing from his eyes, but I don't know what to say. I mean, fucking hell, I never meant to do that. I was just about to let the bastard off.

He's wailing and wailing; and his face, the stump, the hand, all that blood... and I'm breaking into a sweat, mind misfiring all over the shop, and I say: 'Tony, look mate, I never meant...'

'SHUT UP YOU CUNT!' he roars.

And there's no talking to him... I don't know what to do for the man... And suddenly I just need more gear. Don't need all this bollocks now. Just need a shot. Now. Need some of that stash that this cunt fucking swiped off me. I head into the front room, beer cans, mess, fucking trash everywhere. When I suddenly remember...

The gear... back at the flat... I'd hidden it under the loose floorboard... hadn't checked... hadn't remembered... SHIT!!!

I run back to Tony, pure panicking – 'Look, I don't know

what to say. I'm sorry man. Fucking hell, I'm so sorry...' and he's sitting there rocking back and forth, eyes stunned, in a trance of pain...

'GET A FUCKING AMBULANCE!' he shrieks.

'Okay! Yes! Of course!' I'm patting myself for my mobile but I must have forgotten it. 'Shit, Tone, where's your phone?'

'In there,' he gasps, 'on the table.'

'Right, okay...' But then I think, hang on a minute... ambulance... police... questions! No way!! I grab the sword and fling it beneath the stairs.

'Tony, listen, one thing. Let's say it was an accident, yeah? That we were just fucking about... like you slipped or something... I don't know, cut yourself... honest, I never meant this, none of it, I'm just so fucked at the moment.'

'WHATEVER, JUST GET ME A FUCKING AMBULANCE!'

'Okay. Okay!' I run back into the room, grab his phone, dial 999. 'Get your arses over here quick! Right now! My mate's just lost his fucking hand...' But it's like she isn't getting the severity of it, telling me to calm down and giving me instructions like I'm a fucking two-year-old... 'Whatever, just get here fast!'

I'm back by Tony's side. 'They're on their way mate, they're on their way...' He's looking fucking tragic now, staring into the wound and whimpering away while I'm just standing there feeling bad.

I look at the ceiling.... God!... all this shit. What happened to us? We had our own decorating business. Legit. Well, mostly anyway... but it all went tits up. We lost everything...

But fuck that, I need a blast. Can't handle this...

'Tony, listen. I know it's a bad time mate but honestly I need some gear... is there any in the house? I'll pay you back double, honest.'

He looks at me and I can see the disgust, total fucking contempt. 'There's a bottle of green in the kitchen. But keep

156

some for me you bastard.'

Methadone? Anything. I head to the kitchen. 'Now hang in there, yeah. Don't worry, they'll have that hand sewn back in no time, believe me. It's been done loads of times...' Then I remember something. They said to put it on ice, pronto! SHIT!'

Where's the fridge? There's no sign of it. I run back to Tony. 'Tony, the fucking fridge, where is it?' But he's shaking his head. 'What... no fridge? ... we need ice! They said to freeze the thing! Preserve it!'

'There fucking ain't one!'

Then I remember the place is a squat. And a fucking grotty one at that. But no fridge?

'It broke last week,' he says through breaths of pain. 'We flung it out, didn't we.'

So I'm thinking... I'm thinking. Maybe we should put it in water or something... don't know... maybe don't mess with it... yeah, probably do more bad than good. And I'm pacing back and forth. Where's the fucking ambulance!

Then I remember the bottle of green – and I'm straight back to the kitchen searching for it. I find it and belt it down – yes. Lean against the worktop for a while. Try to relax...

'AAAAAHHHHHH!'

I'm up like a shot. It's Tony. Shrieking like a fucking maniac. I run to him. 'What's going on?'

'My h-hand, he stammers. It just fucking m-m-moved!'

'What?'

'I just seen it. It flipped over by itself. I ain't lying!'

I look at it there on the floor. It's been turned over, palm down now, but so what? What's the bloke trying to say?

I get down and put my arm around him, try to sooth him but he keeps telling me the thing moved! It fucking moved! He's clutching on to me and it's pitiful. 'Tony mate, listen. You're in a bad way okay, in pain, you're just seeing things, yeah. It happens. I've been there...'

157

'AAAHHHH! IT JUST MOVED AGAIN!'

I feel for him, really do, wish the fuckers would hurry up, he's hallucinating all over the place. I look down at the hand and... hang on, maybe it does seem in a different place, closer to him now. But still...

'Calm down. You're shuffling about and moving the thing yourself. Just try and stay calm till the ambulance comes...' But he's telling me I don't understand, the thing is alive, and he's holding me tight, petrified, and I look to the hand and... I fucking see it myself... its fingers drumming on the carpet! 'AAAAAAHHHHHH!' Both of us.

Then suddenly it's still.

'See! I told you, I fucking told you!'

'Shut up!' I tell him. 'Shut up!'

We're clutching each other watching but it's not moving. Staring at it for ages. Nothing. Not a twitch.

'Now Tone, look,' I say, wiping sweat from my face. 'We just need to relax okay. We're just both fucked up right now... I mean, I don't need this shit. You're psyching me out man.'

'But we seen it. We both seen it!'

'SHUT UP! – I get up and start pacing up and down. 'We're both in a state okay. Just fucking seeing things alright!' But he's trying to shout me down. 'Shut up Tone, I don't want to hear it!'

I head into the room looking for the phone - Where are these cunts? - when suddenly: 'AAH! AAH! AAAAHHH!' Tony again... I run back.

'What now?'

He's leaning back against the stairs, screaming, and the hand... there it is... crawling up his chest, making its way to his neck, wrapping its fingers around his throat...

'TONY!'

I run over and try to seize the thing, but it's gripped tight, veins bulging, locked in a vice-like hold – My God! Jesus Christ!

– it's squeezing the life out of him and he's choking and struggling and fucking hell, I'm pulling and pulling but it won't budge, and his face is going from red to white to blue – 'TONY! TONY!' – for fuck's sake – I'm using all my strength, his eyes rolling in his head but the thing is stuck like steel, stuck there, it won't move... 'TONY!!!'

I'm still struggling but Tony is still now... limp... lifeless... Oh my God... he's dead!.. I don't believe this. I stand up; the hand still glued to his neck, Tony lying flat on the stairs, eyes wide-open in shock. Then the hand: gently it loosens its grip and topples to the floor.

I'm clutching my head in my hands. Shit... there's blood everywhere... Shit. It's too much to take. It's a fucking... murder scene. I panic. Can't handle this. No way. Got to move. Got to get out of here. Now.

I head straight out into the night, head down, moving fast, and... BAM! I slam straight into somebody. He's shouting and putting his arms out and wanting to start, but I don't have time for this shit, keep moving, threats hanging in the air, one foot in front of the other, don't even know where I'm going, one backstreet to the next, brain fucking scrambled...

'Alright Mikey. What's the rush?'

I turn and see a meatwagon cruising alongside me, a pig hanging out with a big sarky smile on his face. I'm stunned but – relax – stay calm – it'll be alright – just play it cool...

But I don't. I run. And of course they're all piling out like a sewer's just burst loose. SHIT! I dart up an alley, out into the next street and up another alley and yes, I'm making speed on the cunts I swear it, until – BOLLOCKS – there's more of the fuckers charging in from the other end, shit shit shit- but wait, I've got a chance and I take a jump for the fence into the back gardens but God it's a struggle, my coat sticking to a knot of barbed wire and fuck... it's no use, the sound of radios and shouting pigs, a pair of hands grabbing me – 'COME HERE

YOU CUNT!' – I fall and feel a baton cracking me across the skull and I'm down on the ground and there's more batons now, a dozen of them piling into me...

'GET UP!' I'm lifted to my feet. A copper puffing in my face. 'Running from us? NO-ONE FUCKING RUNS FROM US!' Poking his stick hard into my belly. 'YOU'RE NICKED! Now get this shitbag into the van before I fucking cripple the cunt.'

We're travelling through Wood Green and I'm clutching my gut. It hurts. I could skin that bastard.

One of them has my coat and he's ripping the lining to shreds and they're all around me in my face like I'm a monkey in a fucking zoo.

'So what's it been tonight then Mikey? Breaking into houses again, yeah?'

'Or handbags and wallets. That's another one of your pastimes ain't it? You fucking slime.'

'Selling drugs, nicking, making a nuisance of himself, you name it, he's done it.'

'Menace to society, that's Mikey here. Waste of space.'

'Junkies. If I had my way they'd be lined up and shot.'

'What do you say chaps, we just speed up and toss him out of the van, let the hospital deal with it. Don't think I want this dirt even near our nice clean nick.'

Then the cunt at the front who's been checking me on his radio goes: 'Here, guess what I've just heard. This is his second arrest today. They only released him from Edmonton a few hours ago. A shoplifting charge. Nicking razors from Boots!'

'Dear oh dear,' shaking their heads. Then one of them backhands me in the face. 'You fucking twat!'

'It's clean,' the one searching my coat goes. 'Nothing. One thing though,' - looking quizzical - 'there's kind of blood all over this thing...'

They laugh. 'Yeah, I know, we just kicked fuck out of the cunt. Ain't that right Mikey boy?'

'But no,' he says. 'It seems more like... dried blood.'

Something comes through on the radio, their ears pricking to attention.

'Serious incident. All available units. A murder off Turnpike Lane - Burghley Road. Suspect seen leaving house. IS1, dark hair, long leather coat...'

All have turned. They're staring at me in disbelief.

Then they look to each other and suddenly it's like they've scored for England. 'YEEEESSSS!!!' Clenching their fists and rubbing their hands together with glee.

'What?' I ask. 'What are you saying?'

'SUSPECT IN TRANSIT, OVER! We're onto a winner here boys! Struck fucking gold!'

'Well then Mikey, a murderer now, eh? In with the big boys. A-Cat.'

'What was it anyway, a row over a bit of skag?'

'What do you reckon lads, twenty years?'

'Nah, thirty-year tariff on this one. Definitely. Bad news, Mikey boy...'

Tony was my mate. I never killed him. I was there, mistakes happen – but I tried to fucking help him. In court they said evidence showed we must have tussled and I'd chopped his hand off then strangled him.

But that's bullshit. Total crap. But there was no telling the fuckers. They didn't want to know. They locked me up, said I was mentally ill. But you know it and I know it, crazy shit went down that night. Mad shit. Voodoo stuff... Are you listening to me?

SMILER WITH KNIFE

Re: Knife rampage, Edmonton 4.03.19.
Suspect Derek Tucker was interviewed by DC Tony Hedges and
DC Ian Driscoll, Edmonton Police Station, 16.8.19.
Owing to its controversial nature the recording was officially
'lost' but a copy was later discovered. This is an excerpt of the
transcript.

'So Derek, you say you left The Gilpin's Bell, Edmonton, that
night around 8.30pm and went on to The White Horse further
up Fore Street?'

'That's right. Me and Pat Brennan. We were together.'

DC Hedges turns a laptop screen towards the suspect.

'Well, take a look at this. Here's the footage of you leaving
The Gilpin's Bell.'

The screen plays some poor-quality footage of a figure
leaving the pub alone. Suspect folds his arms.

'Was that filmed on a fucking potato? That don't even look
like me. It could be anyone.'

'It's you alright. But the point is, it shows you leaving the pub
on your own. No Pat Brennan. You see Derek, you were never
in the pub with Mr Brennan at all that night, were you? You
drifted from pub to pub alone, and between each you committed

brutal acts of violence on random members of the public. People who simply happened to cross your path.'

Suspect shakes his head.

'Number one, that footage you've just showed isn't me. No way, it's a joke. And number two, let's see some footage of inside the pub, then we can all rest easy, how about that?'

'As we've already told you, the night in question was five months ago so all indoor CCTV footage has been wiped.'

'That's convenient.'

'It is for you, yeah.'

'Look, Pat was pissed. And yes, as we were walking along he started on a few people. You know, swearing at them, pushing and shoving. One or two ignored him and kept walking on, one or two didn't.'

'Let me put it you, Del, that it was you who confronted those men and that it wasn't merely a 'few slaps' or 'a bit of a kicking' as you earlier put it, but that you used a knife in those attacks.'

'No. I was there, yes, but I was pulling Pat away from those blokes and there was no knife.'

'How do you explain this then?'

He's shown a photo of a man's face, heavily bruised with a stitched scar from ear to ear.

'This is the first victim of that night, Andrew Christos. And here's what he looked like before that attack.'

The same victim is shown on his wedding day smiling next to his bride.

'Not a good contrast, is it?'

'It's not a good look, no. But to be honest I don't know how that was even possible because Pat didn't have a knife on him.'

'Let's go back to the beginning. Back to The Gilpin's Bell. So, you leave the pub—'

'With Pat.'

'Okay, you leave the pub with Pat. What happens next?'

'We head up the main road. Fore Street. We're walking along

and he goes up and headbutts some bloke. Just some random guy. Cracks him in the face, laughs and carries on walking.'

'In that instance the victim never came forward, so let's move on. What happened next?'

'We went into The White Horse.'

'You and Pat Brennan?'

'Yeah, me and Pat, we went in for a pint.'

'And you soon got thrown out?'

'Well, Pat was doing lines of sulph right there on the table and the governor wouldn't have it.'

'Amphetamine sulphate?'

'Yeah. I told him to go to the jacks to do that shit. You'll get us fucking thrown out. And that's exactly what happened.'

'The thing is, we spoke to the landlord and–'

'Let me guess. He didn't mention Pat. Not a word. Said there was only me.'

'That's right. So you're noticing a little pattern here.'

'The only pattern is this. Pat's a dangerous man and you know what can happen when you grass a man of his capabilities. The governor's hardly going to go badmouthing him to the Old Bill, is he? You know, safer to say you never saw him.'

'How about you, did you dip into the speed that night?'

'I had a few dabs. One or two. No harm done.'

'So then you proceeded on to The Bull in Silver Street. What route did you take to get there?'

'We went up the alley next to The White Horse, passed the flats, up the steps and along the footbridge over the railway tracks.'

'Let's stop there. Just over the footbridge at the dead end of Bridport Road is where the second attack occurred. Now this one was considerably more serious than the first which you say was a mere headbutt. This was Andrew Christos, the man with the slashed face. Fill us in.'

'It's the same as I told you already. We go over the bridge and

165

this geezer's coming along, Arsenal top, kind of swaggering, maybe a bit pissed – and Pat's on him straight away calling him a gooner cunt.'

'He's punching him?'

'Yeah, and they're kind of wrestling.'

'What next?'

'I manage to pull Pat off, the bloke staggers back, lands down in a pile of bin bags I think, and we're off on our way.'

'What kind of state did you leave the victim in?'

'Pat you mean? Well, he must've left him bloodied but I don't remember no knife. Though to be truthful I was more concerned in just getting Pat away from him. You know, before he fucking killed the cunt. Pat was a brutal fighter. Especially with a drink in him. I never saw him lose a scrap. Not once.'

'Okay, let's talk about Patrick Brennan for a minute.'

Suspect shrugs. 'Whatever you want.'

'How long have you known Pat for?'

'A long time. Years.'

'You did your first job with him in '97, is that correct? The Mayfair jewellery job?'

'Yeah. The one I was later nicked for.'

'Was Pat the accomplice that at the time you refused to name?'

'That's right.'

'And he ran off to Tenerife with your share of the earnings?'

'He did indeed. And I went after him.'

'Did you track him down?'

'Of course I did. He'd bought himself a snazzy apartment out there.'

'With your money?'

'He'd fucking spent it. We agreed he'd set up another job though, and this time I'd receive the lion's share.'

'And did this job ever happen?'

'You know it happened because again I was later fucking

166

nicked for it.'

'Grafman's jewellers in Knightsbridge?'

'Yeah.'

'Well, there's a little conundrum about that one. At the time you insisted that you'd carried out the job with an accomplice. A getaway driver. But all the evidence pointed towards you escaping alone on a motorbike. In court there were photos that proved this.'

'They proved nothing. They were pictures of a bloke on a bike who wasn't me. Even the judge accepted that.'

'Okay, fair enough. But what about the proceeds, did Pat get his hands on it and again do a runner?'

'Unfortunately, yes. He discovered where I hid it and grabbed the lot before I had the chance to get it laundered. He fucked off to Thailand and opened a bar.'

'And again you followed and went looking for him?'

'I did, yeah.'

'And while you were looking you got yourself arrested for slashing a tourist outside a brothel, is that correct?'

'He wasn't a tourist, he was a pimp. So I heard anyway.'

'What happened?'

'Nothing happened. I was arrested but released two days later. It was a case of mistaken identity.'

'The power of money, eh?'

'What money? I didn't have any. Pat had nicked it all.'

'Did you ever find Pat in Thailand?'

'Yes, in Phuket.'

'And you spoke to him?'

'He told me he'd set up another job for me, and this time he wouldn't let me down. He'd let me keep every penny this time.'

'And the job was?'

'A security van in Acton. Don't ask me the details because you already know all about it. It was all there in court. Public record.'

'You netted yourself over three hundred grand in cash.'

'Yes.'

'What happened to it?'

Suspect exhales. 'It was later nicked.'

'Let me guess… Pat Brennan?'

'A group of men burst into my place one night. Balaclavas, shotguns, the works. I knew they were working for Pat straight away. They drove me to a lock-up, got the info out of me.'

'You mean they forced you to reveal where you were hiding the cash?'

'They spent half the night torturing it out of me. Said they were going to cut my fucking bollocks off. But at the end of the day it's just money, isn't it.'

'So you handed it over. Where did you have it stored?'

'My old mum's grave. Some of it was in my uncle's plot.'

'Both in Edmonton Cemetery?'

Suspect nods.

'Pat cleaned me out.'

'What did he do with the proceeds this time?'

'He bought another bar. This time in Spain. Fucking Puerto Banus. Right where I used to take the wife and kids on holiday.'

'Now let me guess. Again you chased him down?'

'I did, yeah.'

'And he promised you another job and said this time, I swear down, no messing about, every pound note will be yours.'

Suspect shifts uncomfortably on his seat.

'Look, you've never met the man. You don't know what he's like.'

'Go on then, we're all ears, fill us in.'

'He has a way about him. A way with words.'

'He's a charismatic man?'

'Yes. I mean, when I walked into that bar pointing a revolver he didn't even flinch. He just smiled, threw the towel over his shoulder and poured me a drink. Next thing we're sitting there chatting and laughing like nothing's even happened. Pat's like that. It's his personality.'

'He has a way of putting you at ease, making you feel good about yourself. Good about life?'

'That's it, you've got it.'

'He makes you feel confident?'

'He has that gift.'

'So, let's say, in preparation for a job, he knows how to fire you up, get you in the zone?'

'One hundred percent. With Pat in on some graft you know things are going to work out, you can just feel it.'

'He's a born leader?'

'Without a doubt.'

'But he was never honest or fair when it came to distributing the cash?'

'No, never.'

'After each score he'd just run off and get himself a big car or a fancy flat in sunny climes?'

'That tended to me his MO, yeah. I mean, once he turned up to my house in a red Porsche Carrera. The very car he knew I was dreaming of. I could've killed the cunt. But minutes later we were going for a spin and I was cracking jokes with the fucker.'

DC Driscoll reaches for some documents.

'Derek. We'd like to show you some files we got hold of. Here's one that confirms the majority share of a bar in Thailand. Here's another for a bar in Puerto Banus. Here's one for an apartment in Tenerife, and here's one for, you've guessed it, a Porsche Carrera. All in your name. That's right Derek, your name. Any comments on this?'

Suspect spends some time perusing the files.

'Well that's the thing. He used to put things in my name. Use my ID. Half the time I wasn't even aware of it. Can you believe the gall of the cunt?'

'And how did he legally do that?'

'Legally? You're joking, aren't you? Bent solicitors, bent accountants, bent fucking bank accounts, you name it. When Pat wants something, Pat gets it.'

'But the bars and the apartment and the car - in the end he lost them all?'

'Well, nothing lasts forever does it. Business goes up and down.'

'How did he lose them exactly?'

'He lost them because he lost his life! Or at least that's what I believed at one point. I actually thought the bloke was dead. That was the rumour going around at the time.'

'What was the story?'

'From what I heard, he was doing some business in Amsterdam. You see he was based out there for a while. Into the coke and pill shipments and what have you. Something involving a Russian firm. So he rips them off on a deal and they put a price on his head. Next thing they're chasing him about all over.'

'Covering what ground?'

'Right across Europe. Down to the Canaries. Northern Cyprus, Greece for a bit, then onto the Costa.'

'Sounds like a man with a lot of contacts. International means.'

'Pat's a man of the world, I'll give him that, no doubt about it.'

'International man of mystery.'

'Well, yeah.' *Laughs.* 'No honestly, he is.'

'Have you ever read any Frederick Forsythe?'

'Crime writer? Thrillers and that?'

'Writes about globe-trotting spies, high-flying criminals, etc?'

'You're humouring me now.'

'We are, yeah, but don't let us stop your flow. What happened next, how did the Ruskies catch up with him?'

'Apparently he was driving home one night from a bar in Fuengirola. They got him at a crossroads. Two men with AKs. Covered his whole car in lead. Wiped him off the scene.'

'But it never actually happened, did it? It was just a story, because of course you were later drinking with him in The Gilpin's Bell in Edmonton five months ago when he unexpectedly walked in and sat beside you.'

'Correct. Out of the blue. Back from the dead. Which in a way didn't surprise me at all. That's Pat. He's that kind of character.'

'Okay. So let's return to that night. You've drank in The Gilpin's Bell, a man on the street has been headbutted, you've had a pint in The White Horse and been ejected because of openly snorting drugs. Then you've taken the back way onto the next pub and en route a man's been seriously attacked by the railway footbridge.'

Suspect gives a slight nod.

'So Del, in your words, describe what happened after that.'

'We turned right down a side street, then through the underpass beneath the North Circular Road and went up Silver Street for The Bull.'

A street map is produced.

'That's a pretty straightforward route. But I'd say you took a circuitous route... along here.'

'No, if we took a different route I'd remember.'

'How? You've already admitted that you spent most of the day drinking. After an all-day drinking session there'd be loads of things I wouldn't remember. At least not until my memory was jogged.'

'Fair enough.'

DC Hedges indicates map. 'I'd say that instead of turning right towards the North Circ, you remained in the backstreets and took a left down Pretoria Road in the direction of White Hart Lane station.'

'No, that never happened.'

'Because roughly ten minutes after the bridge attack another man was attacked on Pretoria Road and received fourteen knife wounds. Yusuf Ahmed, thirty-seven years old. We spoke to him in his hospital bed. His face was badly slashed but it was the internal bleeding of a torso wound that went on to kill him days later. He described his attacker as a burly white man, smelling of alcohol, smiling as he attacked him.'

Suspect emphatically shakes head. 'That had nothing to do with us. I heard all about that one. Read about it. The bloke was a scummy crack dealer.'

'So?'

'Street dealers get into scrapes all the time. Big scrapes. It's an occupational hazard.'

'Mr Ahmed insisted that it was an unprovoked attack by a complete stranger.'

'He would say that, wouldn't he? Trying to throw you coppers off the scent. Speak to his supplier who he most likely ripped off. Or whatever local crackhead tried to rob his takings maybe. The bloke was having you on.'

'He wasn't robbed. He was carrying over four hundred quid. It wasn't taken.'

'And his stash of drugs?'

'Not taken either.'

Suspect shrugs and exhales.

'So you went nowhere near Pretoria Road?'

'Why would we, there's nothing down there but industrial units and that. A fucking shithole. We were going to the pub.'

'Roughly twenty minutes after that attack a witness saw you at The Bull with dried blood on your hands. Said you looked dishevelled.'

'Do you know how many enemies I've got? People who would love to see me put away? Think about it. Now show me the video footage of me with blood on my hands. That would put that to bed, I tell you.'

'Again, as you well know, the CCTV footage no longer exists, so let's move on to the next incident. Pymmes Park. You left the pub around closing, walked back along Silver Street and hopped over the fence into the closed park. Why did you do this?'

'Two reasons. First, I needed a piss and didn't want to expose myself in public. Second, because it's a short cut to where I live.'

'Your late mum's old council flat that for years you'd used mainly for the storage of stolen goods, etc?'

'It's not a council flat. She bought it from the council years ago.'

'And just for the record, it's where you're still living now?'

'Yes.'

'So let's keep moving. You're walking through Pymmes Park and you encounter a man?'

'Yeah, he's coming along, probably just cutting through like us. Maybe he's a homo out cruising, fuck knows. But Pat set on him.'

'This is victim number four, Douglas Adkins. Describe what happened.'

'Pat gets in front of him, calls him a poof to his face, and asks him what he's going to do about it. The man is trying to move on but Pat pulls him back. Then bang, he lands him one in the face, bloke hits the deck and then Pat's laying the boot in, stamping all over the fucker.'

'During the course of this, what were you doing?'

'I was pulling at him, trying to talk some sense into the cunt. Telling him to behave or the two of us would be getting nicked and facing time. I'm telling you now, whisky chasers and Pat just don't mix.'

'Again the victim was stabbed.'

'All I saw was Pat hitting him.'

'With what?'

'His fists and feet.'

'No blade?'

173

'Not that I could see.'

'Mr Adkins received nine stab wounds. One was two millimetres from his heart, and if it wasn't for the close proximity of the North Mid Hospital, he could've well lost his life.'

'Good job I managed to pull Pat off him when I did then.'

'So you leave Mr Adkins behind on the ground and cross the park, head towards the main drag of Fore Street, cross over towards your place in Jeremy's Green, and on Brettenham Road is where you encounter number five. The final victim David Obeyo. Now what happened?'

'We're walking along, almost home, and suddenly Pat's shouting at this guy across the road. What are you looking at, you black cunt? This, that and the other. Really giving it some. Bloke comes over and they go for it, a bit of shoving and a few punches. It was funny really, the bloke calling him a white devil and stuff.'

'Mr Obeyo said you lunged at him with a knife…'

'Me? Pat, you mean?'

'You tell me, that's why you're here. Obeyo said he was lunged at with a blade that slashed through his clothes, drew some blood, but after a struggle he managed to knock the knife from his attacker's hand.'

'That's news to me.'

'But this attack was different to the others, because now unarmed he got the better of you, didn't he? He hit you hard and you staggered back and ran.'

'Never happened. I pulled Pat away and we ran because a load of police sirens were blazing along the main road. On an emergency. The black guy ran as well.'

'How hard did Mr Obeyo hit you?'

'He didn't.'

'A neighbour said he saw you the next day sporting a black eye.'

'Look, fists were flying, and I was getting between them so it's possible I was hit, yeah.'

An exhibit in an evidence bag is produced.

'This is the weapon we believe was used that night. Obeyo told us he dropped it into a drain a few streets away. We retrieved it.'

'When did he tell you that, because apparently he only came forward as a victim last week?'

'That's unimportant.'

'And we all know that if that knife's been lying in water for months there won't be a shred of DNA left to link it to anybody.'

'That may be true. But it was retrieved from the sewer at the very spot where Mr Obeyo said he dropped it. That's good circumstantial evidence right there.'

'Sounds like the bloke's trying to earn brownie points, get into your good books. What does he do for a living? Have you checked his record?'

'Again that's not relevant.'

'It is if he's a fucking drug dealer trying to play victim to get you lot kissing his arse. You need to go back to detective school. You don't understand half the tricks criminals play. I do because I've been in the game my whole life.'

'Nobody said he was a criminal Del, and it wouldn't affect the case even if he was. This is serious shit. We're talking one murder, three attempted murders and a GBH all in one night. Do you know how many years inside we're talking about here?'

'Talk to Pat about it. He's out there, so all you have to do is your job and find him.'

'Well, that could be a little difficult.'

'How come?'

Interviewers pause. One nods to the other.

'Is Patrick Brennan a real person, Derek?'

'Now I know you're having me on.'

'We'll be straight with you, it's no secret that for months we were chasing the wrong suspect, and even now witnesses are few and far between, but of those who talked all insisted you were alone that night. In the pub, on the street.'

'Well they're liars.'

'Okay then, let's change tack. Let's talk about you. Word on the street is you don't have too many friends these days. Would it be correct to assume that, overall, things have gone a little downhill for you in recent years?'

Suspect folds his arms. 'Not really, no.'

'I mean, your wife left you. She said she couldn't stand the violence--'

Leans forward: 'Now look here…'

'Let me finish. And business had all but dried up, hadn't it? You lost the house in Enfield and had to return to your old mum's flat. You got yourself addicted to amphetamines which did your temper no favours and people no longer wanted to work with you.'

'Bollocks. That's not true at all.'

'Word was you'd lost your touch. That you'd become too temperamental to work with. Off your head on drink and speed. A liability.'

'No. No way.'

'Do you know Big Billy Goodman?'

'Of course I do.'

'This is what he told us, in his very words: "Del Tucker used to be alright. A decent geezer. But the drugs sent him off his tree. He's nothing more than a joke now."'

'Goodman never said a thing. He'd never talk to you cunts in a million years.'

'Oh yes he did. We're Old Bill, people talk to us all the time. All sorts of people.'

Suspect stares at the table.

'Derek. You were sectioned a year back. You spent six weeks in a mental facility after threatening to jump from a bridge over the M25.'

Remains silent.

'How would you describe your mental health at present?'

'None of your fucking business, how about that?'

'Here's a psychiatric report from your stay at the facility. Shall I read it to you?'

'That's confidential. You're not even allowed to have that. This is illegal.'

'In a murder case? You need to learn the law mate. I'll read some of it to you. It says here that—'

'I don't want to hear it.'

'You can handle it.'

Raises voice. 'I said I don't want to fucking hear it.'

'Okay.' *Document is placed aside.* 'If we've hit a delicate spot, we can pass on that. But I'll tell you what I think. Pat Brennan is quite an obsession with you, isn't he? Now, would I be going too far, Del, to say he's the man you've always wanted to be?'

'You can psychobabble me all you like. But Pat attacked those men and because you can't find the fucker you're trying to pin it all on me.'

'Not quite.'

'Well what then? You're constantly telling me I was on my own that night, implying Pat's not real, like he's a figment of my imagination.'

'Not at all. The man exists all right, I can assure you that.'

Files are produced.

'In fact, he's in this room right now, staring us in the face.'

A birth certificate is shown.

'Your father was called Patrick too, wasn't he? You were originally named after him. Then when you were seven, he left your mother for another woman and threw the both of you out of the house. A nice big house in Wanstead, and you and your poor mum ended up in a little council flat back in Edmonton where she came from. She changed your first name from Patrick to Derek, and your father's surname Brennan back

177

to hers, Tucker. And you never saw your father again.'

'No... no...' *Suspect shakes his head.*

'But somewhere, let's say, in some dimension, young Pat Brennan stayed behind in that house in well-to-do Wanstead, growing up in parallel. And he became a confident, moneyed, successful man.'

Suspect continues to shake his head.

'Unlike you who were left to rot. Del Tucker who always got the shit end of the stick. And you went on to lose all your money, every business you ever had, your wife, the big house in Enfield, your kids not wanting to know you. While the former Pat Brennan got everything, all the things you wanted and were once destined for...'

'No, you're wrong.' *He slams the table.* 'You're fucking wrong!'

'That's not what this report says. Not what you told the psychiatrist in the nuthouse.'

Tucker jumps up and attempts to assault interviewers. Two uniforms enter the room to help contain him.

'Bring him to the cells. We're talked enough. I've been hearing nothing but shit from the cunt all night.'

'It wasn't me. I'm innocent, I've done nothing. You're corrupt bastards the lot of you.'

'Take him away. Let him cool down for a bit. And if he starts kicking and shouting in the cells get the doctor to medicate the fucker. That or let him keep his belt so he can fucking top himself and save us some bother. Either way I couldn't care less. Be good Del mate, because in the morning you're getting charged with murder.'

REMAINS

After leaving school in 1989 I went to college for a while, but soon dropped out. As for my future I hadn't a clue, and almost surprised myself at not being too bothered either. I'd had a small group of friends, but after school they all disappeared. I was very much a loner. I lived with my mother in a terraced house on the border of Tottenham and Harringay. My mother was sick – she had stiff legs, a bad back, various other ailments that through the years had only got worse - but I tended to her as any son would. She'd had me at forty years old and my dad had walked out on us very early; so early in fact that I couldn't remember him. My mother wasn't without her faults, but I felt a very close bond to her. I loved her dearly.

In all my years at school I never brought friends around. Maybe once or twice but that was all; quickly ushering them upstairs so they wouldn't have an inkling of the family set-up. My mother was based downstairs in the back room, never opened her curtains and rarely left the house. She'd sit in front of the TV until the early hours, then move to the bed that I'd positioned in the same room for ease. She often drank too much, and some days she'd rant and rave - long embittered tirades that I'd close my ears to. Other days we'd sit and talk as if nothing had happened. She'd never remember a thing and, relieved that she was sober, nor would I mention it.

With alcohol her only solace, I felt sorry for her. She had relatives back in Ireland, but we never saw them. Perhaps once a year her sister Bridie would come down from Manchester, and we'd tidy the house, present things differently. But to be honest, it was something we both quite dreaded. Mostly we were left alone.

The recession at the time meant jobs were scarce, but after putting up adverts in shops and through doors I'd get the occasional bit of gardening work - mainly from old people who sometimes needed bits and bobs done around the house as well. I got friendly with one or two, and sometimes I'd drink tea with them, listening to what the area had been like years ago; air raid shelters, bombs falling. They'd tell me stories and show me photographs; they liked the company.

In early 1991 I got a job shelf-stacking at Sainsbury's. I wasn't thinking long term, but it was mindless and easy, offering plenty time to dream, to forget I was even there, and for that reason I quite liked it. My mother never encouraged me to work at all, in fact to do anything other than keep her company, but the money did come in handy. So did the food and alcohol I'd steal.

Despite my lack of social contact, I was a normal eighteen-year-old like any other, and with money in my pocket I decided it was time I lost my virginity. I planned to visit a prostitute. There was really no other choice. I'd always been shy around girls, and previous sexual experiences – if they could be called that - were disastrous.

Back in my third year at secondary school, bored during a lesson, the boy next to me began speculating on who were the most beddable girls in the class. Of one thing, though, he was certain. The ugliest, most untouchable, had to be Amy. Amy was Chinese, quiet. I'd hardly looked at her before, but from that moment on I started fancying her. I'd find myself watching her in class, secretly staring at her. One day passing her in the empty corridor, I stopped to ask her the time. As she looked at her watch I saw one of my hands reach into her blazer to touch her chest. 'What are you doing?' she said. 'Get off me!' I tried it again and she pushed me away and ran off down the hall. It was a moment of madness, and I stood there confused, my heart thumping in my chest. Later at home time when I saw her again, I said I was sorry, it was a mistake. She kept walking.

'You're sick,' she said.

My heart never stopped all day. That evening I bought a magazine, *Oriental Heat*, from the top shelf of a newsagents. Embarrassed, I asked the Indian for a bag. He shouted over his shoulder, then during the wait, folded his arms and stared at me with a knowing smile. I went back to my bedroom and, in between my mother's incessant demands - tea, dinner, fetch me another bottle of sherry - I masturbated furiously, in awe at the crude, shocking displays of flesh, writing AMY in thick marker pen above the various girls that bore her resemblance. By midnight, spent and guilty, I brought the magazine to the bottom of the garden and burned it. Maybe Amy was right. Maybe I really was sick. For the next few days, looking at the back of Amy's head in the classroom, I felt I had truly soiled her in every way possible.

When Friday came around, I noticed three Chinese boys from another school were following me home. I ran, but after a while it seemed pointless; I let them get to me. They punched and kicked me to the ground. One of them demanded I kiss his shoes. As I went to do so, he kicked me in the face. 'You ever touch my cousin again and I'll kill you.' On Monday, passing Amy in the corridor with my face bruised, she gave a tiny smirk. 'I deserved it,' I told her. Later when I saw her looking at me, I thought I could detect a flicker of sorrow.

Another episode happened a couple of years later, when I was fifteen. It was a hot Saturday afternoon and I'd stopped my homework to spy from my window on the girl next door who was sunbathing in the garden with two friends. The girls were scantily dressed and I could hear them discussing boys. I was crouched on my knees, masturbating. One of them spotted me and pointed me out. I froze. 'Oh him, the resident creep,' the girl next door said, but the other two carried on smiling and calling up to me. One of them, a plump girl, flashed her breasts and laughed. I darted away from the window; the room now airless, roasting hot. When I returned a minute later, only the plump girl remained. I stood there by the window, my trousers around my ankles. Looking up, she stared almost in confusion, then she got up and walked back inside. Horrified, I snapped the curtains closed and curled up on my bed, waiting for the inevitable. 'Pervert!' they shouted. The girl next door saying, 'I told you he was a fucking weirdo.' Six months later when the family moved away, I felt a weight lift.

I looked back at these episodes with embarrassment. But all in all, they were youthful misdemeanours; I'd matured since then. Importantly, if I wanted to lose my virginity while still a teenager, I needed to do it now. I chose a place above the busy shops on Green Lanes. As the woman removed her clothes revealing lacy underwear I felt like running back down the stairs. I felt like a little boy again - felt as though I was somehow betraying my mother. In her rants she'd always warned me off women; from having a girlfriend. They'd only use me, she'd say, just like my father had used her. But I wanted a girlfriend more than anything. Nervously I told the woman it was my first time. 'I'll make it special then,' she said. We had an hour. Good job, because on my first attempt I finished within seconds.

I visited several times more, building up my confidence, until in October 1991 I was sacked from my job after being caught stealing. Back to square one. But maybe this was the kick I needed. I could go back to college, take my A levels, do English Lit at uni. Back at school that had more or less been my plan before I'd allowed myself to sink into inertia. I could do it. But as the weeks went by, and I settled back into the routine of home life, such hopes seemed vague.

I'd sign on, go to the shops, take books and CDs out of the library, read the music papers - it was all very mundane. I was eating too much and, though never exactly thin, I really started to pile on the pounds. Meeting an old teacher on the street one day, it took her seconds to recognise me. Afterwards, I stood in front of the mirror and hated myself. Somewhere out there the world was turning, things happening, exciting things, while I hid myself away getting fat and ugly. At night I'd sit in my room re-reading some of the authors I had done at school – Orwell, Hardy, Lawrence. Then I explored Camus and Sartre. I delved into Tolstoy, Turgenev, Dostoyevsky. I was interested in the ideas, but the endless dialogue did my head in. Did I really have that many hours to waste? I suppose I did, but even so. Maybe I just wasn't clever enough. My self-esteem was at rock bottom.

One evening walking back from a gardening job in Hornsey, I passed two casuals sitting on a wall. 'Oi, wanker.' I ignored them, kept walking. 'Fucking cunt, are you deaf?' They were right behind me. I ran, cut through some flats, but they caught up and jumped me. 'Fat cunt. Fat fucking cunt.' The kicks seemed to go on forever. I got home with cuts and bruises to my face, my whole body aching from the kicks. My mother seemed particularly tender to me that night. We drank brandy and stayed up talking until dawn. At times like that I felt so close to her. Several times I broke down and sobbed on her shoulder as she held me. 'I love you,' I said. 'I love you so much.'

After the beating I made an effort to lose weight. In a way, you could say they beat it out of me. By the spring of 1992 I'd started going out to clubs on my own. I'd hardly ever done this before. After drinking myself into another state - which was cheap and easy; a quarter bottle of vodka normally did the trick - I found I could chat quite easily to almost anybody. With my hair now dyed jet black I'd go to places like the Catacomb in

Manor House on a Friday or the Dome in Tufnell Park on a Saturday: indie nights full of people my own age.

One night at the Dome I bumped into an old friend, Miquel. He had come over from Spain at twelve, and on his first day at school I'd befriended him, brought him into my little circle. Greeting cheerfully, we agreed it was terrible we'd lost contact. Miquel was at college and was sad to hear I'd dropped out. He was full of compliments, saying I had been a 'genius' at Art and English, and should definitely take it further. I told him I planned to, but not quite yet; my mother was ill and I was looking after her.

Miquel introduced me to all his new friends - both boys and girls - and suddenly I wasn't on my own any more. On a Saturday night I could walk into the club actually knowing people, talking to people. I developed a kind of weekend confidence, almost a swagger, which was quite a breakthrough for me. I was finally comfortable in my own skin. Being around people, it became evident just what I was missing by not doing college or uni. Still a virtual recluse during the week, I envied all these bright colourful people, apparently carefree, who lived it up at the weekend but spent their weekdays quietly chipping away doing something of worth. I knew I was wasting myself, but still hadn't quite the impetus to do anything about it. Perhaps I feared failure. Or maybe it was something else that inhibited me. Guilt.

Getting home from a night out, my mother would still be up, glum-faced in front of the television. 'Look at you, off galivanting while I'm stuck here hardly able to get off this chair - leaving me here to rot.' I'd try to appease her but she'd sulk and refuse to speak to me - something she knew I couldn't bear. I'd been in the house full-time for so long now, I wondered how I'd ever be able to pull myself away. 'You'll see,' she said. 'One night you'll come home to find me dead on that floor. I'll do it you know.' This wasn't a threat I took lightly. She'd overdosed twice several years before, but both times managed to convince the doctors it had been an accident. I was worried for her. But I didn't stop going out.

One Sunday afternoon in the summer I went to an Anti-Nazi League demo with some of Miquel's crowd. The camaraderie of chanting slogans and shouting at the fascists was great fun; I enjoyed it.

A couple of days later, out of the blue, I got a phone call. It was Catherine, a mutual friend of Miquel's who I'd spent much of the demo casually chatting to - but as everything with Miquel's friends was so platonic, I'd thought nothing of it. But now I got the feeling she wanted to meet; just us, together - she seemed to be dropping hints, prompting me to ask her out. Suddenly I was nervous. There were brief silences and giggles, but after a while it became obvious the moment had passed.

'What's all that racket?' she asked, colder now.

'Oh that's just the TV,' I lied as my mother ranted and raved incoherently in the background.

'Okay, I'll see you around then,' she said. And that was it. I went upstairs and punched the wall. I'd had a chance and blown it. A few weeks later when I saw her again, she virtually ignored me.

In September Miquel went off to Edinburgh University, and most of his friends seemed to disappear overnight. But it didn't matter. I soon met someone who was to change everything. Her name was Hannah.

I met Hannah one night at the Dome. She had dark hair and glasses, was wearing a Sonic Youth t-shirt under a black cardigan, and was painfully shy. I really fancied her. For the first few weeks we'd end up snogging on the street after the club, before she'd get her cab home. Finally she asked me over to her house during the week. She'd never had a boyfriend before, but was somehow under the impression I wasn't so inexperienced. I found this funny because, though perhaps sordidly true, I was as naive to relationships as she was. Hannah was doing her A-levels. She lived with her parents in St John's Wood.

I'd never been over this way before, but coming out of the tube station and walking towards her street, I could see it was clearly quite a posh area. I reached her place, an impeccable white-fronted house. I was nervous. Her dad let me in, and her mum made me coffee. Hannah took ages coming downstairs. Her parents seemed cordial enough, but they asked a lot of questions and I found myself lying ridiculously. When Hannah appeared I noticed she seemed quite sulky with her parents, but I still got the feeling she was showing me off. Whisking me upstairs, I was relieved. A few weeks later, she laughingly told me that when she'd told them I lived in Tottenham, they were 'horrified.'

I'd come around perhaps once a week and we'd listen to music and kiss on her bed. She had lots of vinyl, tapes and CDs and we'd listen to stuff like Suede, PJ Harvey, Lush, The Smiths, Cocteau Twins. We shared much of the same taste, and introduced each other to new stuff also. Sometimes with the music playing we'd just lie holding each other for hours not saying anything. Hannah had a quiet, pensive, almost secretive side that I found really attractive. It seemed as if there were so many layers yet to be explored, but all the time in the world to do so.

Her wall was covered in cut-outs from the *NME* and *Melody Maker*. There were quite a few pictures of Richey Manic - a blow-up of the 'razored arm shot'. Opposite her bed hung a large poster of Joy Division. In black and white, the four members climbed a subway stairs; a quietly paranoid Ian Curtis glancing over his shoulder to face the camera. I'd only heard a couple of their songs before, but Hannah played me their albums. She told me Curtis had hung himself in his kitchen, and was discovered the next morning by his wife. 'I Remember Nothing' was the most chilling song I'd ever heard.

Hannah spent a lot of time studying, and we'd sometimes meet at Swiss Cottage library. I was reading Hermann Hesse at the time, his early novels: *Gertrude, Peter Camenzind, Demian*. They were melancholy, yet radiant and uplifting. I'd read passages over and over, basking in the beauty of the words, feeling light and summery with the winter rain blurring the library windows. Hannah read Virginia Woolf, Elizabeth Gaskell, Emily Dickinson. She was reading to pass exams, I was reading for pleasure. I was the happiest I had ever been.

One Saturday night after we went out, I brought her back to mine. I figured sneaking Hannah up the stairs would be easy, but when we got in my mother was standing in the hallway in her dressing gown. 'Oh, so what do we have here then?' I was surprised to see her smiling quite good-naturedly. 'Are you not going to introduce me to your little girlfriend then?' She seemed in quite a good mood, and I was relieved. She shook Hannah's hand and after a few minutes chat said, 'You two go on upstairs, don't let me stop you. It's time I was off to bed too.'

In bed Hannah kept her clothes on, she still wasn't ready to take things further, but we kissed and did what we normally did, which by now was everything apart from the actual thing. I still hadn't seen Hannah in the flesh; but in the dark she'd sometimes let me touch her under her clothes. I didn't mind, understood there was no rush, but still it seemed very one sided.

In the morning I woke to see Hannah up on her elbow next to me, and my mother's drunken screams coming through the floorboards.

'She's been doing that for hours,' Hannah casually said.

I was horrified. I got up and threw on some clothes. 'Let's get out of here,' I said.

Closing the front door behind us, I grasped the incoherent roar that my mother was screaming over and over. 'WHORE... WHOORE... WHOOORE...'

We went for a walk in Finsbury Park and sat by the lake.

'When you told me your mother was ill I never realised you meant mentally,' Hannah said. 'She's damaged. What happened to her?'

'She's an alcoholic. She sometimes screams, sometimes talks rubbish. It's not her fault.'

'It must be hard for you,' she said. 'Living with a double personality.'

'It isn't,' I said with finality. Hannah lived in a nice area, came from a nice normal family. Things were different for her. I didn't want to talk about it.

One evening kissing on her bed, as she slid down to undo my belt, I said no. 'I don't want to do it like that anymore. I want us to do it properly - together.'

She turned away and sat on the edge of the bed. It was a Sunday evening and we'd spent the day walking along Regent's Canal and drinking cider on Primrose Hill. I felt so close to her, felt it had been one of the best days of my life.

'We've been together for months now,' I continued. 'Are you worried it'll hurt, is that what it is?'

She didn't answer.

'You're always covered up,' I went on. 'You've never shown yourself to me. I don't get it. Why? It'll be beautiful. I'll make sure everything's fine.'

She turned to me over her shoulder, her eyes filling with tears. 'I'm not a virgin,' she said.

She told me she had done it loads of times, hundreds of times, her step-brother had abused her from as far back as she could remember.

It went on until she was fourteen, until he moved out. He'd made her do all sorts of things, and for years she'd thought it was normal, thought it was love, something siblings simply did. She'd been cutting herself ever since. She pulled up her top, revealing thick lacerations on her skin. She'd once told her parents but they'd refused to listen, told her to grow up, told her she was lying.

'Where is this bastard? Where does he live? I'm going to kill him.'

I was serious. I wanted to take a knife to his throat.

'He's dead,' she said. 'He drove a motorbike over a mountain road in Portugal. The coroner gave an open verdict, said it could have been an accident, but I know it was suicide. And I know it was because of me.' She broke down. 'I loved him. I didn't want him to die. It was all my fault. He must have hated what he did to me.'

'It's not your fault,' I said to her angrily. 'I'm glad he's dead. He deserved to die.'

'You can't say that,' she said. 'No matter what he did, he was my brother. We grew up together. We did normal things. We were close.' She pulled a pack of photos from her bedside drawer, spread them across the bed. 'I killed him,' she sobbed. 'It was me.'

I picked one up. He looked normal; smiling, happy. 'Fucking bastard.' I tore it in two. 'You should bin these, every single one of them.'

'Get out!' she suddenly screamed. 'You don't understand a thing. Get out!'

She dragged me to the door, pushed me out of the room.

I was banging to get back in when I saw her dad flying up the stairs.

'What's going on?' he said as Hannah audibly cried in the background.

He walked up to me. 'You leave this house right now. You're not welcome here.'

I walked the six or so miles home in a state of shock. I bought a quarter bottle of whisky, swigging it angrily as I went.

Up towards Finsbury Park I noticed a face outside a chip shop. I recognised him instantly. It was Lee Roberts, a bully from school. He was standing with a portion of chips, biting into a saveloy. I stopped and stared at him.

'What, mate?' he said, not recognising me. 'What are you looking at?'

Back at school he'd seemed menacing and scary, but now I saw him for the long streak of piss he actually was. I felt the hate swell. Head-first I ran at him. No wonder I had done nothing with my life; no wonder so many people were held back, confidence ruined, lives destroyed. It was because of people like this.

I connected and his chips went flying. I wanted to ram him out onto the road, let the cars and lorries deal with him. I wanted to kill him. We were rolling about in the middle of the empty one-way road, traffic waiting to gush from the lights. 'You fucking freak,' he shouted, as we tried to hit each other. The traffic came forward, cars beeping in front of us. Two muscled-up Greek blokes shot out of a BMW: 'What the fuck's going on?' and Roberts freed himself and ran.

One of the men pulled me up ready to hit me.

'He raped my girlfriend,' I said, and he suddenly released his hand. As we watched Roberts run, I realised what they said was true. Bullies really were cowards.

Over the next few days, every time I phoned Hannah her mum said she was out. I knew she was lying. Finally her dad answered.

'She hasn't gone to college,' he said, 'hasn't left her room in days, what the hell have you done to her?' He slammed down the phone on me.

Immediately I called back, but it had been taken off.

I left and got the tube to St John's Wood. Within the hour I was outside her house. Hannah's light was on. I threw stones up at her window. She looked down at me, stared for a moment, then pulled her curtains closed.

I rang the bell. Her dad answered. He tried to close the door on me, but I pushed past him and ran up the stairs.

As I pounded on Hannah's door he appeared behind me and told me the police were on their way.

'Get them,' I said. 'They should have been called years ago.'

Hannah opened her door. Her face was red from tears.

'It's okay,' she said. 'Let him stay.'

We went inside and I held her close. Her body was wooden in my arms. I saw a small knife on her desk, caked in blood. 'Please,' I said. 'You must stop doing that. I'll help you. You can get over this. I love you.'

Minutes later the police arrived. They knocked on her bedroom door saying if I didn't leave the house I'd be arrested.

'You better go,' Hannah said.

Two officers led me downstairs.

'Are you sure you don't want to press charges?' they asked her dad.

He shook his head and pointed at me. 'I just never want to see him again.'

They told me I was lucky to get a warning, but if I ever returned to the house I'd be in big trouble.

Later that night Hannah killed herself.

I found out when the police hauled me in at 8am for questioning. I was shocked, in a daze, the whole world unreal. They asked me question after question - if I'd ever threatened her, if we'd cut each other, discussed suicide, planned a suicide pact, reading me entries from her diary, wanting to clear things up. I told them if I hadn't been dragged away from her, she would still be alive. I told them about the abuse and broke down like a baby. They put me in a cell for a while to calm down, then they let me go.

Hannah had hung herself in her wardrobe. She was cremated on 19th February 1993. The family didn't invite me to the service. I don't think I could have handled it anyway.

I was in a bad way, but my mother showed me little sympathy. There was something about that girl, she said, something not right, and she'd warned me but I didn't listen. She also started taunting me about getting a job - probably because she knew it was the last thing I could possibly handle now. With red wine and kaolin and morphine caked around her mouth, she'd rant that I was lazy, doing nothing, a lazy fucking slug. Why aren't you out there working like every other young lad your age? What's the matter with you anyway?

I ignored her, still told myself it was the sickness, not her. After all, some days when she'd be semi-sober we'd be fine. But sometimes when her tirades became too much, I crushed sleeping tablets into her food - a first for me. I also started punishing her by refusing to run down to the shops for her alcohol or Night Nurse or endless prescriptions. But she knew how to soften me, and in the end I'd always give in. I still loved her, but perhaps a little less devotedly these days.

One-night walking to the shop at the corner, a man jumped out from nowhere and threw me up against the wall. Holding a knife to my neck he told me to hand over all I had or he'd cut me. He was black and his eyes were crazed, and the contrast of his smirking white mate in the background somehow made it all the more menacing. I did what he said, then he knocked me to the floor. His mate stepped forward, kicked me in the stomach and said next time they'd fucking kill me. They walked away, and I picked myself up and staggered home.

The hot summer months brought darkness all around me. More and more muggings were going on. A near fatal rape happened in some garages at the end of the road, and an old woman I had done some gardening for was attacked in her own home. She gave them forty pounds she had stashed in a tin, but still they beat her about the face and broke her hip.

I visited her a few weeks later when she was sent home from hospital. Her resilience impressed me, but she'd become gaunt and thin, seemed to have aged years. I brought her some biscuits and twenty quid from my dole. She refused to take it but I insisted. Six weeks later she died.

I'd always been tolerant, always refused to live with hate, but now I questioned that philosophy. The area was changing, but so was I. It seemed as if I'd lost all my hopes and dreams, and now there was nothing left but reality.

In October I got a surprise call from Miquel. He knew nothing of Hannah, never knew she existed, and I didn't mention her. He was back in London for a week, meeting up with friends, and asked if I wanted to go out. Six of us, a crowd I'd never met before, pub-crawled around Camden Town, then got a bus the couple of miles up to Tufnell Park for the Dome. Though I tried my best playing the person Miquel had previously known, I felt awkward and self-conscious all night. I was downing extra shorts to get in the mood, but by the time we reached the club I was slurring my words and could hardly walk straight. Standing to the side watching everybody sing along on the dancefloor, I realised I may as well have been alone in my room, staring at the wall.

At one point, Miquel passed me on his way to the bar. 'What's wrong with you?' he said. 'You seem different.'

My presence was irritating him. I soon slipped away.

When I got home my mother was yelling my name. She was drunk on the floor by her chair, hand raised, imploring for help. I stood viewing the scene as if for the first time. Empty bottles surrounded her table; her shelf lined in various tranquillizers, sleeping tablets, painkillers, inhalers, cough medicines - all the medication that for years she'd mixed with alcohol to incapacitate herself with. I stood staring at her as she shrieked up at me. Turning, I closed the door and went up to bed.

All night long she roared and screamed, and several times I heard the neighbours banging. As I lay staring at the ceiling, I realised this was my life - I was destined to be alone, with no friends, no girlfriend, no happiness, ever.

'Just wait until you get out into the real world,' the teachers had warned. They were right. My forays in the outside world had been disastrous. All I did was spread seeds of discord wherever I went. If I had never met Hannah, never entered her life, she would most probably still be alive.

I woke up around noon and my mum was on her seat, fresh faced and sober, telling me about a terrible dream she'd had. In her dream I had died - horribly. I'd been abducted off the street and beaten to death; she'd been glad to wake out of it. She'd heard me getting up so had made me a cup of tea. She'd made boiled eggs and toast and had even given the kitchen a clean. She was sitting on her chair smiling up at me. I ate my food then got my jacket and walked out of the house. I sat in the park all day, staring across the green.

When I got home, again she was off her head. She was ranting that she'd ran out of kaolin and morphine and it was a Sunday, the fucking chemists were closed, and what the hell was I going to do about it? I stood there, her voice like a caterwaul, calling me every name under the sun. Suddenly I realised not only what I had been brooding over for hours, but denying throughout my whole life. There was no love here at all. I was living in a madhouse.

I took a bottle of kaolin and morphine from the stash I kept under the stairs, and crushed into the chalky mixture as many Lorazepam and Tramadol as I could find. I brought it in with a bottle of brandy that had been saved for her birthday, and put both down in front of her.

'You're a saint,' she said, gripping my hand with both of hers. Then I went upstairs, lay on my bed and listened to Nirvana's *In Utero*. Four hours later when I came down, she was dead.

I spent the next week or so dissociated from reality. Aunt Bridie came down from Manchester and made all the arrangements while I sat in the back room, completely numb. The days passed fast around me as Bridie made me meals and tidied the house. Uncle Paddy soon followed down. 'Leave the poor lad alone, don't be fussing around him,' he said. I quite liked having the two of them around. It somehow felt normal. As things always should have been. The night before the burial I remember silent tears on my face as we all had a few whiskies in front of the TV.

After the funeral a small crowd gathered back at a local pub. Mainly distant relatives and friends of the family from before I was born. People offering their condolences, shaking my hand. We stayed in the pub drinking all day. At one point Uncle Paddy sat me aside and said there were a few things I should probably know - to help get my head around things. Two decades before I was born, my mother had had a child taken away from her, and was put in a laundry run by nuns. It mustn't have been easy. These things never leave you, he said. I hadn't known any of that. But what difference did it make now anyway? Later I noticed Bridie shedding tears over her brandy and people comforting her.

'Suicide,' I heard someone remark. 'It's an awful thing.'

The next day Bridie suggested staying behind for a while, but I insisted I'd be fine, just needed to move on. I wasn't lying. I'd woken up early, surprisingly un-hungover, with a new frame of mind entirely. In the afternoon I waved them off in their car. I was alone now, completely. But I'd been thinking - perhaps aloneness was only a concept in the head anyway. As I closed the door on the world outside, I felt strangely optimistic, inspired even.

WORDS OF LOVE

Hello Ruth.

You're surprised, aren't you? Me, putting it in writing. Perhaps you thought I wouldn't contact you at all, I'd stay away, crawl under a rock and die maybe. But come on, you know me, I'm not like that. London might be a big place, easy to disappear in, vanish like a ghost, but let's be realistic now, I'm not going anywhere. I mean, where would I go for a start? There's nothing else out there for me, no other life, you know that.

You're just trying to teach me a lesson. Punish me. And fair enough, I see your point. I was wrong. I admit that, I shouldn't have done what I did. Violence is unacceptable, of course it is. I'm not disputing that. But I'm fine now. I've seen to it, I did what you said. You were right: I did need help. Stress, my God, it's like a mind-bending drug. But that's sorted now. It was just a blip. I'm not perfect, I admit that, but come on, we're all human, you're not averse to the odd tantrum yourself; we all are. But no, there's no excuses. None at all.

I just want to say I'm sorry. I've had a lot of time to think about it all. Three months now. That one night flashing through my head like a nightmare. That person, that monster, it wasn't me. Something clicking in my mind, sending me crazy. Wrong, so wrong. I see you lying there in the state I left you… and I just want to hug you and nurse you and soothe you. Kill the person that did it.

Well, listen: I think I finally have. This last week I feel I've woken up and seen the light. I'm ready to put it all behind me. I think we both should. I'm ready for things to be normal again now. As they were. I mean, of course you're still angry, I understand that. But let's call a truce. No more games. No more sadism, Ruth.

Fuck this. This isn't sounding right. I've got to get the words right, explain to you how I feel. Can't fuck this up. Because I know what you're doing. You're torturing me. That's what you're doing. Your little game. Torture.

But listen. I'm close to you, you know. Even now, so close, sitting in our cafe, that place on Kingsland Road - you know, just around from the flat. Our flat, Ruth. You might be at work now – 1.30pm, definitely – but I still feel close to you. This is our place. Where we used to go. All those Sunday mornings here, having breakfast, reading the papers, no rush, just being together. Then maybe we'd have a browse around Brick Lane, the markets, go to a pub, or who knows, maybe go back home, back to bed, the two of us, together.

That's the way things are meant to be. This – life now – it isn't normal. I'm living in a single room, shared bathroom, shared kitchen, hate the place, hate the people. It's nowhere near here but you gave me no time, nothing, it was all I could find. But don't worry, I'm not there much. I've even started taking days off work. Without you I just can't concentrate. They keep calling me in, saying they're concerned, that I've become quiet, remote, telling me they care about me, just want to help me. But I'm not stupid. I know all they care about. Performance. That I'm not buckling down, bringing in the clients. They don't give a damn about me. I'll be out of there soon, I just know it. Who cares.

But it's all so wrong, so unnatural. Like the world has shifted balance, thrown me aside. Laying out your photographs on the bed each night, making a shrine, trying to draw you near, will you to me. It's not normal, Ruth, not normal. It shouldn't be that way. I shouldn't be living like this. Now, for example, hours to kill and I'm waiting for you, waiting for that glimpse. I've started watching you, you know. Did you know that? Every day. Watching you get out of the taxi and enter the flat.

You don't get the bus anymore. Why not? And you've changed your email, phone number, even changed the locks. Too extreme. There's no need for that. I hide across in the bushes of the park, or sometimes up close, in the side alley, and I see you, pulling the blinds, see the lights go on and off, see it all. Do you think I enjoy that, out there in the cold each evening, on my own, creeping about in the bushes, in the shadows like a nonce? Of course I don't. I hate it.

But I can't believe what you're doing. Never thought you'd take things this far.

Even to broach the subject fucking disturbs me, makes me want to tell myself it's all a mistake, it isn't true.

Ruth, listen. I know about him. I've seen him. He visits, two, three times a week, climbs out of a cab, just like you. Or sometimes – and this really gets me – the two of you come out of a cab. Who is this man, Ruth? Do you work with him? Is he a work colleague? But you've changed your workplace too, something else to throw me off, so who knows. Maybe you met him in a bar or a club. He walked up to you, a stranger, and you said yes straight away just to try and hurt me. That makes you a slag, you know that don't you? And you know what happens to slags. They end up slaves, beaten black and blue by these bastards day in day out every fucking time. Look at the statistics: two slags die a week at the hands of a violent partner, violent bastard. I don't agree with it you know, but real life, it happens.

We've had our ups and downs, fair enough, but we're different. We care for each other, love each other. Nobody else loves you. You know that. He probably thinks you're ugly, feels repulsed every time he touches your skin, but he's just using you for sex, using you like a piece of meat. Believe me, I'm right about this. Because you know you're ugly, don't you. Know you're fat. I might not think so – I don't see you that way at all - but everybody else does. They see the truth. Fat, ugly, repulsive. And that stranger, I've seen him, the cockiness of him, getting out of the cab, heading along the path and up the steps. And you, letting this bastard into our home, our bed. Do you honestly think I'm going to let this impostor get between us this way, destroy everything we've got? No way, never.

Don't worry. I know what I'm going to do. I've thought about it quite a lot. It seems the only way – because I know how things go, these kind of people get possessive, don't want to let go. I know what type of person we're dealing with here. First possessiveness, then violence, you wait and see. It's true, men are all the same; most of them anyway. You don't know what you're getting into.

There's only one way. He's going to have an accident. Walking along the path before he gets to the steps. Prick. Cabs everywhere, frightened to walk the streets of Hackney, I'll show him. Get him right on the garden path. Instrument to the back of the head – whack, bash his brains out. Or maybe use a knife, again from behind. No, fuck that: let him see who he's dealing with – he won't be getting up again, will he? There you go: straight in the heart. Grab his phone, wallet, go. It's those youths again, those gangs, seeping out of the estates and bringing terror to the residential streets. Man dead. Terrible. Another Hackney statistic.

I'll do it, Ruth. I'm not joking. I'm thinking about it right now. Relishing the thought. You'll see.

PULSE

I've been letting things slide and it's beginning to show.

The night before, a simple errand had turned into a total balls-up. I'd been sent with two others to pick up someone who owed money, and though we'd been tooled he'd slipped through our hands making us look like cunts. Jack Meehan sent out another mob who luckily caught him quickly, but it was something I could've done without.

On the phone trying to blame the two blokes who'd accompanied me didn't work. Meehan wants to see me in person.

I drive up to Chingford and walk into the pub.

'Look who it is,' Meehan says, turning from the bar, his cronies lined up next to him. 'The court fucking jester.'

One or two of them laugh, but not for long. His face is set rigid, showing no sign of a joke.

'Over there,' he nods, and I take a seat at the far corner, the bastard leaving me fiddling with my phone for a full half an hour.

'So,' he says, when he finally shifts his arse from the bar to sit in opposite. 'It's the man himself.'

'Look Jack, I know things went wrong last night but...'

'I don't want to hear it.'

'But Jack, let me explain...'

201

'Are you fucking deaf?'

I'm not going to argue. Here is a man who only weeks ago bludgeoned one of his own lackeys to death with a hammer, only stopping to proclaim how much he was enjoying himself.

He leans in. 'I give you a simple job and you bollocks it up yet again.'

I go to speak but he puts up his finger, talking quietly. 'If I hadn't known your old man, I wouldn't have you cleaning my fucking bogs. You're useless and getting worse by the day.'

He stares at me for maximum effect, drawing it out.

'Now you better start pulling your weight, I'm telling you now.'

I nod.

'We'll leave it there. All the next shitty jobs, they're yours. You're lucky I'm in a good mood today. Now get out of here before I change my mind.'

I get up and walk.

'Hey, Einstein,' I hear. I turn to see I'd left my phone on the table. I head back, my face burning now.

He grabs me down by the lapel, speaks in my ear. 'You keep shoving that amount of shit up your nose and we might need a little chat about your future - or lack of it. You listening?'

'Yes, Jack.'

'Get out.'

Several of his cronies smirk at me as I pass, blokes who in any other situation I'd have gladly kicked up and down the floor, but I have to grin and bear it. All in all, I'm relieved - it could've been a lot worse. But what he'd said at the end there wasn't funny. I'll have to rein things in. Start slowing down.

I head along the street. Two Yardie-types are pumping music from a parked car; a bunch of Albanians arguing outside a bookies. The area has seen better days, that's for sure. But if one more suburb is turning to shit, what do I care? A couple more years on Meehan's payroll and I'll be kissing London sweet goodbye. There'll be no Herts or Essex for me. No Spain either. I'll be taking it all the way. Down under. Me, Ella and the kids. Good schools, clean streets, decent quality of life. Gather my funds and away we'll go. The kind of living my parents only dreamed about.

My old man had worked most of his life on the buildings only to die penniless. Being a gambler, it wasn't that surprising. But the year he'd spent working for Jack Meehan was his downfall. During a police chase through Hackney he ploughed his car into a wall, leaving my mum with all his debts and four mouths to feed. Growing up in a cramped Finsbury Park council flat with a mother who couldn't cope hadn't been easy. But I have plans now, big plans. It's just a matter of time.

Walking along the street I catch the eyes of several passers-by, and I swear a Turkish-looking bloke in shades is staring at me from a car, but I've got to get myself in check. It's my imagination. Too much stress, not enough sleep. But it's one of those days, I can feel it, the gods up there plotting against me, pushing for a little action, the kind that only ends in tears.

I turn down a side-street towards the car. It's only half-five yet beginning to get dark. I check my phone. Ella has left a message reminding me I promised to read stories to the kids before bed. But it isn't that kind of day. My nerves are shredded and going home I'll only be a pain to be around, and a row with Ella is something I don't need.

I text her back saying I'll be working late when somebody slams straight into my shoulder.

'Watch where you're fucking going, man.'

A guy half my age is standing there arms-open in front of me. White, baseball cap. Bum-fluff moustache. He looks me up and down, then tuts and walks on.

No way.

Without a second thought I lunge for him and pull him back. He looks shocked for a second, but he's quickly shaping up, I'll give him that.

We go straight to it on the pavement, slugging it out, the bloke throwing me at least two good right-handers, one that has me seeing stars for a second. But before long it's all over and he's staggering back against a car, hands drawing blood from his waist, his face a picture. I move in again, the blade low, give him two more quick ones. He slips to the deck. Then with a look left and right, nobody about, I swiftly exit the scene.

I feel better now, foot down on the pedal, within minutes joining the flow of the North Circular, Chingford behind me, a sinking ship that Meehan is welcome to. I've got a throbbing eyebrow and jaw, but I feel great. A score settled, a battle won and about bloody time. Maybe I'd cheated there with the shiv, but with a mouth like that you deserve all you get. Cocky little cunt. No sympathy. He'll live. He'll lose a bit of blood, suffer the inconvenience of a hospital visit, but maybe he'll learn a lesson or two in the bargain. Think twice next time because some of us don't fuck about.

I think of Meehan and the show he put on with the hammer. Gathering four of us in a lock-up for a spot of dark theatre. Dan Flynn tied to a chair. Showing us what happens to those who flout the rules.

Meehan has a few screws missing, of that there's no doubt, but maybe I'm not that dissimilar. Maybe that's what happens after a while. I've certainly done enough of his dirty work. The disposal of Flynn's body for a start, the kind of thing I didn't sign up for, but work is work, something I've never shied from, and maybe the government are right, not enough people applying themselves these days, youngsters the worse of the lot, in need of a firm hand, a kick up the arse every one of them.

It made you wonder what things are coming to. No respect, just mouth, backchat, cunts eyeing me on the street, taking liberties, Meehan hissing threats in my ear, the whole thing fucking outrageous.

I notice my hands at the wheel - they're caked in blood. Christ. I'll have to stop at a garage. Clean myself up.

Within the hour I'm back in Crouch End, parking far enough up from the flat for Ella not to notice, and heading to the nearest pub. Ella has left two messages trying to guilt-trip me about the kids, but being a good reliable family man isn't my priority tonight. I need some downtime. Either that or go off my rocker completely.

'Hard day at work?' the barmaid asks as she pours my pint.

'Always hard,' I smile. 'But I'm winning, that's the main thing.'

It's early Friday evening, the pub slowly filling up. It's a bit of a media haunt, not my usual kind of place, but the sight of young untroubled faces having a good time is just what I need right now. I remember this pub back in the day. Run by an Irish family, the landlord an ex-blagger, the lock-ins legendary. It's hard to believe it's the same place.

I head to the Gents, getting a smile from a young blonde as I let her pass. In a cubicle I snort up a fat one, then by the sinks I look at my face in the mirror. I have the blue eyes of my Scottish mother, the dark hair of my Greek Cypriot dad. I'm not a bad-looking bloke. But these days I make an effort, don't smoke, watch my food, go to the gym two, three times a week. The amount of coke I'm putting away probably isn't doing me any favours, mentally or physically, but that's something I'll have to work on. But on a Friday night? No chance.

A few more drinks and the lights dim, the music gets turned-up and the night is in full swing. The place is rammed now and I end up chatting to a bloke about the merits of Arsenal over Spurs. Friendly banter. He works for the BBC and is with some tasty women, a big birthday party, everyone half cut, and when he asks what I do I tell him I work in security, high up, and next thing we're joking about MI5 - that's the thing you see, I can't talk about it.

Then I'm in the corner chatting to one of his mutual friends, a girl in her early twenties, strawberry blonde, telling me she's temping for a magazine but is trying to break into acting, has done a couple of things already, talking a mile a minute, clearly on the white herself, saying she's recently split with her boyfriend, a bastard who walked out on her, left her having to pay his share of the rent and everything - what, leaving a beautiful girl like you? - and she laughs.

Another drink and she's looking into my eyes, leaning close, and then we're kissing, and I haven't done this in quite a while, haven't touched a woman but Ella, have only ever cheated on her twice, two single nights a long time ago, feeling bad after both, but I'm not thinking of that now, going with the flow, taking whatever the night has to offer. And then it's closing time and we're outside, a crowd on the pavement, people coming up talking about a late place up the road, but she says she's going home, whispering in my ear that I'm coming with her.

A quick walk through the streets and we're there, heading up three flights to an attic flat, and before long we're stripped off and going at it on the bed. Finishing I roll off her and lay back in a sweat. The girl rests her head on my chest, the two of us out of breath. My heart is hammering, refusing to slow.

Then she's facing me, saying something, and I look at her face as she speaks and it's like I'm seeing her for the first time. I can't even remember her name. Who is she? And what am I doing here?

She gets up to go to the fridge, strutting naked across the room, just a skinny young girl, and I think of my wife at home, Ella who shares my plans and dreams, the big move away from London, away from Meehan, away from the rain now pelting down on the attic roof, and the girl is back with two bottles of beer, crawling towards me on the bed saying I'd better have some energy left.

Suddenly I'm on my feet, putting my clothes on.

'What's going on?' she asks.

'I'm leaving.'

'What, right now?'

'I've got to go.'

'Why?' she says, crawling over with a sultry smile. 'Come on, stay. I'm not finished with you yet, lover boy.'

She reaches out to touch me and I whack her hand away. 'Get off me.'

She jolts back, the mood sour now. 'What's the fucking matter with you?'

I throw on my jacket. The answer is I don't quite know. Some men do this kind of thing all the time. But maybe I'm different. Maybe I have standards, feelings. Or do I?

'Small loss anyway,' she says, looking me up and down. 'You're nothing special. So go on then, piss off.'

Suddenly I grab her by the hair. She starts screaming and I put my hand around her throat. At that moment I see myself killing her, packing her into a suitcase, gunning it up to some isolated woodland, just like we did with Dan Flynn, a makeshift grave in the pouring rain, the whole thing over with, dead.

Quickly I let her go. What am I thinking?

She's cowering beneath the duvet now, crying with fear.

'I'm sorry,' I say, repeating it a little louder: 'I'm sorry.'

'Get out!' she screams.

The next day it's bright and sunny, and I get up feeling surprisingly clear-headed. By rights I deserve a banging hangover, but it's just not there. Ella has gone out with the kids and let me sleep on for a few extra hours. Earlier we had a kiss and a cuddle and a chat and things are good between us.

I bang out some push ups, then head for the shower. Yesterday is something I want to forget. I was wired to the eyeballs and the thought I'd gone home with some girl now seems surreal. Things had turned sour, gone badly wrong, but with drink and drugs that's just sometimes what happens. The girl's flat is only half a mile away, but it's a busy area so it's doubtful I'll ever bump into her. And seeing me again she'd probably cross the road.

I let the water spray over my face. Jesus, what was my problem yesterday? I even stabbed some bloke on the street. Good job I'd got rid of the blade because you never know. Coming out of the shower I check my messages. In two hours I'm due to meet Ton-up Tommy in his van for a run up to Felixstowe. A late one. Oh well, no rest for the wicked then.

I sit riding shotgun as we roll up the A12, Tommy happily keeping me up to date on his romantic exploits. He'd met this bird a few nights ago in a club and was giving her one in the bushes of the car park, only to be interrupted by two coppers with torches.

'I was banging her by a tree, trousers round my ankles, and I'm hardly going to stop for a couple of nosey plod, am I? Fair play to them though, they fucked off fast. Even muttered an apology I think. Looked embarrassed more than anything. The good old British bobby, eh? But you should see this other girl I'm seeing. Lives just two doors away as well. Legs up to the ceiling mate, I'm telling you now.'

'Don't you have a girlfriend and a kid?' I say, shaking my head.

'Yeah, but so what?' he smiles, fist pumping by his side. 'More the fucking merrier.'

I laugh. I'm in a good mood. I'd had a morning toot, but nothing since then and don't feel bad for it either. It's time to rein in the gear for definite. Maybe the drink too. Knock it all on the head. Perhaps I'll start hitting the gym more. Start jogging again. Early mornings up and around Ally Pally, make it a daily thing.

'Oh yeah, did you hear about Meehan's nephew?' Tommy says.

'No, what happened?'

'He's dead mate. He got stabbed on the street, didn't he.'

'When?'

'Yesterday I heard. Up Meehan's manor. He was only out of Feltham a few weeks as well. But you know how these kids carry on. All that gang crap. I'd put money down he was a wigga with attitude who went around running his mouth off. Think they're living in America the lot of them. Put them in a ghetto over there and there'd be shit pouring out of their pants. Still, whoever did it, I wouldn't want to be in their shoes I tell you. Meehan's not going to mess about. He'll find him, believe me. Even if the coppers get there first, the bloke will be done inside. Wouldn't be the first time, would it?'

He continues on. 'Remember that bloke from Dagenham who threw a drink in Meehan's sister's face? Nobody could find the guy, he went into hiding, so his wife got targeted instead. She got run over on the pavement. A hit-and run. She's in a wheelchair now, a raspberry ripple. That's the thing with Meehan, if he can't get you he goes for your nearest and dearest.'

Tommy turns to me noticing I haven't said a thing.

'Are you okay?'

'Yeah... fine,' I say, rubbing a hand across my sweating forehead, the need for a line of the white stuff suddenly overwhelming.

209

DIRTY WORK

It was almost noon and I was an hour late for work at the pub. As I walked in, I saw my uncle Frank behind the bar polishing a glass. I was just about to make an excuse for my timekeeping when he turned to me with a face like thunder. Throwing down his cloth he stepped out from the bar. No customers had arrived yet, so I wondered why he had such a strop on.

'Everything all right Frank?' I asked as he approached me.

Without a word he punched me in the face. I staggered back into some chairs and landed on my arse.

'What the fuck?' I said, holding my jaw.

The old Irish bruiser pointed down at me. 'Get out of my pub. You're sacked.'

'Why?'

'You're a thieving little bastard, that's why. Pinching from my till. How long has it been going on for? I'm making a pittance as it is, bills up to my ears and you're trying to put me out of business.'

'I don't know what you're talking about,' I said, rising to my feet. 'You've lost your marbles mate.'

Again he went for me, but I put my hands out. 'Touch me again and I'll have you done for assault.'

'You want the police involved? Go ahead. I've got you on

camera and with your record they'd throw you straight back inside – and it's where you fucking belong. Now out.' He pulled me towards the door.

'Frank, please, don't do this. I need this job - we're family.'

He stopped and looked at me.

'Not any more we're not. You're no relation of mine. Your mother was right, you're just like your father when he was alive. A waster and a pain in the fucking arse.'

That comment was below the belt and I saw red. I couldn't help myself, I lunged for him. Any mention of my dad always hit a nerve, but Frank had gone too far, was crossing the line with insults like that. We tussled across the floor, but before long he had me down on my knees in a painful arm lock.

'Are you going to calm yourself?' he said.

'Yes.'

'Are you fucking sure?'

'YES...' I said painfully.

He let me go and I held my arm, both of us hunched over breathing.

'I'm getting too old for this crack I tell you,' he said, his face red as a Bloody Mary. Then he straightened himself up and went over to pour us each a brandy.

He put a glass down on the bar. 'Drink this then be on your way.'

I brought it to a table and sat down. I stared at the dust motes in the air. What had I done? Two men walked in and Frank cheerfully greeted them, putting on the charm as if nothing had happened. My mum had been good persuading her brother to take me on, but like I did with everything, I fucked it all up. I was plunging fast into self-pity mode when a wad of twenties landed down on the table.

Frank leaned in, speaking quietly.

'There's your wages and a week on top of it. I must be mad giving you a penny but I'm doing it for Peggy's sake. If you've got any sense you'll start looking for another job today. It's up to you. Spend it all on drugs for all I care. But if I hear you're giving your mother grief again I'll come for you, that's a promise.'

I headed out along Caledonian Road. The sun was streaming down but it did nothing to lift my mood. Spotting pub regular Seamus shuffling towards me I swerved down a backstreet because chat and questions was the last thing I needed.

I stopped by a bench outside some flats. The thought of my recent past almost left me in tears. After splitting with Stella I'd hit the gear and gone off the rails big time. I did a few months inside then finally sorted myself out, but burgling my own mum's place was a low I'd never forgive myself for.

'What's up Brian?' My old mate Mario had stopped on his bike. 'Lose on the horses again?'

'Worse.'

'Chin up man, can't be that bad. It's a beautiful day. Look on the bright side.'

Back at school Mario was the class jester, and even after bouncing in and out of prison a few times he'd somehow never lost his spirit.

'How come you're not in the pub?' he said.

'Don't ask. That's a bridge well and truly burnt.'

'Well you know what they say, one door closes, another door opens.'

'The only door I'll be opening today will be the one down the dole office mate.'

He looked left and right, then said, 'You need anything?'

'No way. I've had my fill in that department ten times over.'

Mario was a mobile pharmacy. An influence I didn't need right now.

'Anything at all, let me know. I'm only a message away.' He slapped my shoulder and was off.

*

213

That evening I was round Stella's place in Archway playing with my eighteen-month-old son Ben.

'So what happened then, why did he let you go?' she asked as she stood washing the dishes.

'You tell me. He never liked me anyway.'

'You must've done something to get on his goat?'

'With a man like Frank it doesn't take much, believe me.'

'Whenever I've met him he's seemed friendly. Full of jokes.'

'You haven't seen him when he's pissed off. His pub's not pulling in much money anymore so I was the first casualty I suppose.'

'What are you going to do then?'

'Get something else. Here, what about your brother? Maybe he could sort me out. I could help him fitting windows again.'

'To be honest, Brian, I don't think he'd take you on. Not after everything that happened.'

'Yeah, suppose not.'

Ben was laughing as he shot me down with a large plastic gun. Stella didn't approve of the toy, but it's the kind of thing I'd played with when I was young. I cracked a can of cider and poured it into a glass, then sat back watching Stella at the sink. She was in a tight t-shirt and leggings. She'd put on a bit of weight lately but it suited her. I missed what we'd had together. The way things used to be. I reached into my bag and pulled out another new toy for Ben. A plastic car. Ben was entranced and played with it on the floor. I walked over and held her from behind.

'We should get back together,' I said. 'I'll get a decent job and we'll be a family again, doing things together, good things, going on holiday...'

'Let's not talk about this now.'

'I'm different, I've changed. I'm responsible now.'

'This isn't right. I told you last time,' she said, trying to shrug me off, but only a little.

I kissed her neck, moving up to her ear, knowing she loved that. 'Come on, let's go to the bedroom.'

'What about Ben?' she said.

'Don't worry about Ben. He can watch TV for a bit.'

We were in the bedroom for no time at all when a crash and a scream came from the living room. She pushed me off and was first to the scene. Ben had pulled a lamp off the side-table, my glass going with it, shards and liquid all around him on the floor.

Stella shrieked and grabbed him up. We checked him out and luckily he was unharmed, but Stella was hysterical, shouting that he could've been cut or electrocuted and it was all my fault.

With Ben in her arms, she ran into the bedroom and threw the rest of my clothes at me. 'Get out.'

As I left the flat, my empty can followed, bouncing off my head then clattering down the communal stairs. 'And don't come back.'

The woman next door was already out, asking what was going on.

'Him,' Stella pointed. 'He's barred from this place. If you ever see him again call the police.'

I walked across the estate and back to my lonely box room wondering who I'd killed in a previous life to deserve this. On Hornsey Road I saw Mario whizz past me on his bike giving me a wave, off on a delivery no doubt, and for a second I felt like succumbing. Giving in. Sinking back into that selfish world of not giving a shit.

No way. I had to pull myself together. Times weren't that bad. I'd rather slit my wrists than go back on the gear.

'Natural motherly instinct,' said Graham, leaning by the bar of the Engel Arms. 'Endanger a child's life and basically the mother goes loopy. It's the natural way of things. But the good news is, Bri, she'll get over it. Maybe not tomorrow, maybe not even next week, but it'll happen.'

'You didn't see her mate, you weren't there.'

'That's what I thought when I split with your sister that time, but I was wrong. Good things can happen in this life. Be hopeful.'

Graham was one of the few members of my family, blood or not, who still spoke to me. He was a success in life, with his own business supplying building materials.

'The thing is, that's not even problem number one,' I told him. 'I need work and fast. Here I am, a father with a kid and I'm totally skint. Do you know how that makes me feel?'

I watched him exhale and twirl his pint. He was thinking about it. So far so good. All I had to do now was mute the flashing danger signs that I seemed to emanate and maybe I'd be in luck. I continued on.

'You know me Graham, I'm a straight-up bloke. I've made mistakes, messed up here and there, but who hasn't? All I want from life is to provide – you know, do an honest day's graft, live quietly, hurt no-one.'

I could almost see the wheels of his mind searching for any pros among the numerous cons, and wasn't sure if he was finding any. I was praying for an act of charity here. Finally he turned to me.

'All right Brian, listen. I've got something. I'll give you a start. But any rows or disagreements with anyone, any shit goes missing, any problems at all, and you're out. Is that agreed?'

'One hundred per cent. I won't fuck it up, I promise you.'

It was the height of summer and I was riding around town in a flatbed lorry, out and about watching the world go by, which beat being stuck behind the bar of a dusty old pub any day.

'There you go son, tell me what you see.'

Driver Reg turned from the wheel to hand me his phone, the

screen displaying a writhing tangle of bodies.

'It's a fivesome,' he announced in his West Country burr, grin showing missing teeth.

'Right you are,' I smiled, shaking my head as I handed it back.

Old Reg was barmy. He spent most of the day tapping up total filth on his new smartphone like he'd just discovered the stuff existed. Either that or he'd be spinning yarns of his wild navy days. Wine, women and fights that he never failed to win. He was a right storyteller. Mad as a hatter, but harmless.

One Friday he asked if I fancied a drink later up his manor, free drinks all night. Reg wasn't the type of bloke I'd usually socialise with, but gratis alcohol?

'You gone potty?' I asked.

'It's my mate's pub,' he said. 'I've done him favours down the years so he always stands me and whoever I'm with drinks on the house.'

'In that case count me in.'

The Last Ship was backstreet old-school, situated in the arse-end of Walthamstow. The kind of place you'd expect to see boarded up with a demolition note on the door. Blink and it's been replaced by a block of housing.

I walked in and there was Reg at the bar.

'Here he is, my partner in crime,' he said to the governor. 'Sit in, young man.'

Next to him was his mate Albert, another big old seadog by the look of things, while Les the governor was a sweaty character with a pair of thick glasses that he kept adjusting over his nose. What a bunch. The pub was near empty, another boozer on its last legs no doubt, but Reg hadn't lied about the free drink.

After an hour or two listening to the three of them boast of past drinking bouts, women and bare-knuckle fights, I pointed out a signed picture of a vintage Page 3 girl that was pinned behind the bar.

'She a regular then?' I joked.

Les told me I wasn't far wrong. She was an East End girl who later turned to racier glamour and attended the legendary after-hours party nights that used to be held here.

'Like Roman orgies,' Albert added, booming with laughter. 'Those were the days, eh.'

After a while I joined a pair of teenagers over by the pool table and we had a couple of games. They were a bit sullen about the uninvited company, but I needed a break and apart from a few stragglers dotted about, there was nobody else to talk to.

'You a friend of Reg's?' one asked.

'No, not really,' I said, looking back at the close-talking huddle at the bar. 'He's just a workmate, why?'

'Nothing, just wondering,' he said and they looked at each other.

When they left I returned to the bar.

'Watch out for those two young fellas,' Reg winked. 'Couple of nancy boys.'

I laughed, but Reg continued on.

'I'm telling you, they're a pair of pansies.'

'Reg should know,' Albert laughed.

'Is that right?' he retorted. 'From the man who rode the arse off a transvestite in Hong Kong?'

Albert smiled and winked at me. 'That wasn't me, it was a mate of mine. He knows well, I've told the story loads of times. He picked up a pretty blonde in a bar and you know the rest.'

They clinked glasses and laughed.

The pints kept coming. The men were chatting away, but by now I'd dropped out of the conversation and was zoning out thinking about Stella. The other day we'd talked on the phone and things were looking promising. A pile of photos landed down on the counter in front of me.

'There she is,' said the governor. 'The Page 3 girl. Mementoes of the good old days.'

I flicked through them, the men awaiting my verdict. The woman was in various poses blatantly giving and receiving from mostly pot-bellied drinkers holding pints. Then I stopped at a shot involving an Alsatian.

'You lot are sad,' I said, handing them back. 'Not only that, but sick.'

What was I doing here with these three old scrotes? If I left now and jumped on the tube I could be back in Holloway having a decent pint in some decent company. Then I noticed it was already past midnight. A bit late for starting somewhere else. I looked up and saw all three men staring at me. A stool scraped back and suddenly big Al was on his feet.

'Think you're better than us do you?' he said, taking off his donkey jacket and throwing it aside. 'You've been sitting there on your high horse all night so I think it's time you stood up and proved yourself, young man.' He started rolling up the sleeves of his shirt.

Albert might've been getting on in years, but I hadn't quite realised how huge the bloke was. His fists were like two joints of ham. I turned to Reg and Les for support, but instead they both started banging on the counter:

'Fight, fight, fight.'

'Come on you fucking little weed,' the old Stepney boy said, his face close to mine now.

He was actually game for it and I realised I might have to pull a quick move on him or possibly regret it. I was boxed in the corner and about to maybe pound him one in the gut when suddenly he roared with laughter and threw his arm round me.

'Get the lad a whisky,' he said, shaking me. 'My brawling days are long gone.'

After that I made several attempts to leave but each time another drink would appear in front of me. By the time we stepped out onto the street it was three a.m., Reg and Albert climbing into a cab saying they were off to Chingford to shag a tart called Shirley.

'Yeah, Shirley fucking Temple,' Reg laughed.

I headed off into the night, got lost and ended up taking night buses all over the place. I crashed into bed. Never again.

Back at work, I didn't mention the meet and it was Friday before Reg turned from the wheel to say, 'Good old session last week, weren't it?'

'Yeah,' I muttered, head down tapping on my phone. This weekend I was visiting Stella and Ben. I was no longer a strictly no-go zone. It was official. She was even making a big meal for me.

'After we left you we dropped a load of Viagra and took this tart from both ends,' he said. 'School uniform, the lot. The real deal.'

I paused, cringing at the thought. If he expected me to pry for more info, he was wrong. I imagined some old slapper dressed as Britney Spears, the two grizzled old timers grunting away. If it happened at all, that is. They probably both headed straight home.

'Fourteen she was,' he said.

I put down my phone. Did I just hear that right? I turned to him. 'You shagged a fourteen-year-old?'

'That's right. What's the problem?'

'Well, it's illegal for a start.'

'Are you saying you wouldn't? Have you seen the way these little scrubbers dress these days? And weren't you shagging as a teenager? I was, we all were. I dipped my wick at eleven years old. You've been reading too much horseshit in the tabloids. It's not reality.'

I looked at him. For the first time I realised he reminded me of somebody. His voice, his whole attitude. I couldn't quite place exactly who it was, but I racked my brains and suddenly it came to me. It was my own father.

I remembered how he'd disappear for days, sometimes a whole week, then return home dishevelled, still drunk. He'd give my mum a slapping, then wake me up in bed to say hello. Years later I saw him a few times drinking with the alkies by Finsbury Park. Then at some point I heard he died, knifed in a fight with another waster. I didn't want to think about it. With certain things in life it's best to bury the memories. It's the only way you can move on.

'You alright?' asked Reg.

'Yeah. I'm fine.'

I didn't find Reg a funny guy any more. In fact, I wanted in on a different wagon.

'So he's a dirty old man,' said Graham that night when I phoned him. 'It's his humour, just laugh it off. Reg is my best driver. He's even put business my way on occasion. He knows people, seems to have contacts everywhere.'

'So did Jimmy Savile.'

Graham laughed. Then he turned serious, in no mood now.

'Look Brian, do you want the job or not?'

I did, so I let it go.

On Saturday night I went round to Stella's for dinner. Ben was in his usual chirpy mood and Stella had really made an effort. She looked amazing. Afterwards we watched a film and I made an advance, let my hand stray, but was quickly rejected.

'Let's take things slower Brian. I'm still thinking about it.'

I'd presumed that I'd be staying the night, but it didn't happen. Turning out of the estate I kicked a bin out into the road. A minute later a police car screeched up next to me and I shot off down the backstreets, shaking them off.

*

All throughout the following week Reg was banging on about sex non-stop, pointedly honking at groups of schoolgirls just to piss me off. When he started showing me some very dodgy-looking footage on his phone, I refused to respond. But everyone has their limits.

'Will you fucking cut it out,' I finally said, serious now. I didn't know for how much longer I could stand the man.

He shook his head, turned silent for a bit.

'The thing about you, son,' he said at last, 'is you're too easy to wind up. No sense of humour. I'm not a bad person you know, I'm just a joker. But you take it all so seriously.'

I thought about it. Maybe he had a point. I was wound up tight worrying about Stella, fretting about my future, thinking all sorts when Reg was just larking about, talking nonsense to pass the day like anyone does. Looking at things from his end, I suppose I wasn't a barrel of laughs.

'Yeah, maybe you're right,' I muttered, knowing I needed to lighten up. 'I've just had a lot of shit lately.'

He didn't answer that, and instead turned on the radio. Golden Oldies. At one point when Graham phoned, Reg told him I'd be running the truck back to the depot today as he was hopping off early to some business in the pub.

Clicking off he said, 'That alright with you, young man?'

'Yeah, course.'

I glanced at him as we rolled along the A13. I noted the clothes he never changed, his missing teeth. For a moment I felt sorry for him. I knew he lived in a big scruffy house of bedsits in Leyton and I suppose it must have been lonely. He'd told me that as a boy by the docks in Bristol he'd had to go out with his mother searching the bins for food as his dad would drink all his wages leaving nothing for the family. Things like that leave their mark. My own childhood wasn't great either, but one thing I'd always had was a plate of food on the table. Maybe a laugh and a joke was all Reg had in life.

Even so, I still wasn't sure about the bloke. I didn't like him.

We dropped off our last load of the day, a delivery of shingle to a building site near Rainham. Afterwards we were on a dirt track taking a shortcut back towards the A13, derelict factories and wasteland all around, when we realised we were heading towards a dead end. We turned the truck around and then Reg pulled over saying he needed a jimmy. He got out, approaching a bush and I noticed he'd left his phone behind. Automatically I picked it up. I started searching through his files. For once and for all I wanted to know what the man was about.

'What the fucking hell are you doing?' he said, appearing by my open window.

'Nothing,' I said and dropped it back on his seat.

Suddenly the door flew open and with both hands he wrenched me out of the truck.

'What were you looking for, eh? Pictures of little boys?'

He hit me in the face and I fell to the ground. I could taste blood on my lips, the hot sun blazing in my eyes, dust rising in the air.

'It's time I kicked some manners into you boy,' he said, rolling up his sleeves.

I saw his clenched fists and knew I'd have to act fast. I sprang from the ground and tore into him with a series of punches, then I kicked him in the stomach and he retreated, coughing and laughing in surprise.

Then he righted himself and said, 'Is that the best you've got?'

Again he was approaching me, back on form, dancing about like a boxer, laughing. I wondered if I'd hurt him at all. He was a big solid fucker with a lifetime of brawling experience and obviously I hadn't.

He began throwing a set of punches that got the better of me. Staggering backwards, I tripped on a rock and hit the ground. I rolled in the dust as he pummelled me with his size 12 boots. It seemed an age before the kicks finally stopped. Then I heard him chuckle as he unzipped his fly. A stream of hot liquid splashed over the side of my face and hair. Finally it petered out and he zipped up.

'Take that as a goodbye,' he said.

Everything now went into slow motion. Reg strutting back to the wagon. Me rising up, lifting a shovel off the flat-bed and creeping up behind him. He was still laughing to himself, about to climb in when the spade hit the back of his skull with a metallic thud. Silently he dropped to the ground. Again I brought it down and carried on bashing until only the sight of mashed blood and brains made me stop.

Reg lay face down, motionless. He was dead. I staggered back on my feet. I was in a state of shock and had to gather my bearings. I did a three-sixty. Vehicles were flashing along the distant dual carriageway, but otherwise the scene was barren, not a soul in sight. I stood unsure, the whole thing a complete head fuck. Then I realised I had to do something, fast, or my life wouldn't be worth living. If three months inside had been an endurance, the idea of twenty years plus was unthinkable. I looked down at my hands. I was still clutching the shovel.

Snapping into practical mode, I got to work. I dragged Reg's body across to a large pile of sand, waist high weeds all around, and started digging.

I got through the hard baked earth and before long I was throwing up big sticky lumps of clay. I toiled on, throwing up that muck, sweating in the hot sun until I was almost hallucinating. Reaching five foot deep, I clambered up out of the pit. With two hands I dragged Reg across the ground and dropped him in. He landed at the bottom all twisted up, and as I began to refill the hole I caught sight of his blood-drenched face. His eyes were wide open, staring at me. My heart jumped for a second, but losing momentum wasn't an option now. I kept grafting, desperate to complete the job. Once the ground was almost flat I covered it over with a huge pile of sand.

Finally I climbed back into the wagon. I turned off Reg's phone and hit the A13 back into town. Reaching the industrial estates by Canning Town I parked in the yard and promptly got out of there. I took a bus up to Leyton and from Reg's phone I texted Graham. *Going back to Bristol. Urgent. Personal reasons.* Then I wiped it down and left it on a wall. It wouldn't be there long.

That weekend I hit the alcohol. I spent most of my time in the pub. I needed to wash the thought of what I'd done out of my mind. The whole thing seemed surreal. Like a dream. There I'd be by the pool table laughing and joking when the memory would suddenly hit me. Reg down in that hole. Blue eyes staring out of a blood red face. But like a lot of memories in life, you just have to push them away, blank them out, pretend they never happened.

Turning up at work on Monday, Graham told me Reg was on a sabbatical, he wasn't sure when he'd be back, and he put me working in the yard for a bit, taking in deliveries and stuff. I didn't stay around for more than a few weeks though. My heart was no longer in it. I needed a fresh start.

A year later I was back living with Stella and Ben, and she was expecting. We were in the park with Ben one day when two detectives turned up and pulled me in for questioning. Reg's remains had been discovered during the ground work for new housing and they had opened a murder case.

In the interview room I sat arms-folded.

'This is ridiculous. I'm no killer, I'm a family man. Go check out some of the bloke's dodgy friends.'

'I'd say you two had a falling out. You discovered his past and decided on a little vigilante action.'

'His past?'

'His stretch in prison. In the nonce's wing. Don't pretend you don't know.'

Hearing that bit of info, I exercised my right to silence. And with no evidence they had to let me go.

Stella and I went on to have a beautiful little girl, Tia, a sister for Ben. She was eighteen months old now and I was working in a busy Irish-themed pub in Soho, fiddling more from the pissed-up customers than I was getting in wages. Life was good.

One day two men in cheap suits walked in and sat at the bar. Serving them I noticed it was the same two detectives. I put their pints down and took their money, pretending I hadn't recognised them, but their piercing stares were relentless.

'We'll get you, Brian,' the eldest said, raising the pint to his lips. 'One day, mark my words.'

'For what?' I asked.

'For the man you put in the ground,' his mate said.

I shook my head. 'You've got a vivid imagination, that's all I can say.'

I'd seen the appeal poster a while back and read the details, and knew the police were getting nowhere in solving this one. Reginald Tully was a man with enemies. Apparently after a skinful he would bring the fisticuffs home, picking fights with the other men at his digs. At one point they'd arrested a fellow tenant, thinking they'd got their man, but he was eventually released unconditionally. Their theories concerning me would get them nowhere. They had no real evidence to charge me. They'd have to take it on the chin. File this one away. Case closed.

'Not at all,' the elder copper continued. 'You did it. We know it, you know it, and even if I have to postpone my retirement, you'll do the time for it.'

Wiping the counter in front of them I couldn't help but allow myself a smile. Life was going well these days. It was pretty near perfect in fact. I didn't ask a lot from life, just a job, a roof over my head and a family, and anything else was a bonus - and nobody, especially not these two jokers, was going to ruin that for me.

'Whatever you say gents,' I said. 'Whatever you say.'

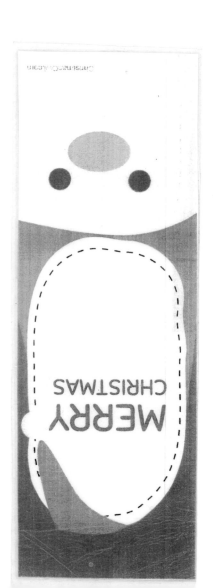

EXILE

Camden Town station at 6.30am and the men would be lined up for the start. If you weren't strong in the back you'd better start believing you were, because when the gangerman's lorry pulled up you had to look like you could work a shovel.

It was 1959 and I'd just come over from County Mayo.

'How old are you?' the ganger said, a hulking Kerryman with a belly on him.

'Eighteen,' I told him.

'My fucking arse you are. Show me your hands.'

I put them out before him.

'Soft as shite,' he said, getting some laughter from the lads around me.

Back home we'd just cut the turf and my hands had seen plenty work, but I was new and green and he thought he'd have some sport with me.

'Alright boys, in the wagon,' he said, choosing a dozen of us. 'And you too.'

We clambered up into the open back and set off into town and over the river to Brixton.

Before long we had shovels in our hands and were digging out trenches for cable.

'How's me little lad doing? Missing his mammy is he?' the

gangerman said, standing over the hole. But by now nobody was laughing because I was throwing that muck like the next man, grafting away. It was hard work, but I was loathe to show it.

He gave me no more stick and worked us on the shovel for six weeks. Then he disappeared owing us several days' pay. I put it down to bad luck, let it go, but the others were fuming. Some of the boys said they knew where he drank, a pub somewhere out past Cricklewood, and planned to bring pick-axe handles and hammers. If they had any joy I never found out, but I asked around for work and luckily got a new start for the next morning; I was sending money home and the landlady needed paying.

Getting the boat had been a necessity. England was where the work was, simple as that. But London was a shock. After seeing the men coming home to visit in the summer dressed in fancy suits and throwing money around, you'd think the whole of London was made of gold, but the reality was quite different. The air was dirty, the streets were crumbling and there was poverty too.

In the cold damp room I shared with two others I spent many a homesick night silently crying into my pillow, but I soon enough got into the swing. After all, having a few bob in your pocket and being able to spend it in the pubs most nights would have been unthinkable back home. Working on the sites soon toughened you up, made a man of you, but as for adjusting to the different way of life, it was just a case of learning as you went along.

I was walking back to my digs after a drink in Finsbury Park one night after missing the last bus. When a man pulled up to offer me a lift, I was grateful. He was a big fella and we were chatting away, then up by Holloway he turned down a backstreet and pulled in saying he needed a piss. Suddenly he leaned over, locked my door, and with his hand on my leg he tried to kiss me. We struggled and he was strong as an ox and seemed to enjoy it, until I got my fingers in his eyes and he screeched like a stuck pig. I slammed my fist into his gut, then ran all the way back to Camden.

The next day at work when I mentioned it to the lads they couldn't stop laughing. They told me I'd just met my first fairy, and you had to watch it, especially a young lad like me, because London was full of them. I found it hard to believe. If that sort of thing ever happened back home you certainly never heard about it.

Camden Town had a reputation. It was full of Irish and a rough old place with fights always spilling out from the pubs, but most of the fights were fair, all fists and no bottles, and usually over before anyone got too injured. But there were always exceptions. One night I was all dolled up in the sharp new suit I'd spent months saving for. I was going around the pubs, the Stores, the Brighton, Mother Red Cap. Then I was just after leaving the Laurel Tree and heading up the alley there, when behind me I heard:

'Hoy, you, cock o' the walk.'

Four Dublin fellas had followed me from the pub. One caught me with a bottle over the head, then they got stuck in punching and kicking - 'Culchie bastard' - and by the time they were finished I was covered in blood and my suit was ruined.

A few days later, I heard that some Connemara lads had given a battering to four troublemaking Dubs round the back of the Elephant's Head. Two they dumped head-first into a big steel bin, the others they left out cold on the road. I hoped it was the same gang. Dubliners were known for their dirty fighting and there was little love for them. From then on I'd have eyes on the back of my head. The prick with the bottle would have to watch himself because I never forgot a face.

The Buffalo was the dancehall to head to after the pubs. They said if you couldn't pull a woman in the Buffalo you might as well lie down and die. I had my fair share of girls from there, but it was a bit of a rough house. You'd get the drunken crowd storming in late with no hope of pulling a woman, so instead they'd cause a riot with the fighting. Years later they changed the name of the place to the Electric Ballroom.

A better class of woman could be found at the Gresham on Holloway Road. It was a proper ballroom and all the showbands would play there. One night I had a great time with a cracker of a girl from Tyrone and afterwards on the street we were doing a bit of necking. She was talking about bringing me back to her room, when from nowhere I received an almighty clout in the earhole.

'Take your filthy hands off her.'

Her brother was standing there, fists up, fuming. I flew at him and we battled it out, a crowd gathering as we clobbered each other black and blue, until it spilled out onto the road and the police pulled in. Two drunken fucking Paddies. Back at the station they threw us into the same cell probably hoping we'd kill each other, but we'd sobered up by then and ended up having a good old laugh about it. I later met the fella around and we'd say hello. I never propositioned his sister again though.

Throughout the sixties I worked all over London - on the building of the Post Office Tower, Centrepoint, countless housing estates that were going up like wildfire, only to be pulled down a couple of decades later. Some of these estates were badly designed and thrown up on the cheap. I lost a mate when we were doing the groundwork for a towerblock in the East End. Willie Gallagher from Galway. We were told it was safe to drill and Willie was only yards from me when he struck a power main and that was him. Dead at twenty-six because of higher-ups who hadn't done their job right. Not long after the block was completed, some of the people living there died when it partially collapsed. Ronan Point it was called.

I was on a site in Neasden once where the tools kept going missing. Big power tools, all sorts. The foreman asked a few of us to have a word with a chippy, the main suspect. When he was pointed out to me I stopped in my tracks - if it wasn't only the fella who had bottled me that time. Without a doubt, it was him. Eight or nine years had passed but twenty stitches and a suit wasn't something I was willing to forget.

'Wait here lads, I'll sort this out.'

I picked up a shovel and walked towards him. His back was turned, just as mine had been.

'Hi, cock o' the walk.'

He turned and the swing of the shovel caught him bang in the face. He fell to the ground, his bloody nose halfway across his cheek. He put up his hands, pleading for mercy.

'No bottle in your hand now is there?' I said, lifting the spade, tempted to give him another walloping, but the boys held me back.

I'd filled out since then and he didn't recognise me, probably didn't even remember it, but he was paying for his past sins and I was happy with that.

I kicked his tool bag towards him.

'Collect your shit and don't come back,' I said, kicking him up the arse as he went.

'What was all that about?' the lads asked. 'Did you know him?'

'We had a bit of history one night, yeah.'

The Dub knew not to return, and it just so happened no more tools were pinched.

Around '69 I was doing some renovation work on a recording studio in the West End. At lunchtime I had a bit of a wander. It was a sunny day and I ended up on the roof, leaning by the railing with a cigarette looking out over Soho. After a while I turned to see a fair-haired lad sitting strumming a guitar. When he finished I told him I used to play the accordion but haven't picked one up in ten years now. He said it was never too late.

I gave him a light and he asked what county I was from, saying he had Irish on his mother's side. He said he himself was born in Brixton, and I mentioned how I'd worked there on my first day in London, digging trenches for the electric cable that had been up on the poles. He mentioned Electric Avenue and said it was the first residential street in London to be lit by electric lighting. I told him I didn't know that, but remembered the street well because it was the very one I was working on. The boss man still owes me a few bob too. Ran off without paying us in the end. He's a millionaire contractor now.

I wished the lad luck with the music and headed back to work. Then a few months later, around the time of the moon landing, I saw him on TV singing away. He went on to become a big superstar, but I always remember that time on the roof, having a chat, him in his fashionable garb and me in my dirty old boots.

I later landed a foreman's job with McAlpine. I also met Marian, the woman I'd marry. In the Gresham we'd spent an hour glancing over at each other until I worked up the courage to walk over. With long dark hair and a short skirt, she was stunning and I was worried she was out of my league.

'Will you look at your man here trying to chat me up,' she laughed to her friends as I fumbled for the right words.

Marian was no wallflower, but that's what I liked about her. We danced the night away and from that day forward we were an item. We were married within a year.

In fourteen years I'd only gone back home twice, to bury my mother and father. My sisters were up in Manchester and Leeds, and our young brother had married a girl from the North and settled in Belfast. Like many who'd taken the boat, I'd never intended to permanently stay, always harbouring the dream of one day returning, but now there seemed nothing to return to, and in reality there probably never was.

We moved to a flat in Archway, close to the Whittington

Hospital where Marian was a nurse. Married life didn't quite bring the happiness for us both that we'd imagined. Marian was a Cork City girl, I was a country boy from the West and our differences sometimes jarred. She'd come home from work stressed and the rows would be fierce. Between us there was a lot of drinking going on, but when I found the gin bottle in the coat Marian wore to work I realised she had a problem.

'Oh go shut your fucking mouth,' she said. 'Are you telling me you never have a drink at lunchtime? It's the same fucking thing.'

There was a difference though. I had control over my drinking whereas Marian was an alcoholic. I wanted us to settle down and start a family. I told her I was willing to give up the drink completely if she'd do the same, and several times we cut right down and things seemed a lot better. But miscarriage followed miscarriage and she lapsed into her old ways. Then Marian lost her job. She refused to admit she'd been sacked for drinking, until one day I confronted her with a letter that confirmed it.

She exploded, screaming and smashing things. I'd never seen her like this. She was hitting me with her fists, going berserk, and I had to pin her to the floor and throw water on her. Later that night we talked. She told me about her childhood. How her father would come home drunk and pull her hair and beat her, and do much worse things that I won't repeat. I held her close and told her it was all in the past, forget about it. You've got me now. I'm your husband and you mean everything to me.

Marian cut down on the drink and eventually got pregnant again. We were delighted. The birth was problematic and Marian was told she couldn't conceive again, but she soon recovered to good health and we had our baby boy Thomas. These were the good times. At work I was promoted and we moved to a garden flat in Finsbury Park. Tom was my pride and joy. I couldn't wait to teach him to play football, bring him to the Arsenal, watch him grow to become whatever he wanted to be. But he'd never have a shovel in his hand, that was for sure. England was a great place, full of good people and opportunities. It was all there waiting for him.

One Sunday afternoon Marian was out in the front chatting to the neighbour and Tom was playing with their cat. Tom must have wandered out on to the road, because Marian only noticed he was gone when she heard the brakes of the car. Thomas died instantly, his skull smashed open across the tarmac, and where was I? Drinking in the fucking pub. Seeing my son in the mortuary battered and lifeless is a sight I wish I never saw. It made no sense. He was still alive to me. How could all that life, all that innocence be gone?

I started going back to Mass, talking to the priest. Marian never set foot in a church again. She turned to Valium and the gin bottle. Punishing herself. Goading me to say what would hurt her even more. That it was all her fault, she'd been a useless mother who let her son be killed on the road instead of being in her arms where he'd be safe and sound, alive right now. And with whiskey in me I'd fall for the bait, releasing the pressure, asking her how she could live with herself, calling her a fucking disgrace. Those words reverberating in my head the day I returned from work to find her dead from an overdose on the living room floor.

I lost my head after that. Lost my job, my home, everything. I drank it all away telling myself I deserved it. I was living in hostels and drinking on park benches, trying to kill myself with alcohol, fights, sometimes standing in the middle of Seven Sisters Road urging the cars to run me down so I could be where my family were. I spent nights in the police cells shouting my mouth off and receiving a kicking, only to call them all English bastards and their mothers' whores so they'd come back for more, hoping this time they'd stamp my skull into the concrete and finish me off for good.

I was with a crew of drinkers in Finsbury Park one day when another crowd started fighting with us. Punches and kicks were flying all over, mine included. I saw a Scottish guy laugh as he ripped a man's face open with a broken bottle, then suddenly he threw his mouth wide and paused stock-still as one of my crowd buried a knife full-hilt into his back. We scattered as he lay bleeding to death. The man who stabbed him got twenty years; I got four for being involved.

In the early 80s, being an Irishman in an English prison wasn't easy. It was after the deaths of the hunger strikers, and the IRA had been targeting England for over a decade now. While I was inside two no-warning bombs went off in Regents and Hyde Park, killing eleven soldiers. Pictures of the horses lying dead were all over *The Sun*. I took a terrible hiding after that. The screws let three cockneys into my cell when I was alone and afterwards I spent a week in the hospital ward. That time I hadn't a chance, but mostly I fought back, fighting all the time and Solitary became my second home.

For a while I was a problem prisoner, shifted around the London prisons. But things settled. When word spreads that you've got a short fuse and aren't scared to fight, trouble-makers tend to look elsewhere. But I still had to watch it. I once saw a man shivved in the neck, blood everywhere. He didn't make it. Another time a queer was kicked to death in the spur below. The guy said he only did it so they'd give him Category A status meaning he'd get his own cell.

A lot of the men inside had been in and out since year dot and knew little else, but I planned for jail to be a one-off. On a good note, it was my first time sober in years and I could finally think straight. What happened to my wife and son was something I'd have to accept, difficult though it was. Either that or continue battling with myself forever.

I'd lost contact with my sisters, but my brother Joe was working over in London for a few months and paid me a visit.

It was great to see him. He told me to pop over to Belfast when I got out, I had a young niece and nephew I'd never seen. I joked saying I'd probably get my arse blown up over there, and he winked and said:

'Don't worry, the country will be united before you know it.'

'Not for as long as Thatcher's in it won't,' I told him.

I laughed remembering that old saying, *We'll give back Camden Town if you give us back our six counties*, and he told me he'd had a few jars down that way the night before.

'How was the craic?'

'Mighty. There was this band at the Bull and Gate, the Pogues. They were mad. A big fight broke out at the end.'

Two months later Joe was back with his family in Belfast. Three months after that he was dead. Two Loyalists burst into his house and shot him in front of his wife and kids. I hadn't known, but he was a member of the IRA. His name and address were most likely passed to his killers by British agents. The war in Ireland was dirty and filthy, but when you think about it, what war isn't? I cursed the Proddies and I cursed the IRA. Joe had been an eejit for joining up, but he was my little brother and I was devastated. I felt for his wife and kids. It wasn't something they were likely to recover from.

As my release date neared, I needed to start thinking about my future. It scared me. If I was to live any semblance of a normal life I needed to stay sober. It would take willpower, an amount I wasn't sure I possessed, but I had no other choice. The doorways and park benches were littered with people who hadn't been strong enough, who'd thrown it all away. Surely I was worth more than that.

When I stepped out of Pentonville the sun was shining down, a beautiful summer's day. This was it, I was free. I set off along the Caledonian Road, and passing a pub I heard somebody call my name. It was Liam O'Halloran from Belmullet who I hadn't seen since before I got married. We shook hands and he asked what I'd been up to.

I lifted my bag and nodded back to the Ville.

'Just got out of the big house.'

'You're kidding me.'

'I am not.'

He slapped my back and told me to get myself in for a drink. If it crossed my mind that I might be doing the wrong thing, the moment passed quickly. Having a pint in my hand felt the most natural thing in the world. We sat having the craic and when Liam left to get back to the wife I carried on drinking. What harm could a few pints do? I took the session down along the Cally, but can't remember anything past the Edinburgh Castle. I woke up the next morning in a doorway, bruised and aching like somebody had stamped all over me.

My bag was gone, my pockets empty, but I tried not to panic. All wasn't lost. I pulled out the crumpled bit of paper with the list of hostels. Arlington House caught my eye. It was one of the few places I hadn't been barred from. I'd get myself over there. I could do it. Start again. I got my legs moving and, trying to ignore my raging thirst, I headed for Camden Town.

SEND OUT THE DOGS

Doing a stretch inside is every copper's nightmare, but at times like this I was seriously tempted. I saw myself putting a Browning 9mm handgun to the bastard's head and pulling the trigger. Maybe the job was getting to me. Or maybe I just didn't like watching child sex offenders walk free.

Up in the dock Sidney Roper had put on his best performance, playing the victim himself, when the abuse meted out to his victims had been horrific. And here I was, outside court, watching the bastard climb into a taxi, smiling at me.

Phil, who had assisted me on the case, held my arm. 'We tried our best, John. There's nothing we can do.'

'I'm not finished on this one,' I told him. 'I'm serious.'

We watched the taxi pull away into the traffic.

'Come on,' Phil said. 'We need a drink.'

We sat in a pub near Islington nick. What with the divorce, the overtime and everything else, my head was in a mess. Only a few drinks in I was pissed, the exhaustion of months weighing down on me. At one point I nipped to the snooker club over the road for some charlie to sober myself up. But Phil, younger and wiser, could see right through me.

'Get off the nonce squad, John. It's not doing you any good.'

I shook my head and headed to the Gents for another toot.

The next day the governor called me in to his office. He pulled me off the team. I was one of his hardest working men, but stress, he said, it happens to us all. Slow down.

He advised me to take a couple of weeks off. Have a break, he said.

'You fucking grass,' I said, passing Phil in the corridor.

He stood there, swearing he hadn't said a thing.

Bullshit. So much for friends.

At home I sat down with a bottle of scotch. Two weeks. I could see myself climbing the walls already. I was a workaholic, kept myself busy, always had done. I'd been in the job almost twenty years, and before that I'd served four years in the army. I wasn't used to this.

But even so, maybe the boss was right. Maybe I did need a break. Perhaps I'd fly off somewhere, forget the lot of it. Or maybe I'd stick around, call a truce with Laura. Try to get on speaking terms at least. Talk about seeing the kids a bit more. But who was I kidding? Laura probably wouldn't even pick up the phone. She hated me.

The past eighteen months with the CSOS (Child Sexual Offences Squad) had been some of the most taxing of my life. I'd been from one squad to another, Murder, Drugs, Robbery, thought I could handle anything, but I was wrong. Viewing child pornography and dealing with the kind of people that made it, required a strength of mind I obviously didn't possess. I was a father for God's sake. It affected me. At times I felt like driving round and kicking Laura's door down, grabbing my kids and fuck the law. The world was festering with every kind of evil imaginable and I wasn't there to protect them. The amount of sickness out there was unreal. Nobody knew. It didn't bear thinking about.

Joining the CSOS had been a bad move. I'd become too

242

narrow-minded, too determined; I made mistakes. The worst was after a 13-year-old girl claimed she'd been raped by a teacher in his car. We pulled him in and I came down hard on him, honestly believed he was guilty. He was bailed and suspended from his job pending the court case. A few weeks later we heard that he'd tried to kill himself. Good riddance, I thought. Then the girl turns up saying she'd made the whole thing up. He'd never even touched her. She'd simply wanted revenge after getting a bollocking in class. She was crying and saying she was sorry. I was stunned. I'd just helped ruin a man's life.

The job pushed me to my limits. Laura hadn't been able to stand it, and the rows would be phenomenal. I'd always sworn to myself I'd never actually hit her, but one day I had her by the hair, fist raised, when I noticed my kids cowering in the corner, terrified of me. 'Go on then, you bastard, punch me.' I let go. Couldn't believe what I was doing. The marriage crawled on for another two years, but from that day on we both knew it was over.

The girls had been four and six at the time, and I wondered if they still remembered it. Of course they did. I thought of my own dad. How the slaps he'd give my mum always shocked me so much. I remember once telling him to stop, and his stunned face as he turned to see me there; hesitating, just like I had. 'It's got nothing to do with you,' he said, pulling back. 'Get upstairs now.' As I grew older such incidents petered out. He probably knew better.

At seventeen I joined the army. I remember the tears in my mum's eyes. Her own father had gone to war and never come back. But this was 1984, different times. Unless of course another Falklands broke out. I lived in Borehamwood, on the edge of London. There were no jobs, nothing doing. The army was my escape.

Basic training was harder than I'd ever imagined. My mates

243

said I wouldn't last two weeks, but that only spurred me on. By the end of it, more than half the recruits had either dropped out or been back-squadded. I made it. Passing out parade was the proudest day of my life. We were soon posted to Germany. It was all exercises and drinking and I loved it. As time went on, the inevitable tour of Northern Ireland was something I both dreaded and looked forward to. But in 1986 when they announced we were being deployed to South Armagh, it was bad news all round.

For a British soldier, the South Armagh region of Ulster was the most dangerous posting in the world. The local IRA were famously cunning, had the support of the people and effectively ran the place. They had forced the army off the roads with landmines – the worst killing eighteen Paras – and all military movement was by helicopter, the area virtually no-go.

The night before our dispatch the mood was unusually quiet. Since the announcement we'd been keeping our spirits up, the bravado high, but now we said little. Lying in my bunk I found it hard to sleep. What had I let myself in for? I was shitting it. We all were.

We flew into Belfast, then got choppered down into Armagh. We were stationed at Bessbrook Mill. The SAS and some Paras were there too, but neither would spare us crap-hats a glance. We were busy from the word go. Often, the chopper would drop us down in teams to set up temporary checkpoints on remote roads, hoping to catch some Provos by chance. With the threat of snipers in the surrounding hills and fields, check-points were extremely dangerous.

One night we were manning a point near Killeavy. The landscape was lonely and mountainous, passing cars few. I was lighting a smoke when a volley of shots took us by surprise. We dashed for cover, and for one moment I remember freezing with fear – but I fought through it. In unison we let rip with our weapons, round after round being emptied into the dark. The feeling was momentous. Nobody was injured and the gunman got away, yet somehow I felt I had passed an important test.

Snipers and mines were a constant threat, and security bases were regularly targeted by mortar fire. Only a year before, a mortar had killed nine RUC officers at their barracks at Newry. Nowhere felt safe. We were fighting an invisible army, being watched and studied and we knew it. In a bid to turn this around, the first of the watchtowers was being built at Glasdrumman. Security was tight, but still the IRA managed to detonate a van bomb nearby.

News came through that two soldiers had been killed in the blast, and we were rushed over to help. The remains of the van lay smouldering by the road, debris scattered far and wide. The shredded rags of their uniforms were hanging from the hedges, but there was no sign of the bodies. We were sent out across the fields with torches. Within a bush I discovered part of an arm. Then further along in the mud of a ditch I saw a single hand, its wedding ring intact. At the far side of the field a soldier was down on his knees crying. In front of him lay the severed head of one of his mates.

I remember vomiting into a ditch, tears streaming down my face. Then I wiped up and never cried again. Not for years anyway. I grew up that day, any remnants of youth left in me destroyed forever.

On the news there'd be violence across Ulster nightly. Riots, bombings, shootings. Gerry Adams and Sinn Fein. Ian Paisley ranting like a madman. The soldiers in the Ulster Defence Regiment could harp on about the subject for hours, talking down to us like we hadn't a clue. But admittedly your average English soldier understood little of the politics or history involved. Some thought the Province should just be handed back and to hell with it. Others pointed out it would only intensify the war, the mad Orange boys willing to prove that. Others, and probably most, saw the whole situation as a mess and just wanted to count the days and get the fuck out of there. The level of hatred and constant threat of death was enough to drive you round the bend.

The NAAFI bar was our only escape. We'd get absolutely shit faced. We'd wind each other up or swap 'war stories' – some I wouldn't want to repeat.

One night I got pally with a sweat who'd seen hand-to-hand combat in the Falklands and was on his second Irish tour. His first had been in Belfast. He told me he'd got so sick of being threatened and spat at that one night he walked into a Nationalist area in his civvies and shot a Republican in the head. Just walked up behind him, slotted the cunt and walked away. It was taken as a Loyalist sectarian attack and a couple of nights later a Protestant got nutted just off the Shankill. He felt a little guilty about that, but that's war.

He pulled out his wallet and showed me some snaps of his time in the Falklands. Fields were strewn with enemy corpses, shot, bayoneted or both. In one picture he was smiling for the camera, propping up a dead Argie, offering the mouth a cigarette.

At the time I laughed along, found it hilarious. Back in the real world, of course, you look back at such things with shame. But having said that, in the real world you're not playing a 24/7 game of cat and mouse with an enemy that wants you dead. You're in a different mindset. I never did find out if that Belfast story was true, but I do know that a couple of years later in Tyrone that particular squaddie took the brunt of a 200lb charge and what was left of him wasn't worth talking about.

One night, after discovering suspicious tools in a car, we dragged out both occupants with force. The men insisted they were electricians, but devices were being discovered all the time, and we couldn't take any chances. We took the car apart but found nothing. Then we decided to wind them up by searching it all over again. The rain was pouring now and both men were getting drenched.

One of them lost his patience and squared up to me, called me a Brit bastard and to get the fuck out of his country. I hit him in the head with the butt of my rifle. I completely lost it and started kicking him on the ground, only stopped when the corporal ran over and told me to calm the fuck down or I'd be on a charge.

The frustration was unbelievable. We had rules; they didn't. Half the time we felt like sitting ducks, just waiting for the sniper's bullet or device that would blow us apart. Some had wives and kids, everyone had girlfriends and family, what the fuck were we doing there?

One night on a four-man country patrol, we spotted shadows through the gorse. We got down, rifles ready. It could be a gunman in wait or someone ready to trigger the command wire of a bomb. Something shuffled and the squaddie next to me suddenly panicked. He charged forward firing his weapon. It turned out to be a stray goat, but he wouldn't stop firing, pelting the dead animal with lead. Finally, he slumped to his knees, crying uncontrollably. He had a total breakdown. He got shipped out that very night and we never saw him again.

As my tour neared its end, I had the almost certain feeling I'd never make it home. A squaddie from our battery had been injured by a device near Crossmaglen and, despite the best efforts of our superiors, we soon found out that he'd lost both legs. Morale was low, tension at breaking point.

On my final night-time field patrol, we heard a gunshot. We hit the ground and another shot rang out. We zig-zagged forward, finally chasing two figures through the gorse. They split off in two directions and I found myself chasing one of them alone. I cornered him by a dry-stone wall.

'Drop the fucking weapon or I'll shoot!' He was already hands-up, the gun by his feet. I came closer. He looked only about fifteen and was absolutely shitting himself.

'I'm sorry,' he kept saying, 'I didn't know you were there…'

I charged at him and punched him to the ground. 'You fucking fired at us, you cunt.'

My rifle was trained at his head. I could shoot him. Fucking kill the bastard. He'd fired a gun and ran; the army would be right behind me. I could do it…

As my mates appeared around me, the thought suddenly seemed insane. They told me everything was under control. They had the other suspect, a girl. Within minutes the Lynx came down and lifted us off to the barracks. All the way the pair were begging us not to tell their parents, and seeing close-up just how young and naive they were, I realised something wasn't right. Sure enough, it transpired they hadn't been firing at us at all. They were a secret couple, Catholic and Protestant. The boy had been showing off with his dad's old air gun, firing at some tin cans lined along a wall. The shots hadn't been anywhere near us.

I'd actually been ready to kill that boy that night. Fill him full of holes and walk away. Maybe it had just been frantic thinking in the heat of the moment, or maybe it hadn't. The thought disturbed me.

The tour ended and the celebrations were huge, but for a while afterwards that incident cast a shadow over the whole thing. That night I'd tapped into a part of myself that I never wanted to see again. Maybe some other men could have gone all the way, lied up in court and carried on quite nicely, but not me. Terrorists were one thing, but If I'd killed an innocent 15-year-old kid just larking about with his girlfriend I'd never be able to live with it.

We flew back to Germany. When the end of my term approached, I didn't re-enlist. I left the army in early 1988 with a certificate of exemplary conduct.

Returning to civvy street was quite a shock. After the intensity of the army it was like I was suddenly living in slow motion. I was back in my old bedroom, back to the same old streets, and it felt as though I'd woken from a mad exciting nightmare only to be greeted by absolute boredom. I'd witnessed so much, done so much growing up, yet the world I'd left behind hadn't changed at all.

A war was going on just across the water, yet it seemed so many people hardly even knew or cared less. It took me a while to get my head around it all. Most of my mates were still aiming low, going nowhere, and sure enough I soon found myself settling into the same slow rhythm, without any real idea of what I'd do next. After six months on the dole or getting whatever labouring work I could find, I wondered which was worse: being one of Thatcher's unemployed millions or humping a hod of bricks on a building site each day.

I applied for the Metropolitan Police.

After training at Hendon, I started my two years as a PC probationer at Harrow Road. Our ground covered Notting Hill to Paddington, and from the off I loved it. We were worked off our feet. Probationers tended to get disillusioned fast, taking all the easy options. Not me. I genuinely wanted to graft. Luckily, I was teamed with some hard-working coppers who taught me a lot. I made as much arrests as possible and it didn't go unnoticed.

Worrying at one point was a knife-wielding mugger who was terrorising lone women around the wealthy enclave of Maida Vale. His violence was increasing with each attack, and when the daughter of a foreign diplomat ended up needing twenty-two stitches, word came down from high to catch the bastard by whatever means necessary. We were issued with photofits, and an operation was carried out involving decoys, but still we had no luck. One evening, passing along Kilburn Park Road, I asked the driver to slow down. There he was. He took one look at me and ran. He tried losing me around the tower blocks, but by now I knew the place backwards.

In the van he struggled and spat all the way, calling me a white-this and racist-that, but I think I held myself back pretty well. Until we got him to the nick anyway. Then it was a free for all. The fact he'd violently resisted arrest was a ticket to do whatever we wanted. In the cells I gave his kidneys such a battering he must have been pissing blood for a month. Coon, wog, nigger. If the bastard had been white we'd have thought of other names for him. That's just the way it was. By the end of it he could hardly stand up. Get up, you cunt. I remember another copper, an ex-Royal Green Jacket, ordering him into stress positions, shouting down at the bastard and cracking him in the head every time he moved. The drunks and thieves in the adjoining cells must have been terrified.

That was a result and I was well pleased. So were the brass. After my two years I passed out with flying colours. I was a full constable now.

Harrow Road certainly had its share of excitement, but if you were hoping for promotion it helped to have experience at one of London's real shitholes. Places like Tottenham, Hackney, Brixton. Grounds your average copper wouldn't want to go near. I was already thinking ahead, wanted at some point to make detective, so when I heard Stoke Newington were looking for PCs I signed up.

Stoke Newington was one of the roughest grounds you could imagine. High murder rate, drugs, guns; the muggers and rapists practically tripping over each other. Being Hackney it was covered in troubled housing estates that, like Broadwater Farm a few years earlier, were ever threatening to explode.

On my first day a policeman staggered into reception covered in blood. He'd been beaten senseless with his own truncheon and had both arms cut to the bone with a machete. It happened in broad daylight, yet nobody had helped. I soon learned that at old Stokey such things were not rare occurrences. The relationship between the community and the police was abysmal. In a way, it reminded me of Northern Ireland. They hated us and we hated them. Attacks happened on both sides and it was a case of constantly scoring points. When a copper was battered with an iron bar by one of the drug-addicts in Abney Park Cemetery, we simply rounded up every one of them and beat the lot rigid.

We often had people phoning the station with threats, but most of these we laughed off. It got a bit worrying however when we started getting messages promising a WPC was going to be snatched and gang-raped, and when they were finished they'd send us the video. We traced the calls to public boxes around the Holly Street Estate, a high-rise shithole in Dalston. Then given the go ahead, we drove round there, grabbed all the usual faces, hauled them in and kicked the living shit out of them. A shotgun was taken from the safe. We shoved it in the top face's mouth, gave him the news. It was gloves-off now, no fucking around. We told him to get the word out or people were going to get slaughtered, literally. Family members, girlfriends, the lot. Message received. The calls stopped.

Stoke Newington was *the* drug hotspot of North London. The frontline was Sandringham Road, a scruffy hive of squats, pubs and cafes, and seriously no-go to any copper in uniform. If an arrest ever happened on Sandringham it was a case of a quick kidnap then burning rubber before the van met a hail of bricks or a gunshot.

What soon surprised me about Stokey was the amount of drug dealers in uniform within the station itself. Dozens of street dealers nightly plied their trade with impunity around the Esso garage just down from the nick. Little effort was made to deter them, and I soon realised why – half their wares were being supplied by the coppers themselves. Any dodgy stuff I'd seen at Harrow Road had been child's play. The level of corruption at

Stoke Newington was unreal.

Crack in the UK was relatively new, and the biggest crack dealer on the block was a Jamaican woman who sold rocks from her kitchen window on Sandringham. One of the Detective Inspectors was not only shagging her, but had actually set her up in business in the first place. It was a good little earner. She handed him up to two grand a week.

Drugs were not only being recycled, but imported by the coppers themselves. A group of detectives had a racket shipping in lorry loads of cannabis from Spain. They'd actually drive it in themselves, the profits running into millions. It certainly kept the local dealers busy. The nick was running all the local gaming machines in the pubs and clubs, and extortion was standard practice. Crims were also being raided for their drugs and cash, all of it pocketed. Put it this way, if there was a local scam, the coppers were in on it.

I'd be lying if I said I was lily-white and hadn't profited from at least some of the dirty cash floating round at the time, but I never got involved in anything serious. It was too risky. Half the coppers at Stokey thought it would last forever. To me it seemed only logical that the shit would hit the fan eventually – and luckily by the time it did I'd got myself transferred to another nick.

The anti-corruption squad flooded the place, and forty-four officers were put under investigation. The desk sergeant, rather than face charges, took a shotgun, locked himself in a cell and blew his brains out. In hindsight, he probably should have taken his chances. The anti-corruption squad at the time were useless. A lot of reputations got blemished, but few jobs were lost, and out of forty-four officers only two ever got sent down.

Luckily, throughout my two years at Cokey Stokey I'd worked my arse off and had the commendations to prove it. A little heroic highlight occurred when I subdued a gunman who hours earlier had taken a shot at a WPC. I recognised him from a description and gave chase down the backstreets off Dalston Lane, cornering him in an empty yard. If he'd been able to shoot straight I'd be dead now. I must have been fucking mad. It got me a bravery award.

After a stint at Kentish Town, I was promoted onto the Crime Squad. This was a big step, and I was out of uniform. I was helping to investigate armed robberies, murders, you name it, and enjoying every minute of it.

One day I heard that police back at Stoke Newington had apprehended a massive IRA lorry bomb driving directly past their nick. Had the three-and-a-half-ton bomb made it to the City there would have been devastation, possibly carnage. Unarmed police nicking an IRA active service unit was no mean feat. One copper was shot but survived. The boys from Stokey were heroes.

On a sadder note, the Met was changing. By the mid-90s, excessive bad press had ushered in more paperwork, petty rules, and rights for just about everybody apart from the copper trying to do his job. Kickings in vans and cells had become a thing of the past. A lot of the old school were being rooted out and forced to resign. If you wanted to remain in the job, it was a case of adapting and going with the flow. As far as political correctness was concerned, you simply learned to keep your mouth shut. George Orwell had it sussed. Luckily some of the more severe changes didn't affect the specialist squads too much – you could still get out there and nick criminals, and if necessary dish out the odd thump or two – but your average uniform practically had his hands tied behind his back, and still does.

By early 1996, I was promoted to full detective. I also met Laura. I'd pulled off several successful operations and meeting the woman I wanted to be my wife seemed the icing on the cake. We married fast, bought a house in Waltham Cross and went on to have two beautiful girls. The marriage was never perfect, and years later when Laura told me I'd never been married to her at all, only the job, I suppose she was right.

In 1998, I took part in an operation targeting brothels in North London. With the sex industry so closely related to drugs and other activities we sometimes garnered good results. Catching the bosses higher up the chain was another story. What was noticeable now in the sex game was a proliferation of East European girls. Most were being promised a better life, then forced on the game and paid a pittance. They were treated like slaves.

With Blair's New Labour in power, immigration was out of control. While packing the housing estates with some of the poorest and most criminal elements from all four corners of the globe, the government was extolling the joys of vibrant multiculturalism, and anyone with any criticism was an evil racist. That government deserved hanging. Having said that, being in the business of nicking scumbags, to say a British scumbag was better than any other kind would be pushing it. Nowadays there was little honour among any kind of crim. Few were likeable.

By 2000, with my marriage weathering its first storms I was working for the Drugs Squad. It was a heady time. I can honestly say that until then I'd never taken cocaine. London at the time was experiencing a blizzard of the stuff – so was my nose. I'd started drinking a lot of spirits too, slipping vodka into my coffee throughout the day. The overtime was non-stop and I was burning both ends. Had it overtly affected my work I would have knocked it on the head, but it didn't. The results just kept coming in.

One night, rather than heading straight home, I stopped off at an estate in Bow where we were planning to mount an operation. The place was a warren of concrete walkways, many of the flats crack houses, others bases for guns, and I wanted to get a feel of the place. It was just getting dark and you could clearly see the scouts dotted at the corners watching for outsiders just like me. I was scruffily dressed, playing the druggy, but within minutes from the sudden whistles and signals I realised I hadn't passed the test. Shit. I was trapped in a walkway, two blocking my way up ahead, four more some way behind. I'd have to play it by ear.

Reaching the two up front, one pushed me in the chest and asked who the fuck I was and what I wanted. I mentioned a well-known dealer and said I had a meet with him, but they didn't believe me.

'He's a fucking pig,' one said.

I acted fast. I hit one in the face, tried kicking the other in the bollocks. Too late. I felt a blow to the back of my head and hit the floor. All six laid into me with bats and feet. As the attack went on, I prayed they didn't have knives.

Then I felt several shocks to my side and back and knew I'd been stabbed. They ran, their footsteps echoing off the concrete and I found myself slipping dangerously close to unconsciousness. It felt so easy to just lie back and give in, but I knew that if I did I'd never wake up. I staggered to the street, blood pouring out of me, and the next thing I remember is waking up in hospital.

I blame that night purely on coke. Nobody had told me to go down there that night, it hadn't been essential, yet I did it. Cocaine had been affecting my judgement, inflating my confidence - perhaps I thought I was invincible. I'd strutted in, copper written all over me, not even wearing a vest. I'd been taking too many risks, and by the law of averages got what was due. I sustained four stab wounds. One was deep and had missed vital organs by a fraction. The doctor told me I was lucky to be alive. I also had a dislocated shoulder, broken ribs, and bruising and scrapes all over me. I looked terrible and felt even worse.

Laura sat by my hospital bed begging me to resign. Banging on about next time dying and the kids becoming fatherless. No way. If anything, it made me want to get back out there and fight the bastards even more. I'd survived the fucking IRA, I was hardly going to let a bunch of low-level street dealers get the better of me. The sooner I was back on the street the better. One thing though, I'd have to clean up my act. The daily diet of powder and vodka would have to go.

I was released from hospital on Tuesday, 11 September 2001. What a day. I heard news of the first plane on the radio as Laura drove me home. Then I spent the rest of the day glued to the screen. The whole thing was surreal.

During my months off, things with Laura picked up. I got some equipment and exercised at home, and spending time with the kids felt great. At Christmas we all holidayed in the Canary Islands, and Laura and I even talked about trying for another baby.

It never happened. Back at work I soon found myself shuffled onto the Camden Murder Squad. I was back in at the deep end, and in hindsight it probably wasn't a good idea. I was involved in an investigation into a man later dubbed 'the Camden Ripper'. He'd befriend and bring home prostitutes from King's Cross who all too often ended up sawn apart by power tools on his kitchen table.

The man was a mental outpatient and the best argument against care-in-the-community I've ever come across.

In Camden, this was a particularly grisly time for murders all round. Only streets away, in a separate case, a man was found chopped up in bin bags left by the side of the road, only discovered when a tramp went looking for scraps. The victim was gay and had picked up a stranger from a nearby pub. On top of that, women's bodies were being found in the canal and linked to similar cases dating back to the 1970s. It was an intense time, and as a result, a new, more violent me began to present itself.

Only two of my attackers were ever caught and prosecuted, and the sentences dished out were pathetic. That bothered me.

During a row with Laura I smashed up our newly-fitted kitchen. I ripped the cupboards off the wall and tore away the worktop, badly cutting my hands. Afterwards, viewing the devastation, blood smeared across the debris, I was shocked. Laura took the kids to her mum's that time for six weeks. But it wasn't the end. One night in a pub I got into a fight over a spilt drink. I beat the bloke to the floor and was about to finish him with a chair when my mates jumped me. I probably would have killed him. I was losing the plot.

I got help. Privately. I was suffering post-traumatic stress not only from the attack, but events stretching all the way back to my tour of Ireland. In particular, they'd wanted to talk about the explosion at Glasdrumman, where I'd helped recover the human remains. I also talked about the time I'd almost killed the boy.

Several times at these sessions I found myself crying. It was strange for me. Afterwards I'd wonder if my mental condition was improving or if I was totally falling apart.

Progress happened though, because eventually I felt more myself again. My marriage, however, by this time was finished. I'd moved out of our house and was living in a flat on my own, and have been ever since.

The tube and bus bombings of 7 July 2005 - 52 dead – was the big surprise we knew at some point was bound to happen. A fortnight later, four more suicide bombers took to the tube for a repeat performance. They failed, but got away, sparking a manhunt of proportions never before seen. The next day police shot dead a suspected terrorist at Stockwell tube, in what turned out to be a case of mistaken identity. The bombers were rounded up after nine days. It was a hectic time.

With the terror alert permanently high, a lot more cops were walking around with firearms. But so, unfortunately, were London's criminals. Gun crime, especially amongst youngsters, had shot right up. Gang violence was becoming a real problem.

In 2006, I fronted a new street crime squad in Haringey. After years in investigations I was back to frontline policing, zipping up and down Tottenham High Road nightly, pulling in offenders by the scruff of the neck.

It reminded me of what had drawn me towards coppering in the first place – action – and I found the whole thing quite rejuvenating. Around this time, Tasers were introduced and I got to premiere the gizmo on a bloke who was cornered and swinging a needle. Another time we were chasing someone who had just stabbed a pensioner. It looked like he was getting away until a car zipped out from nowhere and ran the bastard over. I enjoyed it. Certainly for the first few months anyway.

Sadly it soon became a case of always pulling in the same toe-rags, watching them get bail, and sometimes even picking them up the very next night. By now, the politicians had the bastards laughing in our faces.

London was a very different place to the city I'd started to police in the late eighties. Most of the high rises were now low-level estates, a lot of the pubs had shut down, and the criminal underworld was speaking English as a second language. After years of a so-called socialist government the gap between rich and poor had never been wider, and it showed. Whole areas had completely gone to the dogs.

One night we came under a hail of petrol bombs thrown from the roof of a four-storey block. When we got our hands on the cunts they were all around sixteen, well-schooled in anti-conviction techniques, and quickly crying physical and racial abuse. We'd hardly touched them, yet suddenly we had every bleeding-heart lawyer queuing around the block to lose us our jobs. The investigation dragged on for an age. It caused a lot of resentment.

We were eventually cleared of wrongdoing, but as for the bastards who'd tried to burn us alive, all were acquitted. All we could do was shake our heads.

One night we stopped a BMW near Seven Sisters. Down came

the window.

'Is there a problem, officer?'

All three occupants were sporting an array of submachine guns. We were forced to step back, watching them go. That was hard for me. It spoke volumes. If people weren't frightened of us, then what power did we have? Zero. The force had been turned to shit.

By 2008, I was seeing my kids once a week and Laura, in another relationship and intending to remarry, was demanding a divorce. There was no point living in a dreamworld, I knew it would happen eventually. I still took it bad though.

One night, after chasing a burglar out of my flat, I decided to buy a gun. As it was, I was a fully-trained firearms officer with a Glock in the vault at Scotland Yard for whenever the official call came, but for personal possession, of course, a firearm was completely illegal.

I contacted an old army mate who worked in the trade. I chose a Browning 9mm automatic handgun. The SAS favoured them in Northern Ireland. I love Brownings, always have. I take it apart and clean it every day. Then I tuck it back beneath the floorboards.

Funny really, if a burglar came calling it would probably take me five minutes to retrieve the thing. By then of course the bastard would have a baseball bat across the skull and be on his way to hospital. Sometimes I wonder why I bought the gun at all. Power maybe. A little thrill. I don't know. Sometimes I wonder if deep down there's some hidden intention to do what at least three of my old army mates have tragically done. No way.

Baby P happened a stone's throw from the Spurs ground, around where I'd be working nightly. My mate worked in the same area, except for the police's Child Protection Unit. While I'd be bundling shitbags and addicts into the cage, he'd be picking up the helpless mess they'd often leave behind – their children. On raids I'd see how some of these kids were treated and it affected me. Baby Peter was all over the press, but a lot of similar cases were ignored completely.

Around now, my job satisfaction had reached near zero. I felt I was banging my head against a wall, and unless I began to feel I was making some kind of difference, I was going to pack in the job completely.

When a new squad was formed dealing in underage abuse, I volunteered. I threw myself in headfirst. The hours were crippling, my divorce was ongoing, and I'd sometimes still hit the coke and booze - ironically though, I felt like a worthwhile copper again. We were cracking a lot of cases. Doing good. People were being brought before the courts and taken out of circulation. I was achieving the aim.

Then came Sidney Roper. He was cocksure and arrogant, slippery as a snake. Roper had enticed two twelve-year-old girls into his home, blindfolded and cuffed them, and put them through hell. An ex-lab tech, he'd taken every forensic measure in the book. But still we pieced together a case on him.

Along came the trial. Roper had previous sex convictions, but none of them could be mentioned in court. His lawyers slandered the witnesses and portrayed the victims as devious liars. The whole thing fell apart. Roper was a free man.

I'd promised those girls so much. I'd failed.

Bringing us back to the present – to where our story started. Given a talking-to at work. Then alone in my flat, drinking whisky and beer all night.

In the morning I woke fully clothed on the sofa. My head was throbbing, the room a tip. I rushed to the toilet to vomit. Then I brushed my teeth and splashed my face with cold water. I looked in the mirror. I looked like a wreck.

I made coffee. I switched on my phone.

Immediately it rang. It was Phil.

'John… just tell me it wasn't you.'

'What are you talking about?'

'Seriously John, tell me.'

'What the fuck are you on about?'

What Phil then said blew my hangover away in an instant. Roper had been shot last night on his doorstep. He was dead.

Both girls' fathers had rock solid alibis. Neighbours weren't talking. Witnesses non-existent.

I was speechless.

'John, are you still there?'

'Yeah...'

He wanted an answer.

'Of course it wasn't me, I haven't left my flat since yesterday afternoon. Fucking hell Phil, what do you think I am?'

When I clicked off, I sat back on the sofa in shock.

Then I noticed the Browning 9mm handgun sitting there on the table.

Acknowledgements

Thank you to everyone who took the time to read this book. I hope you got something out of it. If so, feel free to leave a review on Amazon. Feedback is much appreciated.

A very special thanks to Paul, my brother, for all your help.

A big thanks to Joe England who featured many of these stories in his legendary PUSH mag. 'Sold on the street literature.'

Also thanks to John King from *Verbal*
Derek Steel from *Razur Cuts*
Ian Cusack from *Glove*
Joseph Ridgwell from *East London Press*
Mike Head from *Tangled Lines*
All of whom have featured my writing in their brilliant grass-roots publications.

Until next time…

Also by Michael Keenaghan…

LONDON IS DEAD
A Novel

A fierce and gripping portrait of society's criminal underbelly, LONDON IS DEAD wields a cast of flawed but colourful characters as they cross paths and swords in the streets of the capital…

Terry Hart's straight lifestyle has got him nowhere – no money and no respect from his family. When he's viciously robbed in his mini-cab by two younger men, his self-pride hits a new low. As the temptation to return to serious crime bites hard, out come the demons from a brutal and tragic past. Suddenly in East London there's a new Ripper on the loose…

Bigz is a street hustler in a world of hard knocks. He's haemorrhaging friends and inflaming enemies, which lands him at the desk of feared local don Hot Iron Mike, a man for whom an apologetic explanation is never enough. Hired as a 'pitbull on the payroll' Bigz is paired with Lil Killa, a dangerous loner with a side project: offing the men who abused him while growing up in care. They make quite a team.

Meanwhile across town, the Kilburn Mob, a resurrected armed outfit from the 90s, have a lucrative job on the cards – and they're hiring. But all is not well between old trusted friends. As past acts of betrayal resurface, not everybody will survive…

'Excellent flow and pace. This debut novel is alive and kicking'
JOE ENGLAND, *3AM Magazine*

'Keenaghan's love for his city shines through in this driven, thumping novel'
JOHN KING

Available in paperback and Kindle. 370 pages.
ISBN-9798354201891

Printed in Great Britain
by Amazon

42409610R00152